Praise for th

"*Yeshua's Cat* has a charm that most religious fiction doesn't pull off — it's an original idea that works well in its genre and will appeal to Bible readers and cat lovers alike. The day-to-day detail of what it was to be alive in such an ancient culture is intricate and visually stimulating . . . Through the eyes of a cat, details of Yeshua's life and times are elegantly described. *4⅓ stars!*"

~ Self Publishing Review

"[*Yeshua's Cat*] is a thoughtful, loving, and gentle portrayal of the life of Jesus . . . An ideal balance for a theological book . . . The author's view of Yeshua and his teaching is supported by rational, philosophical and theological argument and founded in love . . . *4½ stars!*"

~ Indie Reader

"Enchanting, poetic, engrossing, and vivid, *A Cat Out of Egypt* is simply a delight, and highly recommended for Christian readers who would gain a different, fictional cats'-eye perspective on Jesus' early experiences."

~ D. Donovan, Midwest Book Review

"*A Cat Out of Egypt* is an imaginative and thoughtful take about Jesus' years in Egypt . . . Not only is the author raising theological issues, but she's describing environmental and historical forces, and she does so without forcing beliefs on the reader . . . without dumping a lot of facts at once, which is the way historical fiction should be written . . . an entertaining and captivating story that will delight Christian readers . . . *5 stars!*"

~ Self Publishing Review

"*The Cats of Rekem* is an intriguing and beautifully written consideration of the life of Jesus and the meaning of his teachings, offered from a novel perspective. The writing is poetic and lush, with moments of tender emotion, spiritual ecstasy and sorrow, enlivened by touches of humor . . . *5 stars, Best of 2015!*"

~ Indie Reader

"*The Cats of Rekem* is a wonderful addition to historical fiction . . . a fascinating interpretation of Jesus, his life, and how he impacted those around him . . . clever and magical . . . well-balanced with a twist . . . a powerful lesson for today! 4½ stars!

~ Self Publishing Review

Cat Born to the Purple

A Sequel to Yeshua's Cat

4th volume in

the Yeshua's Cats series

written and illustrated

by

C. L. Francisco, PhD

ISBN-10: 1537605569
ISBN-13: 978-1537605562

for Don,
whose steady faith and support
have kept my feet—and my spirit—on the path

TABLE OF CONTENTS

Prologue

*T*he Grandmothers named me "Purple Gleaming in Shadow," because of the way sunlight picks out purple highlights in my black fur. Rarely do the elders name a kitten after the purple dye that so enthralls humankind, but at my birth the Mother of Cats sent the Grandmothers a dream, and they saw my days rolling out like a tapestry woven of all the rainbow hues of the pebble-purple shellfish. Indeed, the mysteries of royal purple have wrapped me round all my life, for I am descended from the noble cats of the fallen temple of Acco—where skilled dyers and weavers still create the most vibrant purple cloth in the Roman world.

Wherever the pebble-purple snails are pulled from the sea along the white sand beaches of my homeland, cats tell this same tale:

Once, in the long, long ago, when the Mother was walking along the beach after a storm with her cats gamboling at her side, one cat danced down between the shallow waves, scooped a buried snail up with her paw and carried it in her mouth to the Lady. Crouching before her mistress, she hooked the flesh of the snail with her claw, pierced the vein with her teeth, and dropped it onto the sand at the Mother's feet . . . where the snail's blood seeped out into the sun and air and worked its magic—turning from yellow and green to blue and finally purple. The Mother's

1

cat had simply reminded her of one of the many small wonders of her creation, and in time the Lady shared it with humankind.

Yet my story does not begin with purple. It begins a full year before my birth, far away in the land-locked hills of the Galilee. So for a while I shall speak through the memories of Wind on Water, a wise cat who once traveled with Yeshua ben Yosef, the human known among cats as He Who Brings Life to the Earth, beloved of the One.

Part One: Spinning

Spinning involves both twisting and drawing out the fibers of raw material into thread. The twisting and stretching is tediously slow, and the new yarn is always trying to tangle, untwist, or perform any of an amazing variety of other nasty feats the moment you let go of it. The thread must be kept under constant tension until the twist is permanently set.

paraphrase of E. J. W. Barber,

Prehistoric Textiles

1

A Fine Phoenician Border

Wind on Water speaks

The wildfire raging on the mountain called Tabor filled the world with a choking haze, blotting out the stars and burning my eyes.[1] Cats might not cry for grief, but I could feel the tears now, scalding and blurring my eyes, pooling at their corners, doing what they could to wash the grit away. My throat scratched and itched like a goat's after eating thistles. Even crouched down in my sling beneath the son of Earth's mantle, I wheezed and gagged . . . and found no relief. How could I escape something that flowed back into my body on each new breath? I whimpered and pressed closer to his breast.

I knew if I raised my head up into the foul air, I'd see what I'd seen ever since the sun had set in the brown sky: fiery explosions in the distance where the southerly wind swept flames up over the next hill, and the next, into yet another stand of summer-dry forest. Only my love for the son of Earth kept me with him instead of fleeing like every other beast in this blighted land. Simon, James, and John stayed

---

[1] Read the original story in *The Gospel According to Yeshua's Cat*, pp., 69-81.

with him as well, their coughs muffled by the mantles wrapped around their faces. They didn't try to speak.

Strange noises filled the night. All around us winds spawned by the flames gusted through the wadis and dry oak woods, rattling the leaves like empty seedpods, peppering plant and fur alike with grit and ash. At length, with the drab dawn approaching, I felt ben Adamah's steps begin to slow—as if he were suddenly unsure of his way. Reluctantly, I raised my head to look around, but I saw only more smoky outlines of rocks and trees before he veered up a small path that branched away from the road and up a rocky hill crowned with a straggling oak grove. Then I heard what he must have sensed already: the exhausted whimpering of a beast in pain.

Uncertain what to expect, I watched from my sling as he climbed the hill. Just under the hilltop he turned toward a massive boulder as big as a small cliff, with a shallow depression undercutting its base. There he found the source of the cries: a human female, trying to press herself even further under the rock's shelter as we approached. Her breath came in ragged gasps, as if the very act of breathing shredded her breast with invisible claws.

Not wishing to come between ben Adamah and the injured woman, I leapt down and crouched nearby, pressing my mouth as close to the ground as I could. My nose twitched with distaste both at the smoke and the rank odor of fear that filled the small clearing. The woman's clothing clung to her body in tattered ribbons, almost glued into the oozing paste of blood and dust coating her flesh. I could see that her hands were shattered, as well as much of her face. The Mother only knew how much damage I *couldn't* see.

Yet what I couldn't see didn't matter. I could already feel the son of Earth pouring his strength into her body, soothing her spirit with his voice. The sullen red glow of the reeking dawn faded behind the clear light flowing from his hands and enclosing her flesh. Then to my surprise, I sensed a struggle . . . almost as if her spirit were a piece of cloth, seeking to loosen its spun thread and revert to the fleece that had formed it, unraveling at his touch, streaming away into his light to lose itself in the love flowing through him.

"No, child," I heard him whisper, "not yet. Stay a while, even if the world has treated you cruelly. You are strong, and joy will come in its own time. Your attackers meant you harm, but even now the One is weaving their evil into good."

Slowly the threads began to weave themselves together again in his hands, until her spirit came to rest in the light holding her close. She breathed a small sigh, like a child curling into her mother's arms after a long day, and fell asleep. Ben Adamah bathed her body with the water we'd been carrying, and cut strips from his own robe to bind the worst of her wounds—or perhaps to prevent her unraveling again. Who can say what things are possible? Last, he wrapped her in the ruin of his robe and took her hand in his, settling down to wait beside her while she slept.

But these things all happened a full turn of seasons ago. I recall them now only because she has touched our lives again.

Ben Adamah told me that the young woman had been the victim of an angry mob hurling stones at her, punishing her for violating one of their many laws—and that her own husband had probably been the one to rouse their fury. I was still new to the cruelties of humankind then, and this was my first meeting with the human frenzy that feeds on the lifeblood of its own kind. For a long time I didn't understand it. How could I? As a cat, I knew nothing of such evil.

By the time she awakened, the wildfire had burnt itself out. The son of Earth gave her a new name then: Eliana, because the One had answered her prayers. Finally, after making arrangements for the three disciples to bring her safely to his friend Eli in Cana, ben Adamah and I went into the wilderness for a time of prayer. That was the last I heard of her—except for the warm mantle she sent to ben Adamah, woven with her own hands—until Eli's message arrived.

A chill wind whipped ben Adamah's robes with the promise of bitter cold to come as we left the shelter of Capernaum's streets and set out on the road to Acco. I'd endured the disciples' complaints for days, until I wished I could sink my teeth into their tongues. The people of Acco were treacherous, the men insisted, and they hated Jews. We'd be murdered as we slept. Slavers would snare us in their nets. On and on they grumbled—all but Maryam. The son of Earth listened patiently, but held to his plan: he would travel first to Acco and then up the coast to Tyre and Sidon, taking advantage of the mild coastal winter to preach to the Phoenicians. The others could come or not, as they chose. If their fears saddened him, he gave no outward sign, but I could sense his disappointment. Now, as we climbed the brown hills under heavy skies, the twelve straggled along behind us, unwilling to reject ben Adamah's lead, yet making their resentment clear. Maryam walked beside him.

We weren't even out of sight of Capernaum when I heard a messenger running up behind us, his long strides eating up the distance like a bounding lion.

"Lord!" he cried out as he approached. "Please wait!"

Dropping to one knee, the young man took ben Adamah's hand in his and gasped his message out between heaving breaths. "Your friend Eli begs you to come to him. The woman Eliana whom you entrusted to his care is in danger. He fears for her life if she remains in Cana. You must not delay!"

Then the messenger dropped ben Adamah's hand and looked up into his face, his eyes pleading.

"You know Eliana, my son?" the son of Earth asked.

"I do, Lord, and I would not see her harmed, whatever the reason."

"Has word of her presence in Eli's home reached her enemies?"

"We fear it, Lord. There is little doubt."

"Then I will come. Tell Eli that I'll join him in Cana by midday tomorrow. And do not fear. All will be well."

Yet although he'd recovered his breath, the man still knelt in the road. I watched without surprise. Even a cat could lose herself in the son of Earth's eyes, slipping down into the light-filled depths of his heart. At last the messenger rose to his feet, moving awkwardly at first, but recovering his balance as his pace slowly increased, as if he recalled his errand only gradually.

So we turned back toward the caravan road that ran along the shores of the sea toward Magdala and Sepphoris. The disciples seemed cheered by our change of plans, but most still followed at a distance.

"Yeshua?" Maryam called, hurrying to catch up with ben Adamah at his quickened pace. "Who is this woman who needs your help?"

I could feel his smile as he looked at her. "You weren't with me when I met her," he agreed. "Eliana is a rare woman, Maryam. She survived being stoned long enough to crawl away to shelter—long enough for me to find her. I healed her body, but the scars in her mind and spirit needed time and gentleness, so I sent her to live with a friend in Cana, where I hoped she would be safe. I couldn't keep her with me, but I've always held her in my heart, remembering her to my Father's care."

He paused, and I could imagine the memories rising in his mind.

"She was little more than a girl, Maryam, and I sensed no evil in her, only such foolishness as a child might devise. But the path I hoped she might follow has come to an end. I must help Eli take thought for another . . . until she is strong enough to walk free."

I remembered the child's smile when she'd first opened her eyes to find a cat sitting beside her under the trees. No, there was no evil in Eliana.

"They stoned her?" Maryam murmured, and then she was silent, her steps slowing until she lagged behind all the others. Soon after that I fell asleep, lulled by the silence of the mist-bound lake and the son of Earth's rapid stride.

His sudden swing away from the main road woke me from a pleasant dream of Maryam's house, with its warm hearth and soft beds. The dream was shattered against the rocky ledges of the small track the son of Earth followed now . . . up the gorge and away from Magdala. Instead of guiding us to Maryam's warm house, he'd chosen to spend a miserable night tramping among Arbel's rugged cliffs. He didn't even apologize.

Lake fog mingled with the clouds shrouding the cliff tops until I could hardly see the rocks along our way. Worse, the higher we climbed, the less like mist and the more like rain the clouds became. At length the humans were slogging through running water, heads bent beneath a heavy downpour. Even tucked against ben Adamah's breast, I was cold and damp. I wanted to stop. I growled my displeasure, but the only response I got was a soft chuckle.

We walked all night. Hardly anyone spoke. I grumbled now and then in pointless protest, and tried to sleep. Finally, as the low-hanging clouds began to brighten with a dull dawn, the son of Earth turned off the highway, toward Cana. In the growing light I began to see familiar landmarks, and then, at last, the walls enclosing Eli's house and garden.

Journey's end! At least I wouldn't be expected to greet our hosts. I abandoned the humans and slunk off to find a snug corner for a nap.

Except for several women going about their own business, the courtyard was empty when I emerged from my storeroom. I couldn't tell for sure how far the day had advanced, since the same heavy clouds still hung over the hillside, but I sensed that the sun had climbed almost to its full rising. With my belly protesting breakfast's long delay, I wandered into the garden, where a fat ground squirrel grown slow and foolish with the approach of winter practically stumbled under my claws. By the time I finished meal and bath, angry voices were drifting from the house. I stretched and wandered inside to see what trouble had been brewing in my absence.

The voices led me to a room painted to resemble a summer garden and furnished with fine wooden furniture. The son of Earth sat on a chair close to his friend Eli, while Simon, James, and John leaned against the wall behind them. I saw Maryam sitting on a couch with Eli's young wife Rachel, who looked as pleased with married life as she'd been with her wedding . . . if you didn't count the look of delicate distaste flitting across her face, apparently in response to an older female and a young male facing her across the room. Eliana was nowhere to be seen.

Not knowing these two guests' feelings about cats (chances were good that they'd consider me an abomination), I crept into the room and crouched in the shadows behind their chairs. I could see little of the male, but the old female reminded me of a desert vulture, with her wrinkled yellow skin and stringy grey hair barely visible beneath an astonishing number of coins and jewels dangling over her forehead. The regular tremors that shook her body set her heavy gold bracelets clinking in time with her headdress, and a faint odor of decay drifted into the closed space under her chair. I hissed softly and moved as far away from her as possible without calling attention to myself.

I couldn't help noticing that her shimmering robes merely mocked her age as they slid away from the talon-like hands clutching the chair. Why would such a one choose the soft silks of a young woman? I'd met aged humans often enough, and like the Grandmothers, the wisdom of years often lay in their eyes. But this woman repelled me. Something unclean dwelt here. I could feel the prickling along my spine as my hackles started to rise. From the male I felt nothing. If these were Eliana's enemies, then perhaps ben Adamah should rethink his idea about whose hand lay behind her attack.

But the old woman was speaking now, and I forced myself to listen.

"You can't deceive me, Eli! I know you've hidden her here. I call upon the Holy One of Israel as my witness! Return her to us for the justice we are owed!"

The woman *did* hiss like a vulture, but it seemed due more to the absence of teeth than to a vulture's beak. I could see flecks of spittle beginning to spot her fine robe.

Eli leaned forward, one hand on his knee, and replied mildly. "Shabtit, mother of Aner, I must ask you to calm yourself. I've told you already that there is no one by the name of Dena in my house. If you have nothing else to say to me, then our conversation is at an end. My patience has its limits."

I cocked an ear at Eli, impressed by his calm. He was a human male of ben Adamah's age, much the same as my friend in height and bearing. Before this day, I'd encountered him only as an ordinary man engrossed in his own wedding. Now I perceived the merchant whose shrewd judgments had amassed the fortune that had built this house.

But Shabtit wasn't finished.

"And you!" she seethed, turning toward Rachel. "How can you pretend that the embroidery on that travelling cloak is the work of your hands? How would you, a village wife, know the secrets of Phoenician needlework? I tell you, I know this wanton's stitching like my own! You will return her to me!"

"Do you insult me as well as my lord?" the young wife asked softly, looking up from her folded hands with barely concealed anger. "Why should I pretend anything to you, mother of Aner? I know little of you, and you know even less of me. Have you ever sat with me and my women as we stitch and weave? When have we ever shared our handwork with you? Is this poor dead girl the only seamstress in all the Galilee who can embroider a fine Phoenician border?"

Then after a pause, she spoke again as she started to rise. "Your rudeness is not welcome in my home."

"Oh, no, neither of you will dismiss me so easily!" Shabtit raged.

Her son Aner said nothing. He only sat rigid in his chair, fists clenched at his sides.

"I will have what is mine!" she shrilled. "You'll see! I'll have the Sanhedrin down on your heads! You'll be shamed in the marketplace . . ."

Ben Adamah's voice cut across her abuse, sharp as flint. "Have you not already had what is due you, woman?" he asked. "Do you not have the child's bride price, and her parents' legacy? Have you not already sold her land and the kilns her father left her, without yielding her any profit from their sale? And with all else gone, have you not stolen her good name and even her life as well?"

There was absolute silence in the room, until the son of Earth spoke again.

"Take care, woman, how you call upon the Holy One to witness what you deserve!"

Then Simon pushed away from the wall, walked across the room and stopped before the two guests, scowling down at them like some rustic angel of destruction. I remembered then that he had cared for Eliana during her journey to Eli's house.

Cat tales and purple snails

Apparently ben Adamah found this pair as repellant as I, which was unusual. I was accustomed to his sadness when confronting cruel humans, and sometimes his anger as well. But his voice had cracked like a whip across this woman's rage, silencing her with a cold distaste I'd not often seen in him. In fact, the only time I could remember hearing anything like it was when he spoke to the evil spirit binding the man in Capernaum's synagogue . . .

2

Reminder of Grace

Wind on Water speaks

I leapt up onto ben Adamah's shoulder as Rachel led the way to Eliana's room. No one else went with us. The others had followed a servant to the large room set aside for visiting travelers.

It seemed to me that of all the sleeping chambers in Eli's house, Eliana's must be the most private. Set in a corner at the end of a long dark hall, her room was hidden from all but those intimately familiar with the house. Whoever had chosen her room had done well by her. The young female I remembered wouldn't easily welcome the closeness of strangers, nor relax without a sheltered den of her own where she could feel safe . . . at least not for a while.

Rachel called softly from outside the room, knocked, and then pushed the door open. "The teacher has come, Eliana," she smiled, and then stood aside.

Eliana spun away from a loom where she'd been weaving with an older woman, her sudden movement setting the small clay weights at the bottom dancing. I wouldn't have recognized her. Of course, the bloody bruises and cuts had healed, leaving only faint lines to mark their passing. I wasn't even sure that I saw lines at all; they were more like faint traces of light leaking out from within. She was taller than I'd remembered, too . . . which was nonsense, since I'd never seen her on her feet. Mostly her face confused me: even I, a cat with limited appreciation for human beauty, could see that this young woman would be difficult to hide. I dimly remembered a child's plump features from our first meeting, but that child had vanished. Her face had molded itself to her bones, taking on the contours she would bear all her adult life. I couldn't say what struck me so, but I knew with some greater-than-feline instinct that this young woman was lovely beyond the wont of human females. Perhaps the Mother's own grace had touched her in recompense for her suffering. No doubt ben Adamah would know.

But Eliana only had eyes for the son of Earth. No more than an instant passed after she'd turned toward us before she fell to her knees, her hands stretched toward him—hands that carried no sign of the ruin visited upon them.

"My Lord," she whispered.

The son of Earth squatted on the floor facing her, taking her hands in his. I jumped down and wandered over to the loom to watch the swaying threads settle back into stillness. I'd seen looms before, but only from a distance. My toes itched with the possibilities that leapt to mind.

"All is well, my daughter," I heard ben Adamah say. "You're safe, and no one will harm you."

Then he rose to his feet, pulling her with him. The other woman bustled from the room, leaving us alone, although I could sense Rachel hovering in the hall.

Ben Adamah led Eliana to a bench along one wall and gestured for her to sit beside him. Now that her shock had worn off, she was drawing into herself, overwhelmed with shyness. She sat and stared at her white-knuckled hands, without even a sidelong glance at the son of Earth. The silence lengthened. I decided it was time to introduce myself, since apparently no one else was going to. I sauntered across the room and stopped just in front of her feet, composing myself neatly, my tail curled around my toes. Then I stared.

It always works. Humans have *no* resistance. Even the smallest kitten can stare down an ordinary human, and Eliana was no exception. I drew her gaze like a lodestone draws an iron nail. As I watched, her eyes grew large and the beginnings of a smile appeared.

"I remember you!" she cried. "I thought you were just a dream. I had so many . . ." Her voice slowed and lost its delight as other memories rose into her mind.

"Eliana?" I whispered, and rose up onto my haunches, placing one paw lightly on her knee.

She looked around the room, seeking the source of the voice. Ben Adamah smiled and raised his eyebrows at me.

"It's me . . . Mari," I said. *"The cat,"* I added impatiently when she failed to understand. "The one you call Teacher gave me the gift of human speech."

For a moment I feared she would panic like Maryam when we'd first talked, but then she looked at ben Adamah, and he nodded and smiled. She reached out a shaking hand to touch my shoulder. Slowly she smiled as well, but hesitantly.

"Here, Mari," ben Adamah laughed, "come sit on my lap, where Eliana can see you."

I thought she could see me perfectly well where I was, but the son of Earth always had his reasons. I jumped into his lap and settled myself comfortably.

"You see, Eliana, Mari is my very good friend. She travels with me everywhere, in a sling under my robe. No one notices her there, and she can come and go as she pleases."

I purred loudly, happy to be the center of his attention for as long as it lasted.

He laughed again, and I felt his body shake. "She makes that noise when she's happy. It's called purring. And," he added, "she'll always give you fair warning if she wants to be left alone, so you needn't fear offending her. Cats are like little lions. They're direct—and they can be very fierce—but only when they feel angry or threatened. Or perhaps if you're a mouse, and dinnertime is near."

I felt Eliana's hand creep over to stroke my back, and I purred louder. Several pleasant moments passed before her hand strayed to a fold of ben Adamah's mantle. She fingered the wool lightly and smiled up at him.

"You were pleased with my gift, Lord?" she whispered. "The robe has served you well?"

"The kindness woven into it has kept me warm through many a cold night, child," he smiled. "You're a very gifted weaver, Eliana. And I see that your skill with a needle is no less."

He smiled as he nodded at Eliana's own robe, its edges bordered with brilliant woven bands, embroidered flowers trailing across it in rows of wavering vines, almost as if the stitching had been added to disguise mended tears. I leaned out of his lap to look more closely at her robe, sniffing the worn fabric deeply. I knew this mantle! Surely it was ben Adamah's own, the one he had cut to bind Eliana's wounds, then wrapped around her to protect her from the cold!

She ducked and tried to hide her face, but the son of Earth caught her chin and lifted it up. "You did well, Eliana," he smiled. "You've transformed an evil memory into a thing of beauty and a reminder of grace. I'm pleased that my robe brought you comfort."

I could see the anxiety building in Eliana's breast, threatening to send her flying out the door . . . although I wasn't sure why. But I needn't have worried: the son of Earth was already reaching out to soothe her.

"Now, daughter," he said in a tone of firm authority, "tell me about your life. Are you happy here with Eli and Rachel?"

She met his eyes uncertainly, but whatever she saw there reassured her.

"Oh, yes," she smiled, and color began to spread back across her cheeks. "Rachel has been so kind to me, and Eli as well! Not everyone would welcome an orphaned stranger into their home," she added.

I licked her hand, and she jumped with surprise. "Your little tongue could card wool, it's so rough!" she laughed.

"Eliana." He spoke her name like a blessing. "Do you remember what I told you when I gave you your name?"

"Yes, Lord," she whispered. "You said it was mine because the One had answered my prayer."

"And do you recall what that prayer was, child? What happened to you before we met? Shall we look at it together?"

The sudden panic in her eyes reminded me of a flock of doves beating their wings in a desperate frenzy to raise their heavy bodies into the air and out of the reach of a predator's claws.

"Hush, child," ben Adamah whispered, laying his hand gently over hers. "Don't be afraid. You're safe now."

Her confusion was plain, but as I watched, the fear sank away as if it had never been. She smiled at him like a trusting child, the tense cords in her neck relaxed, and her eyes grew calm. *She's forgotten!* I marveled. *She's forgotten that she was stoned.*

Was it possible? She remembered the son of Earth—she even remembered me—but the rest was lost. Yet I could see that the threat of remembering hung over her head like a boulder suspended from a fragile thread. Part of her knew the horror was there, but she was unable to admit its presence, or to flee from it. What would happen if the thread unraveled and the memories broke over her?

"Ben Adamah?" I whispered.

"Wait, little leopard," was all he said.

Cat tales and purple snails

Later that evening, Ben Adamah told me that Eliana just needed time, that once she realized her own strength, the memories would return. Until then, the One would hold them for her in a small pouch spun of spider's silk. I think he might have been making up that last part.

But he knew that I found Eliana's lapse disturbing. She'd mislaid a chunk of her life, a part of who she was. What if she never got it back? Would her mind be pocked with empty holes where memories used to be? More than a few times while we were in Cana, I dreamed that I walked through a wilderness riddled with black pits echoing with nothingness, waiting to swallow me up if I missed a step.

Even cats have nightmares.

3

Memories

Wind on Water speaks

"How much does she remember, Eli?" the son of Earth asked.

"Almost nothing," Eli replied.

The rest of our company had gone to their beds, and we three sat alone beside the banked embers of the cooking fire in the courtyard. I didn't understand. I merely watched the sky from the safety of ben Adamah's lap as the north wind drove the clouds before it, carrying the chill tang of forested mountains and far deserts. The solitary keening of a high-flying bird only deepened the silence.

"I thought from what Simon said when he first brought her here that she remembered everything, and would be her normal self—whatever that may have been—quickly. But when she awoke the next morning, she remembered nothing, at least nothing to do with the stoning. I've been able to put a rough story together from what she's said and from the gossip in Sepphoris, but you heard Shabtit's version . . . and I know that Eliana is no more capable of adultery than my own Rachel!"

Ben Adamah shook his head. "I'm not surprised, my friend. Eliana wanted to die when I found her. I healed her body and soothed her spirit, but I could tell that her mind was very nearly shattered.

I had hoped that time and love might heal that as well, but if she won't allow me to touch the scar, I can't help her."

He sighed deeply. "Tell me as much as you know, Eli."

Eli ran his fingers through his hair, and then rose to his feet, facing away from us out into the night. I curled more tightly into ben Adamah's lap and prepared to listen.

"Eliana remembers nothing of her marriage, or even her betrothal. But she's always struggling to cover the gaps in her mind, trying to offer plausible explanations—so her versions of the story keep shifting."

He sighed again.

"She was only a child, Yeshua!" he exclaimed. "How will she ever come to terms with this?"

He expected no answer, and the son of Earth offered none. Eli turned and started pacing back and forth in front of the fire.

"Her grandparents were respected weavers of fine linen and wool, the best in Sepphoris, and Eliana's mother Sarah had already begun to learn the craft when the Romans came. Fortunately the grandparents weren't among the rebels in the uprising, so when the Romans razed Sepphoris, the grandparents weren't killed, but they were taken off to Acco in chains with the rest of the city's people to be sold as slaves. I'm not sure how Eliana's mother escaped. Sarah told Eliana she hid in the woods, but she was just a child, maybe seven or eight, and I suspect the Romans just didn't bother with her. After all, they were teaching us a lesson, not setting up a slave market. Once Eliana came to us, I tried to find out what had happened to her grandparents, but too much time had passed.

"Anyway, a kindly woman from Shikhin—you know, the small potters' village near Sepphoris—found Sarah and took her in. From what I can tell, she treated her like a daughter, and taught her the skills she needed to help with their pottery workshop . . . they made oil lamps and amphorae mostly, for shipping oil and wine. They had their own clay pit, and kilns and workshops. It was a good business, and they made good pots. Well, Eliana's mother still did her weaving and embroidery when she could, and Asella, the potter woman, was pleased to have the cloth she wove.

"When Sarah grew up, she married Asella's son Eshkol, and eventually they ran the pottery workshop together. Eliana was their only child and heir."

Eli paused again as if to gather his thoughts.

"Do you remember, Yeshua, when the tetrarch moved his capital to Sepphoris after the uprising? And merchants came from all around to set up business in the new capital?"

Ben Adamah nodded, and Eli came back and resumed his seat.

"Well, Shabtit and her husband were among those new merchants. They dealt in oil and wine. They were among Eshkol's best customers, so when they kept pressing him to agree to a marriage between their son Aner and Eliana, Eshkol finally agreed. Eliana was twelve. Maybe if her parents had known them better they wouldn't have agreed. You saw Shabtit. Her husband was much the same. They were greedy and grasping, and resentful that the capital had moved off to Tiberius almost as soon as they came to Sepphoris. But they betrothed Eliana to Aner, and eventually the marriage was consummated.

"Then maybe a year later, we had a small earthquake, nothing serious. It caused some fires, and a few old walls collapsed. But Eliana's parents were firing amphorae that day, and the fire pit under the big kiln was blazing. When the ground began to shake, stacks of wood and brush were lying all around, ready to feed the fire. From what Eliana told us, the kiln was probably old. It had been there as long as she could remember . . . made of bricks, and bound with iron bands to keep it secure. Just an ordinary kiln. The earthquake must have shaken the bricks loose. Or maybe the bands slipped. But it burst apart, hot bricks and jugs tumbled everywhere, sparks went flying up from the pit, and the piles of brush caught fire. Before anyone could do anything, fire had spread to the potter's shed and the storage buildings. No one was sure how it happened, but her parents were trying to put out the fire in the building where the amphorae were stored when the roof and shelves collapsed on top of them. Flames roared up, and the men were afraid to go in after them. By the time the fire burned itself out, her parents were dead and all the buildings were gone, even their home.

"Eliana remembers the fire—or she remembers how it was described to her, since she wasn't actually there—and she believes that we took her in afterwards. Perhaps she confused the fire that killed her parents with the fire burning through the mountains when you found her."

He shrugged and looked down at his hands. "We let her believe it. Why not? But from the little I can glean from friends in Sepphoris, the fire was the beginning of the end for Eliana. She grieved terribly for her parents, and withdrew into herself, shutting out Shabtit and Aner almost altogether.

"I was told that Shabtit had pushed for Aner's marriage to Eliana because they knew she'd inherit the workshop when her parents died, bringing wealth and prestige to Shabtit's family. But when the workshop burned, almost everything but the land and the clay pit was destroyed, and suddenly Eliana was hardly more than a pauper. Shabtit might sell her weaving and embroidery for a nice profit from time to time, but it wasn't enough to satisfy her.

"So Aner sold Eliana's property to another potter in Shikhin, and as you know, never gave Eliana any of the proceeds. It was right after that that the rumors started in Sepphoris about Eliana's loose ways, and her unfaithfulness to Aner.

"I believe Shabtit used Eliana's grief and withdrawal as an excuse to point at her and say that she was disappearing all the time, no one knew where."

I could hear Eli's teeth grinding.

"I don't actually know if Aner knew what was happening or not. But the whole thing blew up in a very unlikely way. On the day before the Shabbat of the Blowing of Horns one of the new merchants who had come to Sepphoris about the same time as Shabtit—a weaver, like Eliana's grandparents—came screaming out of his workshop, saying that he'd caught a whore plying her trade among his bolts of cloth. A crowd gathered, as they will, and Aner was called. The woman the merchant dragged out to the street was Eliana (the man had locked her in a storeroom). Then Aner and the mob took her out and stoned her."

Eli's breathing was growing ragged, his words pressured and harsh. I could feel his rage rising.

"Rachel heard through some of her women that Eliana had gone to the shop that day on an errand for Shabtit, and had been looking at a new loom in a room by herself when the trouble started. And the men who were supposedly with her mysteriously disappeared before anyone but the merchant could speak to them.

"Shabtit arranged it, Yeshua! I have no doubt. Eliana was no use to her anymore. She was penniless, with no family to defend her. She hadn't borne Aner a child yet. Shabtit decided Aner could do better. So she set it up. Only you came along, and Eliana lived.

"What makes it worse is that it was a simple gift of love that betrayed her presence with us here, Yeshua."

Eli shrank into himself with these words.

"She wove a cloak for Rachel as a gift for the baby's birth, and embroidered a band of flowers all around the edges. Rachel wore it when we took the baby to the priest for his circumcision. Apparently Shabtit saw it and recognized Eliana's work. Rachel had heard that

Shabtit had always been jealous of Eliana's skill. The woman has eyes like a vulture."

I blinked in surprise.

With that last remark, Eli finished his story. He slumped down on his seat, his face in his hands. But when the son of Earth didn't speak immediately, Eli surged to his feet again.

"How do you keep from hating, Yeshua?"

His body was vibrating with the rage he struggled to subdue.

"You know I do my best to follow the law and the prophets, but this pair tempts me to murder!"

He hunched over, wrapping his arms around his chest, his face drawn with worry.

"They come into my house demanding justice, Yeshua! *Justice*! Oh, my friend, how I wish I might give it to them!

"I thought I could never love Eliana more than I did when she first came to us—she was so sweet and frightened, like a baby hedgehog . . ."

He shrugged and laughed at his own words. I tried to fit his image to the human I'd seen, without success. Eliana was no hedgehog.

"But then my son was born," he went on, "and somehow my heart gathered her in with little Sameus, as if she were truly mine, and my love kept on growing."

He stopped again, his eyes now searching the night sky.

"That's when those two appeared at my gate with their tongues dripping lies and venom . . . And I understood how a man might kill in anger. When I don't guard my thoughts, Yeshua, I imagine Sameus' tiny body falling beneath that rain of stones along with Eliana's, and I find my feet already at the door, ready to carry me to Sepphoris to wreak bloody vengeance on Shabtit and her vile whelp."

His breath rushed out of him in an angry wave. "You see, Yeshua? Even as I confess my hate to you it overwhelms me again!"

When the son of Earth spoke at last, he reached out and gripped Eli's hands, his eyes full of peace. "I hope you won't have to face anything like this again in your life, Eli. But let me answer your first question before we speak of that: 'How do I keep from hating?'"

"I don't hate because the One has shared his love for humankind with me . . . all humankind: I feel his love for his children, like yours for Eliana and Sameus. In each poor twisted human wreck I see the child who was, and I grieve for their suffering. Love drives out any possibility of hate. Each time I touch my father's sad children, I feel his pain, pain as bitter as your own hate . . . except his pain is born of love; it doesn't warp and ruin those who feel it.

"But Shabtit and Aner . . . even I am hard-pressed to care for them, my friend. I'm sure you noticed the anger that darkened my words when I spoke to them. Not even a parent could look with love at a child's empty husk, eaten out from within by evil, until nothing but illusion remains. Shabtit chose to yield herself to greed and tyranny long ago; the human child she was is long gone. And what chance did her son have beneath the lash of such a mother? No, all I see looking out from their eyes is the evil that consumed them . . . not even a tattered remnant of humanity remains. Still, who can plumb the depths of the One's mercy? All times are in his hand.

"Your hate, Eli, is another matter. Although it has its roots in righteousness, and is not wholly evil, the result will be the same if you allow it to keep burning. For a fire must have fuel, and what fuel does hate feed upon if not the spirit of the one who hates? You're building a pyre and binding yourself upon it with your own hands, fueling your own agony with the hate you nurture."

Eli was staring at the son of Earth with horror. "Yeshua, what must I do to escape this trap?" his voice rasped out.

Ben Adamah held his friend's eyes with his own, as if calling him across the vast depths of space, and said, "The answer is always love, Eli: your love for the One and for his creation; your love for your family and for yourself. Love is at the heart of all healing. See the One's love in my care for you. Look and know the Creator's pain as you confront your own corruption. Is your hate worth the price we will all pay? What of Rachel and Sameus? Human darkness carries contagion on its wings. Would you bring this evil home to them?

"You're a man who loves freely and without fear, Eli. Don't let your passion blind you now: hate never serves love—it only destroys. If loving Shabtit is beyond your ability, then turn your back, and walk away, always keeping your eyes on the One. You know that Shabtit will never accept your love; there's no sin in recognizing that. Don't throw your pearls before swine, my friend, where they will only be trampled into the slime. Let it go."

The affection uniting the son of Earth with his friend burned in the night like a steady flame, warming me in its glow. In time the intensity faded, and a companionable silence returned.

"It is Eliana whose hate concerns me, Eli," the son of Earth said at last. "Rage cripples her spirit. Her mind may not remember, but her heart has not forgotten . . . That she should have been so betrayed by those she trusted is a burning agony to her—one she isn't yet strong enough to bear. So by the One's grace, those memories wait in the shadows for a day when she stands in her own strength. But until she remembers her pain, I cannot help her heal."

Neither of the two friends had anything more to say after that. We went to bed at last.

Cat tales and purple snails

Hate: the son of Earth had wrestled with it himself through more than one bitter night. Maybe the hardest time came after the news of his cousin John's beheading. If I hadn't been in my sling, I might have been left behind, so abruptly did he quit the disciples' circle. We were already in a night fisherman's small boat, well across some dark inlet of the Galilee's great sea before I heard the disciples' first cries from the shore.

Ben Adamah didn't speak until we'd climbed high onto a desolate hilltop above the lake, and then his words were a torment to us both. I'd never felt such anguish in his breast before. Almost he repented of his refusal to claim power in the world, so furiously did his anger rage against John's murderers. But his fury was itself a prayer, and as the hours passed even I could feel the One's presence falling like gentle rain on his fury, leaving only grief and exhausted peace in its place.

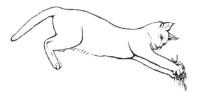

4

Names

Wind on Water speaks

*E*li's face paled the next day when a servant brought the news: Aner had been seriously wounded in an accident, and Shabtit was already wailing at her gates. I guessed that Eli feared he'd ill-wished them. Such notions were among the more peculiar human ideas I'd come across; the son of Earth abhorred them.

The servant told us—with many dramatic pauses and grotesque expressions—that after Shabtit and Aner had left Eli's house, they'd gone to meet the last autumn caravan passing through Sepphoris for Ammon. Aner was loading amphorae filled with olive oil and wine onto the resentful camels when he wandered too close to one of the beasts—and the camel turned on him and nearly tore his arm off. According to the caravan leader, Aner had whipped that same camel needlessly the year before when the jugs in its load had arrived cracked, with their contents drained away.

"Camels never forget a cruel man," the driver confided to the crowd drawn by Aner's cries. "They have the patience of the desert. They may bide their time, but they always take their revenge."

Each day Eli's servants brought new reports of Aner's suffering. His arm was swollen and inflamed. He screamed aloud, caught up in the terror of waking nightmares. His body rejected any food he managed to swallow. Fever burned in his flesh, and his breath grew rapid and shallow.

I kept expecting Shabtit to send for the son of Earth, begging him to heal her son, but no messenger came to our door. And if ben Adamah was listening for footsteps that never came, he said nothing.

After a few days, Aner died, leaving Eliana a widow.

"Where shall we send her, Yeshua?" Eli asked.

Eli and the son of Earth were sitting together in the sun on Eli's roof the day after Aner's funeral. None of us had gone to pay our respects.

"I have in mind to take her with me to the coast," ben Adamah said slowly. "Shabtit will not let this matter rest, Eli. Once her grief grows less crippling, she'll seek someone to blame for her son's death, and who is she more likely to choose than Eliana, no matter how absurd the accusation? No, we must find some place of safety that lies beyond her reach, where Eliana can be free from fear."

"But the coast, Yeshua? Hardly any Jews live there at all! The cities are gentile entirely—Phoenicians and Romans. The Holy One of Israel is scorned among them. And if we hid her with one of the few Jews I know there, word would reach Shabtit's ears even before I returned from the journey."

The son of Earth stood and joined me at the roof's edge. Together we looked out over the olive groves, watching their branches rustle with unseen harvesters.

"Do you have any contacts with gentile textile merchants of good character, my friend?" he asked at length. "In Acco, perhaps . . . someone who might accept her and value her skills? I know you've already spoken to her about going away to learn her craft with a master weaver. She might be safer in a gentile workshop . . . although I'd choose that course only as a last resort."

Eli's brows rose in consternation, but I could see that ben Adamah's idea was nudging its way past his original objections.

"Let me think on this, Yeshua. I'll need to send messages to Acco to make inquiries—quietly—even if I don't go myself. Give me a few days."

"Eliana!" Eli's voice came echoing down the hall.

She was weaving at her loom, while I worked at spinning thread. I'd watched enough women doing it in my life, and Eliana had given me a fluffy wad of wool on a forked stick to experiment with. How hard could it be? Snag the wool with my claws, chase it around the floor a few times, pull it out thin, and then snag some more. Eliana seemed pleased with my efforts. She was smiling a lot.

"Eliana!" Eli called again, now from just beyond the door. "How would you like to weave purple robes for the emperor?"

Then he was bursting into the room, smiling hugely. Rachel and the son of Earth followed close behind. I squirmed backward into a corner, shaking my paws to unhook the wool. Getting odd bits disentangled from my legs and tail took more effort than I would've liked, but no one noticed. Finally I sat down and curled my tail around my paws, prepared to listen to these new developments.

"I heard back from a purple merchant who says he'd be pleased to train you!" Eli beamed.

Eliana seemed to shrink into herself as Eli spoke, her hands straying toward the familiar touch of her loom.

"You know your skill is too extraordinary to waste here in Cana, weaving clothes for a merchant's family!" Eli exclaimed. "Well, I just heard back from a friend in Acco named Ebed Ubasti. He'll welcome you into his home as one of his family, and they'll teach you things you could never learn here—not even in Sepphoris. I know him and his daughters well. They're gentiles, but kindly people, with an immensely successful business in dying and weaving. His cloth is sought after all across the empire. Not even the dyers of Tyre and Sidon can match the richness of his purple! To be accepted as an apprentice with such a man is high honor indeed!"

"Ebed *Ubasti*?" Eliana repeated in a small voice. "I don't know the name Ubasti. *Whom* is he servant of?"

The son of Earth laughed, and we all turned toward him in surprise.

"This merchant is named for Bast, the great cat goddess of Egypt," ben Adamah smiled. "Mari's many times great grandmother, Daughter of Fire, who traveled with me when I was very young, was once a sacred cat at Bast's temple in Bubastis.[2] I suspect that this weaver chose his name for himself, because Bast has all but vanished from the Phoenician coast. Perhaps your friend visited her temple in Egypt, Eli. Her cult is powerful there—as once it was along these shores.

I looked at ben Adamah oddly. That curious bit of family history was still strange to me, although a year had turned since I first heard the tale.[3]

Eliana's soft voice broke into my thoughts. "I would feel strange living in a gentile house, sharing my bread with worshippers of strange gods. Is this truly your wish, Teacher?"

"Ah, child, wait! We haven't finished explaining! According to Eli, this weaver's father bought a slave many years ago—a devout widow from Sepphoris named Tirzah, enslaved by the same Romans who carried off your grandparents. She still makes her home with the

---

[2] See *A Cat Out of Egypt*.

[3] See *The Cats of Rekem*, pp. 21-23.

weaver, where she is beloved of all, both for her ability as a weaver and for her kindness. According to Eli, she lives as a widowed sister might, under the merchant's protection, but in her own small house. She has invited you to share her home. She's blind now, and doesn't go far from her own hearth, but she'll be delighted to pass on her skills to a daughter of her own people."

Eliana's face had brightened as the son of Earth explained these details, but fear still shadowed her eyes. "But Acco, Lord? Surely it's a cruel city, with its face set against Israel."

"Do not fear to walk among the nations, Eliana," he said. "They are children of the One just as you are. Only remember your birthright. You are a child of the One, and he will not abandon you."

"I wonder if any cats live with Ebed Ubasti?" Eliana murmured, smiling at me.

A mere paw's count of days passed between Aner's death and our departure for Acco. Eliana was quiet and anxious as the early morning mist closed behind us, hiding Eli's house from view. The small donkey sent along to carry Eliana's few possessions—and the many gifts Rachel had heaped upon her—stayed close behind her; perhaps they each found comfort in the other on the strange road. The promise of a definite goal cheered the disciples, and knowing that Eli's friends waited to welcome them eased their fears. We walked slowly on the busy highway, spinning out the time before Eliana would have to step through the gate that would sever her completely from her old life.

Ben Adamah, Simon, Eliana, Maryam, and I gathered around a campfire a little way off the road, on the edge of the Galilee's last line of low hills, where the uplands began to slope down into the plain of Acco. The other disciples sat apart at their own fire, in deference to Eliana.

The torches of a Roman outpost flared from a hill nearby, and the dim glow of a village broke the darkness between us and the mountain called Carmel. The lights of Acco glittered in the distance like a cluster of stars fallen to earth. Beyond them, I could see nothing but the empty darkness of the great ocean.

"Once more we must find you a new name, Eliana," the son of Earth said softly. "This time, we must choose a name that will fit into the Roman world."

Eliana tried to smile in answer to ben Adamah's remark, but I could see that this was a loss she hadn't expected. Already the road at her back was strewn with the ghosts of things she was leaving behind: the curve of a hill; a favorite spring; her parents' house, now ash; village streets; the laughter of women at the loom; even Rachel's chubby Sameus. All lost to her, except in memory. The skills her friends urged her to pursue came at a high cost.

"Master, why must I have a new name?" she said at last. "I don't understand."

I watched Ben Adamah closely. He was walking a difficult path here. I knew he wouldn't lie to Eliana, yet neither would he force her to confront a truth she wasn't ready to see.

"The name Eliana has served you well," he said slowly, "and it might have served you all your days if we'd been able to find a place for you in the Galilee, but I believe a new name will smooth your way in this gentile city. My heart urges me to find you a path into the Roman world, where your skills will bring glory to the One . . . and joy to you."

Eliana sighed, and then asked, "How shall we choose this new name?"

"I have an idea," he replied.

I thought he might.

"You will need a different name, but it need not be unlike your old one: *Aeliana* you shall be among Greeks and Romans, which means 'sun' or 'sunlight.' *Aeliana* sounds so much like *Eliana* as it falls upon the ear that after a while you'll hardly notice the difference. And are you not a young woman walking into the sun of a new day, lit from within and without by the light of the One's love?"

Eliana's lips trembled in the firelight, as if memories stirred in the darkness around us. The son of Earth leaned in closer before continuing.

"I also offer you another name, Eliana, a name between you and the One, a name I drew from one of my father David's psalms of praise:

> Wonderful are your works, O Lord!
> You know me through and through:
> how I was made in secret,
> and woven together in the depths of the earth . . .

"I give this name to you alone, child, a name no one has ever borne before: you are *Tirakemah*, 'God is weaving.' Speak it on your bed at night to remind yourself that the One is also a weaver, and that he has not yet finished with you. Never forget, Tirakemah: the One weaves true! Thread may seem tangled, the weft snagged and loose, but his warp is firm—and the Weaver will always gather his threads together in beauty at the end."

He was silent then, waiting for Eliana to consider her answer. I watched the firelight dance across her face, now casting it into light, now shadow. Her eyes were as fathomless as the night sky.

In a way, ben Adamah was asking her to be her own Grandmother, reaching through the invisible currents of time for a name that would bring her joy and good fortune through the years to come. What a weight lay on the givers of names! How great was the

Grandmothers' wisdom in penetrating these mysteries! I was content to have no such responsibility fall to me.

"I thank you for your gift, Yeshua ben Yosef," Eliana whispered, her eyes moist with tears. "To receive three names from your hand is grace beyond my imagining."

Cat tales and purple snails

Names seem to mean less to humans than to cats. Human kits are often given the names of dead grandparents, without regard for the kit's personality or appearance. And constantly reusing the same names means that many humans have identical names, which is confusing. Of course, special signs or blessings are sometimes recalled in a human child's name, but still these names have little to do with the young human herself.

With cats, names always point to something unique in a kit's presence. Just so, I am Wind on Water because of the way my fur ripples in a breeze. My foremother was Daughter of Fire because she defeated a lethal snake considered by many to be a demon of darkness. A cat bonded to one of ben Adamah's friends was named Lion of the Mountain because of his large mane and extraordinary size. The Grandmothers meditate carefully before naming kits. A name must have dignity and substance enough to carry a cat proudly through all her days.

I've often wondered if humans don't feel diminished by the hosts of strangers bearing their names. I was pleased that Eliana would have one all her own.

5

Ebed Ubasti

Wind on Water speaks

*E*bed Ubasti did indeed live with cats. They sunned themselves on the walls of his garden and slept in the shade of his trees. They crouched in the courtyard, eyes following the women as they prepared food. Kittens careened underfoot. I learned later that the only place cats were *not* found was in the weaving rooms. And not because the doors were closed against them: they weren't. It was simply a condition of their lives, handed down from mother to kit. The weaving rooms were the domain of humans, source of the wealth that made everyone's lives possible. Ebed Ubasti considered the cats partners in his enterprise. For their part, the cats were descendants of the sacred cats of the Lady's temple that had once stood on Acco's high hill, and they understood the discipline of forbidden spaces.

But by the time we reached the weaver's house, I was in such a panic that this new surprise merely confused me. I might have been a milk-blind kitten, for all my foresight: it hadn't occurred to me to brace myself for my first encounter with the ocean. *Ignorant cat!* I remembered the terror that had nearly flung me hissing from my sling in a frenzied attempt to escape my first glimpse of the sea of the

Galilee. And that was merely a lake, as the son of Earth had been quick to explain. I was an older, wiser cat now, veteran of many towering cities and crowded highways . . . but I'd never seen an ocean. Nor ocean-going ships. Nor Roman soldiers darkening the land like hosts of migrating birds.

The ocean stretched into forever, a featureless desert of water waiting to swallow the unwary into an even deeper abyss than the one I'd glimpsed beneath the lake of the Galilee's waves. Thank the Mother of Cats that ben Adamah had no plans to step onto one of *these* terrifying ships and cross *this* water!

Our path led us along the shore outside the city, past the harbor and into the curve of a large sandy bay, where the weaver's house sat above the dunes, overlooking a walled compound. I wanted to see where we were going, but after my first paralyzing glimpse of ships and ocean, I shifted around in my sling until I faced away from the shore, resolutely refusing to heed the ocean's growl. Following Eli's directions, ben Adamah guided us to a gate that opened toward the city. A phalanx of cats escorted us into the garden, some of them clearly aware of my presence. But before I had time even to consider the choices presented to me in this strange household, our host emerged, hands outstretched in greeting.

I breathed deeply, reaching out toward the comfort of ben Adamah's embracing calm. I felt his smile, and relaxed into the peace that flowed from his breast.

"Welcome!" the strange man cried. "Many times welcome, esteemed Teacher! Your fame flies before you! You and all your companions are my most honored guests for as long as you wish."

I studied the man closely, certain that any human who chose to live among so many cats must be unique among his fellows. His robes were costly, and arranged in the Roman fashion, but his Phoenician origin was clear in his dark skin and pointed beard. Last of all I noticed his eyes. They were sharp, yet gentle and amused, the eyes of a man one might trust. Perhaps I would like this human who shared his life with cats . . . and who built high walls around his house to block out the sight of the sea.

Finally my attention was caught and held by a nagging presence I'd ignored until now: the odor of rotting fish. I knew it well from our previous winter in Magdala, where humans brewed a noxious sauce of decaying fish for rich men's tables. This odor was less pungent, but, if possible, even stronger. I'm fond of fish, and the smell of fish, but this stench appalled even me. Perhaps the other unpleasant odors overlapping the heavy miasma of fish aggravated the offense.
I sneezed, and then looked around at the others. Maryam and Eliana wore strained expressions of polite greeting, but the twelve seemed to be in pain.

"Ah," our host sighed, looking at their faces, "I *am* sorry. The smell is something visitors always have a hard time getting used to. It's a nasty combination of the odors from the dyeing vats and the rotting purple shells down by the beach. My house is upwind of both when the wind blows from the north, but winds are variable. Still, without the dyes and the snails, we would have no work. So we're grateful to the gods for their blessings. Please, come into the house. The odor will be less once we're inside with a fire in the hearth."

He stretched out his hands again, this time to direct us into the foyer. Then we were filing into the welcoming darkness, the disciples jostling each other in their eagerness to escape the open air.

After relaxing briefly in our sleeping rooms—one for the son of Earth and me, a second for the two women, and a kind of barracks room for the twelve—we all gathered in a closed and shuttered banqueting room, where many lamps burned scented oil and a fire blazed in the hearth. A parade of what appeared to be a select group of cats followed us in, arranging themselves around the room's edges, wherever humans didn't settle. I took up my place in ben Adamah's lap, waiting for introductions. To walk into the midst of a large community of strange cats was a chancy proposition for a cat alone, especially a female of uncertain standing. But if the master of the house acknowledged me, my acceptance would be assured. Otherwise I might find myself clinging to the son of Earth like a blind kit to its mother for as long as we stayed here.

Ebed Ubasti was right about the air inside the house: the odor of fish was hardly noticeable. His smile embraced us all as we found places on the softly padded couches. Then at last he turned to Eliana—now Aeliana.

"Child, you're very welcome here. Your friend Eli has told me of your skill with a loom and needle. After we've all spoken together, there will be time for you to settle in. But for now, please tell me what we should call you, here in this strange Phoenician city."

He smiled warmly, as any human male might smile at his own kit. Eliana glanced shyly at the son of Earth before answering.

"I am Aeliana, sir," she murmured."

"I welcome you, Aeliana," he smiled, "and I pray that the gods will guard your steps."

He bowed ever so slightly, and I felt Eliana-Aeliana relax.

"I'll introduce you to Tirzah soon," he added, "but for now she asks to be excused. Her joints are aching today, and she'd prefer to greet you at her best. Perhaps tomorrow."

"And now," he smiled again as he turned back to the son of Earth, "to a matter of the most pressing urgency!"

He looked straight at me. I merely blinked and stared at him through slitted lids.

"Rabbi, you have an unexpected—and very welcome—companion of the bosom." He chuckled at his own joke and continued. "Will you introduce her to us?"

Ben Adamah looked around at the assembled cats and inclined his head. "This is a young female descended in a direct line from the Great Cat Who Is Bast, she who rules in the temple of Bast in Bubastis. My friend's name among her own kind is Wind on Water, but among humans she is known as Mari. She and I have been traveling together since the days of her youth."

As soon as he stopped speaking, a low rumble filled the room, a rising flood of feline comment that swirled around like water in a rocky pool. I didn't sense hostility, but I was only half-attending: the son of Earth's recital of my family line had caught me off-guard. Descended from the Great Cat Who Is Bast? *This* he had never told me!

Ebed Ubasti's soft words broke into my reverie. "My Lord, you are an animal speaker!" he exclaimed. And then he said to me, "Noble one, be welcome among us. You will find no enemies here."

"I thank you for your courtesy, Ebed Ubasti," I replied . . . and he surged to his feet.

"You speak the language of men, noble Cat?" he asked in a voice trembling with emotion.

The son of Earth raised his hand as if to calm our host. "Yes, and yes," he smiled. "I've always been able to speak with animals, and I've shared my gift with Mari, so that she might speak clearly with me—although it's true that many cats descended from the One Cat have this gift already."

Ebed Ubasti shook his head as if he were dazed and then closed his eyes, raised his hands, and began to speak rapidly in a language I didn't understand. But since he wasn't speaking to anyone in the room, I supposed it didn't matter. He seemed to be praying.

The disciples stirred uncomfortably, but ben Adamah only waited, a slight smile on his face.

When our host finally opened his eyes, the son of Earth spoke to him in the same strange speech Ebed Ubasti had just used, except that now I could understand it.

"I have long been familiar with the Mother of Cats, Ebed Ubasti," he said. "I lived in Egypt as a young child, where my tutor was a priestess of Bast, and my closest friend a daughter of the Great Cat."

Cat tales and purple snails

The son of Earth once explained to me, early in our days together, that the One might just as easily be called "Mother" as "Father," because the important relationship was that of parent to child. He spoke of a father more often than a mother because the humans of Israel were firmly convinced that the Creator was male. Cats are equally certain that the Creator is female—that is, the Mother of Cats. Ben Adamah considered it a matter of little importance.

I was not so clear about those he called "little gods," like Bast. He seemed to regard them as small spirits of the created world, who owed their existence—and obedience—to the One. But some of these small gods were greedy for power, and sought to divert human worship to themselves, away from the Creator. They had grown dark over the ages, working evil and chaos among humankind; ben Adamah named them demons. Others, perhaps like Bast, took human worship to themselves, but only as intermediaries of the One. They used what power they had for good—or at least not for evil. These, ben Adamah tolerated more easily.

6

I Was Hungry . . .

Wind on Water speaks

After sunset a breeze began to blow off the land toward the bay, sweeping away the stink of dead shellfish, and the servants of the house opened the windows to the night air. I'd been exchanging formal compliments with the cats who'd joined our meeting, but now I was ready for dinner. Unlike the resident cats, I didn't care for dead food chopped into a bowl. It was one thing to accept treats from ben Adamah's hand, but a bell summoned these cats to a common dinner, served in bowls on the stone floor of the courtyard. I wasn't impressed. Strolling past the courtyard into the garden, I climbed a tree leaning over the top of the wall and surveyed the grassy dunes and thickets rising away from the beach. Ben Adamah's promise that the ocean breezes would blow mild, even with winter approaching, proved true. I decided to explore before seeking my dinner.

Although darkness hides little from a cat's eyes, starlight softened the ocean's terrible glare. I could sit in the darkness facing the water without feeling the panic stirred up by the ranks of brilliant marching waves. After a few moments, I crouched low and made my way toward the beach, senses alert to every smallest change in this alien landscape. In spite of the fresh breeze, the scent of the sea—and rotting snail shells—still blotted out most other smells. And with the constant whisper of the waves foaming on the sand, how could I sense danger approaching, or prey either? I felt vulnerable and off balance.

Darkness also brought a new uneasiness: a strange glow flickered in the froth of each new wave and then retreated back into the sea, leaving glittering blue sparks stranded and finally winking out on the bubbling sand. I kept a careful distance from this cold fire. I did notice that the nearer I came to the water's edge, the less I could see of the distant ocean, but I wasn't sure which left me more unsettled: the endless horizon or the risk of burning my toes in the foaming blue flames.

I was still considering this question when a long-legged shore bird came running along the beach toward me, its attention focused blindly on the sand between its toes. All thoughts of the strange fire fell away, and I tended to more practical matters.

Sometime later, dinner and bath complete, I emerged from the sandy hollow where I'd been dining.

"Hello," a small voice piped. "Who are you? You're not from the big house, are you? I've never seen you before."

I turned to study the scrawny kit who'd addressed me, applauding myself for not jumping out of my skin at the sound of her voice; I hadn't sensed her presence at all. She was small and very black. Unlike me, she showed no hint of stripes beneath her dark fur.

"No," I replied. "I'm a guest at the house with my human."

"I didn't think you could be from there!" the kitten laughed, and then spun around chasing some invisible bit of beach clutter. "Those house cats couldn't catch a runner-bird if it was dragging a broken leg! They can't hunt at all. They eat out of *bowls*," she added with disgust.

I was enjoying this bold kit's cheeky company.

"Where do you live?" I asked.

"Oh, anywhere," she shrugged. "I'm almost grown, you know, and my mother has new kits, so I take care of myself."

"What do you eat?" I asked. I was curious.

"I really like runner birds," she said wistfully. "Did you have leftovers?"

"Help yourself," I shrugged.

It had been a fat bird.

Judging from the kit's feeding frenzy, she wasn't as savvy a hunter as she wished me to think. I watched as she crunched the bones to paste, even gnawing off bits of flesh still clinging to the feathers.

"Yummm!" she purred at last, settling back on her haunches before starting to groom her fur, spitting out gobs of sand as she went along.

Once finished, she showed no signs of wanting to part company with me. Wherever I wandered, her quick footsteps pattered along behind, her unending stream of conversation assaulting my ears. Any and every thing that came to her mind rolled out on her tongue: the cats in Ebed Ubasti's house were cruel and abusive; they wandered the beach in packs and attacked the cats living wild whenever they found them; they'd even severed their ties with the Grandmothers, setting up elder females of their own in their place. This last dereliction stopped me in my tracks, and I turned to stare at my small shadow.

"Little one, surely you must be mistaken! The Grandmothers stand over us as the hand of the Mother herself! No cat would dare reject them."

She merely stared at me, her eyes full of reproach. "How do you know what happens here? You only just arrived. I told you the truth."

After that I thought she might turn away when I started off again, but the footsteps followed faithfully. I even felt vaguely guilty when I leapt up onto Abed Ubasti's wall. I glimpsed the flash of her small body crossing the sand as I slipped over the wall and dropped down into the garden.

I awoke to the growls of angry cats beneath our window, and reluctantly uncurled myself from ben Adamah's warmth to investigate. Traveling with the son of Earth, I'd lost the knack of ignoring the background noises that were part of living among other cats: I could no longer just roll over and go back to sleep. So leaping to the window ledge, I peered down into the garden. Noises indeed! At least three cats were yowling together, their voices rising and falling in anger, definitely not in love.

The warning growls escalated, and even as I looked, a large yellow male launched himself at a small black shadow pressed against my wall.

"No!" I screamed, and dove onto the brute's back, driving my claws deep through his fur to pierce the flesh beneath, biting hard into the back of his neck. I'd caught him in mid-leap, and he twisted as he fell, so that his full weight hammered me against the ground. I lay still, badly winded.

"Peace!" The word rolled like thunder from the window above. Ripples of power sang through my body, turning my muscles to jelly and emptying all thoughts of violence from my mind. Apparently ben Adamah's command was having the same effect on the other combatants: the cat on top of me slid off and lay still, while the other two collapsed in place.

I struggled to my feet and staggered toward the kitten. She was frozen into a tight ball, apparently unmoved by the son of Earth's call. After all, violence had never been on her mind.

I licked her fur, and she unrolled slightly, daring to peer over her tail with one wide eye.

"Is it over?" she squeaked.

"Mari?" the son of Earth spoke in his normal tones.

"I am well, ben Adamah. A new friend came to visit me and was set upon by the night watch."

He studied the scene below the window and then disappeared, emerging shortly from the courtyard to join us. The males slunk away into the night, but he'd already dismissed them from his mind. He knelt beside my small friend and reached out his hand.

"Kitten of purple shadows, will you let me touch you?" he murmured.

Her eyes grew huge as only a kitten's can, and she crept toward his outstretched hand. I hummed to myself, remembering my first meeting with the son of Earth. He stroked her head and then carefully picked her up and held her against his breast. She was almost small enough to sit in his hand. I could hear her purring quietly.

He turned to me and raised an eyebrow. "Well, Mari, shall we invite your new friend inside?"

"Do you have a name, little one?" the son of Earth asked after watching her bolt every scrap of food he'd brought for her breakfast. She seemed to be suffering no scruples about eating from a bowl.

She paused in her bathing and bowed low. "I am called Purple Gleaming in Shadow, mighty one. The Grandmothers just gave me my name not long ago when we celebrated the balancing of day with night.

"I was born of the eve of the longest day . . . gracious lord," she added.

"Don't call me 'mighty one,' or 'gracious lord,' purple kit. Mari calls me son of Earth, or ben Adamah. You may do the same."

The kit bowed again.

"And you don't need to bow either," he added.

She glanced sideways at me, and I laughed. "He's just teasing you."

"Oh," she said thoughtfully, and then sat up straighter. "That's alright, then," and went back to her bath.

Bath completed, she walked over to the son of Earth and sniffed his hand. She seemed to be making great strides toward overcoming her shyness of this first human she'd ever seen up close.

"Tell me, small Shadow," he said, "why did you follow Mari back here last night?"

She thought for a moment and then replied, "I was hungry, and she fed me. No one but my mother ever did that. I didn't want to be alone again."

The son of Earth nodded seriously. "You are very small to be all alone in the world. Have you no aunts, or uncles, or brothers or sisters to share your life?"

"No, mighty . . . son of Earth. The house cats came and killed my brothers and sisters, and some of the Grandmothers led the other cats further away where they could be safe. But I came back. My mother had stayed behind grieving for her other kittens. Now she has new kits, but they'll probably be killed too."

Ben Adamah was looking sharply at our little guest now, and I spoke into his thoughts. "She told me that the cats living with Ebed Ubasti have decided that they're some sort of aristocracy, far above the lowly cats of street and shore. Apparently other cats don't deserve to live. They've even rejected the Grandmothers' authority and set up females in their place. I've never heard of such a thing."

"No, Mari, Daughter of Fire would be sorely distressed. Such behavior is unacceptable for any cats, particularly for those who serve in the Mother's courts, and I'm certain that Acco's cats originally came here as temple cats of Bast . . . Yes, to reject the Grandmothers is a thing unheard of!"

He sank into his own thoughts for a time, and then rose to his feet. "Take care, Mari. Keep the kitten close, and out of the way of the others. I'll seek my father's will in this matter. Something is very wrong here."

Then he reached his hand down to the kitten and smiled. "Stay with Mari, small one. I'll send a friend to keep you entertained."

Then he checked to be sure the shutters were secure and left to join the other humans in the day's business.

I'd hardly fallen asleep on the bed, the kitten curled against my belly, when the door opened and Aeliana entered.

She stopped abruptly, hand to her mouth, eyes huge, and whispered, "Oh, it *is* a kitten!"

Cat tales and purple snails

I'd never felt the bite of ben Adamah's discipline before, and I didn't enjoy the experience. Not that I blamed him. If disabling all attack was the quickest way to rescue us from those slavering hyenas I was all for it. Still, I'd never thought about it before: what it might feel like to be one of those wild dogs he'd rescued me from . . . or one of the men he'd walked away from in Nazareth . . . or, for that matter, the waves in the lake of the Galilee (that is, if waves can feel). Each time he must have reached out and changed something that was part of us: strength? will? sight? power? It made me dizzy to think about it. I was just a cat. How could I understand?

But, wait! The son of Earth had healed me, twice. Wasn't that the same thing, only different? I'd felt him reach into . . . well, whatever I called "me," and mend what was broken, seal what was torn, ease what was hurting. Was that so different from what he did tonight? Like the difference between digging a hole in the sand—and filling it up again.

I sighed and gave it up. My head felt strange.

I wondered if the twelve got headaches when he tried to teach them. Maybe that's why they seemed to have such a hard time learning.

7

Daughter of the One

Wind on Water speaks

Aeliana hadn't been in the room for very long before Ebed Ubasti came knocking on the door to take her to meet Tirzah.

"May I bring Mari with me, Master?" she asked softly, but then added quickly, "Or perhaps Tirzah doesn't like cats?"

"Oh, never fear that in this house, daughter!" he laughed. "Tirzah will be delighted to meet Mari. I've been telling her for years that these cats can talk!

"Come, now, Tirzah is waiting for us. The Teacher will join us there if he can, as soon as he returns from his walk by the sea."

I shrugged and leapt onto Aeliana's shoulder, followed closely by the kitten. Ebed Ubasti led us across the large courtyard where the cooking was done, and into a narrow hall on the far side. At the hall's end, he stopped at a wooden door, which opened almost before he finished knocking.

At first I thought I was looking at ben Adamah's friend Keturah, so similar was this woman in age and dress—until I saw her pale milky eyes and the stout stick she leaned on as she stood in the doorway.

"Aqhat, is that you?" Her voice had the sweetness of a silver bell, although quavering and weak. "Have you brought the child?"

Aqhat? The man had a name after all!

"Yes, mother, I've brought Aeliana, and a blessing for you from far away!"

He looked at me briefly before clasping the old woman's free hand and laying it on his arm to guide her away from the door.

To my surprise, what must surely be a separate house opened up beyond the door. A roofed passage continued all around the small sun-filled courtyard where we entered. I saw that Tirzah had her own cookfire and oven, with all the usual things found in human kitchens, and storerooms as well. In one corner, stairs ran up to a flat roof, where two open rooms faced away from Ebed Ubasti's courtyard toward the Galilee's distant hills. Ebed Ubasti led us to Tirzah's small sitting room and helped her settle into a cushioned chair. Aeliana came slowly after.

"A blessing, Aqhat?" the old woman murmured, responding to Ebed Ubasti's greeting at the door. "The child at your heels is all the blessing I could wish."

She turned her blind eyes toward the courtyard where Aeliana hesitated, and stretched out her hand as if her blindness were no impediment at all.

"Come, child, and let me touch you," she smiled. "Sound and touch are all I have now. I hope you won't mind if my fingers see for my eyes."

"You honor me, my mother," Aeliana said softly, and paused to let me jump down before she entered the room and approached Tirzah.

I breathed a sigh of relief. Once I'd nearly been the cause of an old woman's heart failure while travelling unseen in ben Adamah's robes. I had no wish to test my luck with this blind woman.

Tall as she was, Aeliana dropped to her knees so that Tirzah could reach her face. Hands twisted with age and labor reached out to touch Aeliana's own.

"Your hands are strong and supple, child, truly the hands of a weaver," she smiled. "I must ask, would it distress you if I called you 'Eliana'? 'Aeliana' is so much like, and yet unlike, the familiar name 'Eliana,' that I fear I'll stutter and fumble whenever I try to speak your name. As I'm sure you know, in our speech Eliana means 'God has answered my prayer.'"

"Of course my mother," Aeliana smiled. I *have indeed come home,* I sensed her unspoken thought.

I watched while Tirzah traced Aeliana's arms and shoulders to reach her face.

"And what a lovely young woman you are!" Tirzah exclaimed, letting her fingertips move gently across Aeliana's face.

But then she drew in her breath sharply as her fingers—incredibly sensitive they must be—found the first of the tiny lines that were all that remained of Aeliana's injuries. Aeliana froze, but after a pause almost too brief to notice, Tirzah's fingers moved on . . . and touched Purple Gleaming in Shadow.

Both of us had forgotten the kitten, hidden under Aeliana's hair since we left ben Adamah's room, but I needn't have worried. Tirzah laughed aloud, and turned to Ebed Ubasti. "Is *this* your surprise, Aqhat? *Another* kitten?"

But instead of dismissing the kitten, Tirzah paused and let both hands rest on Purple Gleaming in Shadow, while her eyes closed in thought.

"A surprise indeed, Aqhat," she murmured softly, while, to my surprise, the kitten purred. "Here is a cat among a thousand, my friend, with heart and vision far beyond her small size. She will bring beauty and grace wherever she walks."

I could see the kitten's huge eyes, peering out over the old woman's hands. Then Tirzah laughed, opened her eyes, and let her hands fall back into her lap.

"Forgive me, Eliana," she smiled. "These moments come and go with me. My blind eyes sometimes see further than I did even in my youth. Is this kitten yours?"

"She is no one's, Mother, as far as I know," Aeliana replied. "She came in last night from the beach with the Teacher's cat, Mari."

"Well, whatever her future may bring, when she finally decides to, she will speak. Be careful what you say around this one—she understands!"

The temptation was overwhelming: I had to see how this intriguing woman would respond to my voice.

"Tirzah," I whispered, barely a wisp of a thought, too thin for most humans to perceive.

"Who spoke my name?" The old woman said abruptly.

Ebed Ubasti looked confused, although I thought Aeliana might have sensed something.

"No one spoke, Tirzah," he replied with awkward good cheer, as humans do with those whose advanced age has confused their wits.

"*I* spoke," I said more loudly now, so that all could hear. "My name is Mari, and I travel with the Teacher, Yeshua ben Yosef. I believe I may be the surprise your friend Aqhat mentioned."

But before Tirzah could respond, I sensed ben Adamah's presence behind me in the courtyard. At the same instant Tirzah turned her head, as a flower turns toward the warmth of the rising sun. Gripping her stick fiercely, she pushed herself to her feet and limped toward the door, oblivious to everyone else in the room. Her hands began to shake with powerful emotion as she tried to hold onto her stick. I believe she would have fallen had the son of Earth not reached out to steady her.

"My Lord," she whispered, "have you come indeed? After all these long years, have you come?"

"Yes, daughter, I am here," he replied and smiled down into her sightless eyes.

The old woman sank slowly to her knees, dropping her stick and raising her hands toward the son of Earth.

"Sing to the One a new song," she cried, her voice as sweet and true as a shepherd's flute, "you who go down to the sea, you islands, and those who dwell on them!" She paused to catch her breath, and then sang on:

> For the people who walk in darkness
> have seen a great light—
> a light shining for all the nations!
> Behold, he is come,
> the one in whom the Lord delights!
> Like a shepherd he tends his flock,
> he gathers the lambs to his bosom,
> in his pasture the calf and young lion
> lie down in peace.
> The One has satisfied my soul's hunger.
> Even now my days are complete,
> for with my own eyes I have seen his salvation!

Then before she could fall forward on her face, ben Adamah caught her hands and raised her to her feet. His joy rolled through the small house like a mighty wind, lifting our hearts as a breeze lifts the eagle's wings. Following close on the wind came the flash of power that rides the storm. Light sparked like a rainbow host of fireflies, and I could almost feel his mirth bubbling in my blood.

"Welcome, daughter of the One! Enter into the delight of your Maker!" he cried. "You have walked a long hard road to meet me here."

Tirzah's eyes swam with tears and glowed like crystal, settling at last into the clear green of a desert pool. Her limbs slowly straightened, and she rose to her full height, holding onto the son of Earth as if she would never let go.

Slowly the light faded into simple sunlight filtering through latticework. The tumbling power ebbed until it was no more than a restless tingling in the tip of my tail. Tirzah stood straight and clear-eyed before us, her gaze still lost in ben Adamah's own. At last he turned to me and held out his hand. I leapt to his shoulder and curled around his neck.

"This is my friend, Mari," he smiled to Tirzah.

Tirzah inclined her head in acknowledgement, and then looked around at Aeliana and Ebed Ubasti. She looked bemused, as if only just remembering their presence.

Aeliana's face shone with joy only a little less intense than Tirzah's own, and tears flowed unchecked down her cheeks. Ebed Ubasti looked stunned, his mouth hanging open at an unattractive angle. The kitten merely purred.

Aqhat had left to tend to his business, leaving the son of Earth and me alone with Aeliana and Tirzah, and the kitten, of course. Tirzah could hardly sit still, overflowing as she was with energy—and sight— that she'd thought lost forever. First she climbed the stairs to the roof, where she'd been unable to go for too long, exclaiming over the sad disrepair of her favorite loom, and finally bustled around her neglected pantries to see what food she might offer her guests. But ben Adamah's presence eventually reached out to calm her, and she settled beside him on a bench, releasing the frenzied gaiety and allowing her habitual peace to flow again.

"May I call you son of Earth, like Mari?" she asked at length. "It's such a lovely name!"

"You may," he smiled. "That is my name as much as any other, and more so than many."

"Little Purple has told me that she shared a sad truth with you, son of Earth. All is not well with Ebed Ubasti's workshop. The cats of this house have lost their balance. I've known many, many generations of Aqhat's cats, and it was not always so. He is a kindly man, and a lover of beauty—which has served him well in his chosen trade—but on a long-ago journey to Egypt he fell under the spell of the beautiful Bast, who once had a temple here in Acco. This he had always known, but he had never seen her in the flush of her power, surrounded by her priests and gilded temples. So he returned to us, determined to make a temple of his house, and to rescue her sacred cats from their hard lives.

"He meant nothing but good. This I know. But none of the Creator's children flourish when they are treated like gods."

Tirzah shrugged, and paused for a long moment, losing herself again in ben Adamah's presence. Then shaking herself almost like a cat, she continued.

"You see how they are. They've embraced human vices, and now they've even thrown off the yoke of the Grandmothers. Only a furtive few dare to speak to me anymore."

She sighed then and held her hand out to the kitten, idly tracing imaginary circles before the kitten's fascinated gaze.

"I've always been an animal speaker, although Aqhat doesn't know it. He dreams of speaking to one of his "sacred" cats some day . . . and all the while they've been listening to him and pretending they couldn't understand. I'm pleased that Mari has made his dream come true. But I fear for the hearts of his cats."

She paused again.

"Be careful, son of Earth. The cats in this house do not love interference. Keep Mari and little Purple close beside you."

I shivered at this unexpected warning.

Cat tales and purple snails

So much gladness in this strange house! Seeing the son of Earth meet Tirzah was like stepping straight into that deceptively tranquil pool of joy that lay in his breast, and watching it scatter through the house like a rain of liquid light. I don't think I or the others—nor the fabric of the house itself—would ever be quite the same. How had they known each other? Whence that welling up of long-anticipated joy? Neither one seemed inclined to speak of it. They only smiled.

8

Do You Remember?

Wind on Water speaks

When ben Adamah finally came back to our bedchamber, night had fallen, and the house was quiet. He had closed us in the room long since, soon after our visit to Tirzah. He said little when he returned, only opening the door and extending his hand in invitation. I leapt to his shoulder, and he bent and scooped up the kitten. Moving quickly out the door, he strode silently into the clean evening air, pausing at the gate to speak a word of restraint to any cat who might try to follow. Then he walked up the shore until a band of scrubby trees separated us from the ocean's murmur.

At last he sat down on the sandy bank of a small river and spoke into my thoughts.

"I brought you out to hunt, little leopard; I didn't want you to go alone . . . There is malice abroad in that house. Take your time, but not too much. We have an appointment to keep."

Then he leaned back, bracing himself on his arms, and studied the sky.

After watching the kitten's enthusiastic pursuit of every slightest flutter of beach grass, I drew her aside and whispered in her ear, "Why don't you wait here and keep ben Adamah company, little Shadow, while I find us both something for dinner?"

Purple Gleaming in Shadow trotted obediently to the son of Earth and settled on his lap. I crept into the tall grass with hardly a rustle.

One fat water rat later, the kitten and I were both perched on ben Adamah's shoulders, making our way through the dunes to a meeting with several female cats from Abed Ubasti's house. They had suggested our meeting place: the tumbled ruins of some forgotten building lying upshore from the harbor. Since it was officially the territory of the harbor cats, males from the house rarely ventured there.

The son of Earth sensed them before I did, and stopped a polite distance from the concealing shadows. The kitten and I jumped down to the sand beside him.

"Good health and long life to you," he said, and bowed formally. "I thank you for meeting me."

I could sense the strange females' nervousness, but ben Adamah was reaching out to them with a gentle flow of calm. One by one they slunk out into the dim light of the stars.

"You wished our help, human. Who are you that we should lend you aid—other than one who speaks with the tongue of cats?"

There was a moment's charged silence before the son of Earth responded, and when he spoke the very air crackled.

"I am one known among your people as He Who Brings Light to the Earth. The Creator of all sent me as her messenger, and I bring her words to any who will hear. I am friend to the sacred cats of the temple of Bast at Bubastis. I have never harmed one of your people, and many of them have known my love. I ask your help because evil has fallen upon your house."

Rarely did the son of Earth reveal himself as a figure of power. He preferred subtler ways into the hearts of his listeners. Perhaps cats required a different approach, I don't know. But as he spoke, a glow spread out from his body like a ring around the moon, lighting the sand and stones at his feet and reflecting back from the cats' eyes.

"Lord, we listen," the leader whispered, flattening her belly to the sand in submission.

The next night, beneath the fragile bow of a new moon, every cat from Ebed Ubasti's house had gathered on the broad expanse of sand between the house and the tide's low ebb. The males paced impatiently, some lashing their tails and cuffing stray kittens. Others shifted quietly, awaiting whatever might come. The females clustered together, shielding the younger kittens. Higher up the shore, where the first grasses clung to the sand, Ebed Ubasti stood with Tirzah and Aeliana. Purple Gleaming in Shadow and I sat beside them. The other humans stood on the walled terrace above us, watching.

At last I sensed ben Adamah approaching. Like the alien general of an impossible army he led them: rank upon rank of the cats of Acco. From markets and houses, harbor and alleys, temples and factories they came, pacing behind him soundlessly, starlight glimmering on the restless flow of their glossy coats. Immediately behind the son of Earth walked a line of elders, their power palpable: the Grandmothers of Acco, those whose authority Ebed Ubasti's cats had renounced. And spreading over the entire shore I could sense an aura of peace enclosing us all—whether we wished it or not.

Ben Adamah stopped a little way above the waves. The cats who had followed him settled onto the shore like spectators in an amphitheatre. The Grandmothers seated themselves in an arc mirroring the new moon's crescent and spanning the ranks of both house and city cats. The house cats' numbers appeared very small indeed beside ben Adamah's host.

For a few moments the son of Earth stood looking at his audience. Then he raised his hands in a gesture of welcome . . . and the ocean's blue fire gathered itself and rose from the waves in a sparkling cloud to eddy gently around him.

No sound broke the stillness. The waves foamed in silence. The only movement I could see among the cats was the faint stirring of fur in the evening breeze. Even the kittens seemed spellbound.

"My greetings to you all, cats of the Mother!" ben Adamah's voice rolled through my mind. "The children of Bast are not my usual care, but because of my long friendship with your people, the Mother of Cats has laid this night's task upon me. Indeed, I was sent to humankind alone, to recall them to the love of their Creator, but to my great grief I have seen that the evil corrupting human souls has begun to twist the Mother's beasts as well. So I stand with you tonight."

His eyes, coldly blue with the glow of seafire, scanned the faces before him.

"I call you to remember," the son of Earth said, " . . . to remember the lost days, now fallen into mist. The sacred cats of the temples of Bast were once a mighty lineage, wise beyond the wisdom of their kind. The Mother of Cats had gifted them with unique understanding of human beings so that they might call men and women back into balance when their steps faltered.

"Do you remember?" he whispered, and his whisper penetrated every ear.

"Life was simple, because you walked in the Mother's will. The mighty rhythms of nature beat clear in your blood. You were *miw*—Cat—and you bowed only to the Mother of Cats.

"In the time before time, when all things were new, the Creator stood in the listening silence and looked within. There in the glow of her own thoughts, she perceived that which would become *miw*. She smiled, and her joy bloomed like a star's light in the darkness. A faint image of *miw* shimmered and settled on her face. For the briefest of moments, she looked upon her yet unborn creature with the tender smile of a cat beholding her newborn kit. For the briefest of moments, the Creator *was Cat*. And the Earth saw and remembered. Then the seeming fell away, and the Creator's thoughts moved on.

"*Do you remember?*

"The Earth has never forgotten the many likenesses that rested on the Creator's face before they dissolved away. Such memories, formed in the days of the Earth's infancy, live still in the stones and rivers, in the air and fire. The one we know as Bast is such a living memory, a moment aglow with a spark of the Creator's fire.

"In the Lady Bast, her sacred cats knew the purity of the Mother's heart, her righteousness and mercy, her love and her justice. You once walked in the light of that knowledge.

"*But you have forgotten.*"

A sigh breathed through the silent host.

"Alas, the violence of humankind rolled over you, shattering the gracious pillars of the Lady's temple. The blind frenzy of religious zealotry mingled human blood with your own, and you were cast out upon the shores of a cruel sea.

"*Do you remember?*

"But many cats have suffered fates like yours without losing themselves. Perhaps you lost your balance when the priests brought you to these shores as strangers, far from your native land. Perhaps an unseen evil has taken root in this land. I do not know all the reasons, but I do know that as time passed, the worst of all possible fates overwhelmed some of the sacred cats of Acco: you welcomed human hate, greed, and arrogance into your hearts. You forgot who you were.

"Today you same few refuse all conversation with humankind, although it lies in your choice to accept it. For you have *not* forgotten human speech: no, some of you listen still to human thoughts, but you dissemble with blank stares and dumb tongues. You hug your knowledge to yourselves, refusing the responsibility that the One bestowed with the gift.

"*Do you remember?*

"In the beginning of days the Mother set the Grandmothers over you to remind you of your path and to be her guiding hand among you. But some of you have refused even this. Who has ever heard of such a thing, that the sacred cats of the Mother should forget the touch of her hand?"

At these words, the Grandmothers turned and faced the cats of Ebed Ubasti, their steady gazes penetrating every shrinking breast.

"Perhaps saddest of all, you who dwell in this house have taken advantage of the one human who reached out to you in kindness, the one who still remembered the beauty of She Who Is Bast. He had hoped to build a shrine to her beauty and grace, but you have created an abode of demons, preying on your own kind and lusting always for more power . . . power that will only turn to death and ashes in your mouths.

"Hear me, cats of the Mother! You were not created for power or for greed. You were not born to hate and sneer. You were formed out of the Mother's love and passion, out of her wisdom and grace, to enjoy your days in the beauty of creation, and to add your song to the harmony of life. You have exchanged the truth for a lie! And if you cannot bring your hearts to remember, you will go down into darkness as the faceless servants of nothingness.

"*Remember*, children of the One.

"I offer you my peace. If you are wise, you will embrace it."

Then he bowed his head, and walked away. The throb of the sea burst upon my ears again with sudden violence, followed by a rushing wind that swept even the odor of snails away. No glow relieved the darkness of those ocean waves.

Cat tales and purple snails

I remembered. I remembered the flow of ben Adamah's power as his love burned through me to heal Keturah. I recalled the windswept mountain where the Mother who wove the cosmos on her loom smiled at me in welcome. Perhaps I hadn't been present in the mighty tumult of creation, when the Mother of Cats first gazed upon her unborn children . . . yet nevertheless, I remembered, and bowed my head as the golden images flowed from ben Adamah's memory to mine.

9

The Balance Is Lost

Wind on Water speaks

The burst of wind shredded the spell holding us enthralled, and suddenly I found myself on a desolate shore, where neither my glowing memories nor the son of Earth walked the dark beach. Ben Adamah had disappeared into the night and left me behind! I leapt from the top of the dune down into the jumble of palm fronds and fish bones that marked the ocean's highest tides, calling over my shoulder to the kitten, "Stay with Aeliana!" Then I was running flat out, loose sand dragging at my feet, my mind reaching ahead for the warm glow that was ben Adamah. He'd covered quite a distance before I found him, walking rapidly along the packed sand close to the water. The pale seafire had returned to the waves. He was no more than a shadow passing between me and its uncanny glow.

"Son of Earth!" I panted. "Wait!"

I could feel the smile tugging at his mood, his steps slowing.

"I should know better than to try to outrun you, little leopard," he sighed, holding out his arm for me to leap up.

"Why would you want to outrun me?"

"I wished to be alone, little one."

"You can always be alone *with* me," I replied, stung by his desire to avoid my company.

"I know that, Mari," he replied, and reached up to settle me around his neck more comfortably. "I wasn't thinking. The heights of Carmel were calling me, and I answered."

The mountain lay ahead of us in the distance, its long bulk a black shadow blotting out the southern stars.

"Why should this mountain call to you?" I asked.

He was silent as his long strides carried us along the curve of the bay.

"The last few days have left me feeling unsettled, little Shulamite. I am dabbling in matters that lie outside the task set me by my father. Although he asked me to heal the brokenness of Ebed Ubasti's house, still I feel the need to speak to him, alone and apart from the busyness of human—or feline—crowds. And from of old, Mount Carmel has been a place of prayer."

"But this mountain lies in the land of the Phoenicians," I objected. "How could your people pray there?"

"Oh, many battles have been fought over it through the years!" he sighed. "Long ago one of our great prophets challenged the priests of the Phoenician god Ba'al there, and won a bloody victory, but it was short-lived. Today a temple dedicated to Ba'al stands there once more. Yet I yearn for the sweeping winds of a mountaintop, and the knowledge that only the stars lie between me and the heavens, even though my father hears my voice wherever I stand."

I sensed that he would say no more, so, secure on his shoulder, I turned my attention to the glittering tide.

Even under the pale sickle of the new moon I could see a distant temple on the mountain's spine, with what looked like a small village clustered around it. On the mountain's face, where it fell away toward the sea, a fire blazed on a Roman tower, lighting the rocky shore far out into the water—a beacon for passing ships, the son of Earth said, to warn them off the rocks. He seemed unconcerned by its presence. He merely walked on until he reached a pile of boulders ringed by twisted trees and cut off from the beacon's light by the mountain's slope. I jumped down from his shoulder, and he climbed to the topmost boulder, where he stood for a long time, feeling the cool wind blowing from the inland mountains.

I left him to his thoughts and went in search of a late dinner. Mountaintops aren't the best places to find a quick meal, but eventually I caught a mouse, small but tasty. When I returned to ben Adamah's rocks, I found him lying on his back watching the stars. I made my way up the tumbled stones and settled on his breast. After a while he lifted his hand and stroked my back.

"The darkness spreading among your people disturbs me, Mari," he said. "I've always assumed that the beasts of the Earth were immune to human evil, except when it simply destroyed them. But now I wonder if the contagion of human hate might have found some way to take root even in the hearts of the beasts who live among us. Not all, by any means, but some."

I lay thinking while his hand ruffled the fur around my ears. At length I answered.

"If the evil presence who visited you in the desert can overthrow the minds of humans—and speak into *my* thoughts—then why could it not twist the minds of beasts, as it tried to do with you?"

"Because, little leopard, like you, beasts have no place in their minds where such evil can lodge. It's nonsense to them."

Again he fell silent, perhaps searching the stars for an answer.

"Do you suppose," he began slowly, "that when animals live close to human beings, they change? That the wild nature they were born with is dulled, and the Mother's voice muted? Perhaps the balance is changed, even lost, so that some beasts become placid and dull, while others grow in wisdom: like you, sweet Mari. Perhaps still others grow crafty, modeling their thoughts after grasping masters. A dull and plodding man might inspire dullness, a wise man might inspire wisdom, and, likewise, a cruel man might inspire cruelty. When the Mother's balance is lost, something will always move into the emptiness it leaves behind. That is the way of emptiness; it seeks ever to be filled."

I waited while he examined his idea for flaws.

"It has always been within the power of beasts and humankind to enrich their understanding of each other: beasts to share with us the balance of the Mother, and humankind to teach wisdom in return. But what if humans fail in their obligation, and their darkness infects the beasts, so that in the end neither ennobles the other? Both are diminished, and darkness spreads.

"Most of the cats of Acco who survived the temple's fall grieved their loss, yet found their balance again without violating their nature or the law of the Grandmothers. But these few who were drawn to Ebed Ubasti were offered something unexpected: 'You are divine,' he told them, 'offspring of the gods! You have been deprived of your rightful place, and I will restore it to you. Come and take your thrones as rulers over your own kind.' And just as their foremothers in the temples had bequeathed to them understanding surpassing that of many beasts, so his words—unintentionally—warped their suffering into a cold malice that grew ever more cruel . . ."

"Ah, Mari," he cried aloud as he rose to his feet, "I weep for the One's children, human and beast alike! The balance is lost! How can it ever be regained? If so few listen neither to their own hearts nor to the One, how can I hope that they will listen to me?"

I leapt to his shoulder and curled under his chin, seeking to offer what comfort I could. Together we stood unmoving while the stars turned in the sky. At length I noticed a change in the air. The wind had died away, and in its place a grey wall of nothingness was creeping across the sea toward the land, blotting out water and stars alike as it approached.

"See, gentle Mari, how a blinding fog overwhelms the land, just as doubts blind my spirit!"

The fog advanced until the whole mountain floated in a ghostly sea. Yet the sky above us remained clear, and the stars burned like jeweled fire. Fog swirled around ben Adamah's feet, but drifted no higher. His breast rose and fell with a mighty sigh. Then as if borne on that long shuddering breath, voices came whispering up through the darkness, curling away in the mist—weeping and laments, groans of pain and anguish, voices calling out in despair. Hoof beats pounded dimly in the depths, and the mists shook with the tramping rhythm of marching feet. Wailing, inconsolable grief, shattered the night, and I felt my heart quail in my breast.

"Ben Adamah!" I cried. "What is happening?"

"Forgive me, little leopard," he whispered, plucking me from his neck and cradling me against his body. "It was unkind of me to let my pain touch your spirit. What you felt was but a taste of the Earth's agony pressing in on me. Only when I am near to despair does it venture so close."

"You are near despair?"

"I am, my little Shulamite. The time grows so short! Yet the needs of those around me only grow greater. My enemy is subtle and cunning, and to the unwary his snares breathe the very perfumes of Paradise. Am I not overmatched? How can my words turn that tide?"

"Not your words, son of Earth," I replied, "but your love, and the love of the One speaking through you. You told Eliana that the Mother never loads her children down with burdens too heavy to bear, that what she asks of us is a joy, never leading to despair. If you are near to despair, then perhaps you've been listening to the counsels of the evil one. Will you not turn aside also—and remember?"

For a few endless moments I feared I'd gone too far. But then ben Adamah gripped me with his hands and lifted me high above his head.

"See, my Father!" he cried aloud, his delight rising up like a fountain until his hands throbbed with it. "See the companion you have given me! See her loving heart that knows no holding back, and her wisdom that puts my own to shame!

> "Oh, my Father, I will praise you with all my heart,
> you whose majesty is as high as the heavens!
> Out of the thoughts of cats—
> yea, out of the thoughts of the Mother's own kits—
> have you called forth wisdom to rebuke my folly!"

At last he let his hands fall back to his breast. I dug my claws deeply into the folds of his robe and squirmed out of his grip before he could decide to point out any more of my virtues to a Creator who seemed to be seated in the highest heavens tonight. I was delighted by ben Adamah's joy, and greatly relieved that he had shaken off his sadness, but I preferred those times when he sought the One's presence in the firmness of the Earth. After all, I was not a bat, that I should fly in giddy circles through the night sky.

"I apologize, sweet Mari," he said at length, as he roused himself from depths of prayer that I could only imagine. He tousled the fur on my breast and smiled. "Did you say something about bats flying in the night sky?"

I didn't answer. He'd been eavesdropping on private thoughts.

"Come, small bat-winged cat, let's go down," he laughed. "The dawn isn't far off, and we must return to the others."

The son of Earth was sure-footed as a mountain sheep in the fog, and he never lost his way. He strode through the clinging mist as if he were walking along a broad highway under the noonday sun. Yet the fog still hadn't lifted when we reached Ebed Ubasti's house. I could see the clouds brightening above us as dawn approached, but no more. The stench of rotting snails hung heavy in the air.

We were climbing the stairs toward the terrace when a tiny body collided with ben Adamah's legs.

"Son of Earth, son of Earth!" the kitten's voice shrilled. "Please come! Aeliana is weeping and won't stop!"

Ben Adamah stooped to pick up the kitten before letting himself quietly into the house. As soon as he closed the door, the kitten squirmed down and raced along the hall, squeezing through the cracked door into the room Aeliana shared with Maryam. Maryam was sitting on the edge of Aeliana's bed trying to comfort her, but without success.

"Oh, Yeshua!" she cried in a harsh whisper, "thank the One you've returned! I don't know what to do for her."

Aeliana sat huddled in the corner, knees drawn up to hide her face, arms clutching her legs tight against her. Her whole body shook with tremors so fierce that I could feel their vibrations in the floor.

"Ah, child," he whispered, and Maryam hurried to rise as he took her place.

"There's nothing to fear, remember? I'm here now, and I will always come when you need me."

He stroked her tangled hair gently, plucking it away from her face, smoothing it back again and again until the tremors lessened. Then he cupped her chin in his hand and raised her face until her gaze met his.

"Now, Tirakemah, you who are also Aeliana and Eliana. I'm here. You must tell me what distressed you so."

"I dreamed," she said, gulping strength from his presence like a nursing kit. "I dreamed that you were lost to me forever, lost in a heavy fog filled with wailing and despair. I even heard your voice among the others, crying out in anguish, in pain beyond bearing. Then hail started falling from a black sky, but it struck me like stones, shattering my bones and tearing my flesh." She took a shaky breath and added, "You were gone, and the world was a never-ending torment."

Cat tales and purple snails

The expression that crossed ben Adamah's face at Aeliana's words was grim, but quickly gone. If he'd been an ordinary human, I'd have looked for signs of guilt, or withdrawal, for surely she'd blamed her pain on his despair. Instead, he turned to Maryam, and bade her bring Tirzah, so that she might better understand the child's suffering.

I had never thought about the consequences the son of Earth faced when he allowed other humans to get close to him, especially clear-eyed humans, like Maryam, and now Aeliana, and Tirzah. Their love for him opened them to his own pain in ways he couldn't foresee, or control, causing them pain in return.

And their pain was a torment to him. Yet he didn't pull away. I wondered if he *could* pull away, and still be who he was? If he came to humankind as the love of the One for her children, *could* he close himself off? Love, as he had begun to show me, came with pain, and pain with love. Perhaps refusing to cause pain because of the love he bore a human being would be refusing to love. Because disguising the heart created a lie. And love couldn't live in the midst of lies.

But I suspect ben Adamah already knew that.

10

Ordinary Cats

Wind on Water speaks

Leaving a now-calm Aeliana with Maryam and Tirzah, the son of Earth transferred me to his shoulder.

"Come, Mari," he hummed, "let us discover where our host has hidden himself."

As we strode through the halls, I saw that the house was almost entirely empty of cats. Only a few females huddled in corners with their kits, trying to be inconspicuous. Apparently the Grandmothers hadn't released the others yet. When we found Ebed Ubasti, he was slumped over the terrace wall in the reeking fog, his head bowed, his misery palpable. The son of Earth walked up to him and laid his hand on his shoulder.

"My friend, we must talk," he said.

"What is there to say?" Aqhat laughed without humor. "My life is a fool's delusion, and I am the fool."

"Do your elders not teach you that the first step in acquiring wisdom is to realize that you are a fool?"

Aqhat merely snorted.

"You have indeed been foolish, Aqhat . . . Yes, I call you by your birth name," he added, noticing Aqhat's frown. "Do you really wish me to call you 'Servant of Bast?'"

Aqhat had no answer to that.

"Hear me, Aqhat! The cats have not yet returned to you, except for a few young females with their kits. Whether the others may return in time has not yet been decided. Their lives lie in the paws of the Grandmothers, where I have placed them. But the Grandmothers await your decision as well."

"My decision, Teacher?" Aqhat repeated, his puzzlement plain. "What decisions are left to me? I did not expect you even to speak to me after last night."

"Yet, here I am," ben Adamah smiled. "And many decisions do await you, my friend. But first, let us go in and break our fast. I know I've had nothing to eat for many hours."

Aqhat made no complaint as ben Adamah preempted his privileges, guiding him, the host, into his own dining room, where his servants were just laying out the morning meal.

Choosing a secluded corner, the son of Earth sat down with Aqhat, and waited until the merchant had managed to force down a few mouthfuls of bread and fruit before speaking. I ate some crumbles of soft cheese just to be sociable.

"Now, Aqhat," he said, "why don't you tell me how all this came to be? Eli described you as a respected merchant and weaver of fine cloth, which are notable accomplishments in any man's eyes. But why Bast? How did you come to fill your house with the descendants of her temple cats—even to the point of taking her name? These things I would like to hear. Will you open your heart to me?"

I wasn't sure Aqhat was going to speak. For some time he alternated between staring down at his plate and glowering at the son of Earth. But I've noticed that humans find pleasure in telling their own stories, especially to someone whose good opinion they value. So after a reasonable show of reluctance, he spoke.

"I used to go up on the hill when I was a child," he began, "and wander among the fallen columns of the temple, imagining the days when it towered over the city. Even though more than a hundred years had passed since it was thrown down, the paint was still bright on some of the stones. Cats lived among the ruins, and I'd heard the stories about the goddess that people once worshipped there, but she meant little to me. Just stories."

He looked up to see if ben Adamah was giving his account the attention it deserved before continuing. He must have been satisfied, because his voice dropped to a more serious tone, and he went on.

"As a young man I accompanied one of my father's shipments of fine embroidered wool to Memphis. While we were there our hosts insisted that we accompany them to Egypt's great harvest festival at the temple of Bast in Bubastis. From all across Lower Egypt people sailed the rising waters of the Nile to celebrate the goddess' bounty.

"Oh, Teacher, it was a glorious sight!"

Aqhat stopped then, his eyes grown distant with memories. Ben Adamah only nodded.

"Not many of the festival-goers were allowed into the temple itself," Aqhat smiled, "but our hosts were prominent people, and we were invited into the great Festival Hall. I was entranced. The common people were enjoying drunken revels outside the walls, but even there I could feel the power of the Lady moving in their excess. Late in the day one of the priestesses noticed my rapture and offered to let me sleep on the roof of the holiest chamber of all, above the shrine of the goddess, in hopes that I might receive a dream from her hand.

"And a dream came—to me, Teacher, to Aqhat of Acco! The goddess came to me in all her beauty, clothed with the holy crown and brilliant jewels of Egyptian divinity, her face like that of the loveliest of cats, her grace beyond description, her head even higher than the stars of the summer sky. She came to me, leant down, kissed my brow, and in kissing me, spoke.

"'Rescue my children,' she said to me, 'and restore my worship to your distant land. I hear my kits' voices crying to me in the night, and I would ease their pain.'

"That was all she said to me, and all I needed to hear. I returned to Acco to do her bidding, and took her name, as befits one to whom a god has spoken. I've done my best for her, but the people of Acco care nothing for Bast of the Egyptians, nor for her cats. They laugh at me and turn away. At least they buy my fabric, for upon that our support depends. To my neighbors I'm merely an eccentric merchant with a peculiar obsession.

"So I've done what I could, but it's never been enough.

"And now I see that not only have I failed, but I've increased the Lady's pain, and made her children vulnerable to humans who would pass judgment from afar."

"I pass no judgment on you or your cats, Aqhat, that you have not already incurred," the son of Earth replied sadly.

"You are not a priest, my friend, nor is your house a temple. The old rules are not in place here. The power of your small god, however limited, no longer rests on these cats, and they cannot communicate her presence without it.

"You tried to create a goddess from your own dreams, and dressed her in royal purple, dyed and woven by your own hands. But Bast is gone from here, her priests slaughtered long ago by zealots from my own country. She was a strange spirit in an alien land, and she fled back to her own native earth, where her praises are still sung. She was a spirit of love and life, of the hopeful dawn and the brilliant noontime, a defender against darkness and chaos, but she is gone. You call out to her, begging her to return, but she does not hear. Even in

Egypt her time is short. Her memory among humankind will barely survive the Romans' rule before fading into the mists."

Ebed Ubasti looked at the son of Earth as if he had pronounced a death curse, and in a way I suppose he had. But ben Adamah went on, pity in his eyes.

"Here is where you find yourself, Ebed Ubasti: You told these cats that they were holy, superior to all others, and they believed you. Yet you were wrong—and so are they. Without spiritual guidance, without the discipline of an enlightened priesthood structuring their lives (mistaken as it was in many ways), belief in their own holiness has become a cancer in their souls, corrupting what was good.

"No one is holy but the One Creator of all, Aqhat.

"Unless these cats, whose line was once noble and wise above other cats, choose to turn and remember who they truly are, they will never be more than mindless beasts in the Mother's pastures: the One has given me authority to seal this fate in their flesh.

"What will you do, Servant of Bast, to ease their way?"

In the end, Aqhat accepted ben Adamah's authority, and spent much of the day with Tirzah and the Grandmothers, seeking some path that might bring healing to both cats and humans, but in the end we all knew that each cat would have to choose. The sun was sinking low over the endless sea when the son of Earth rose from his pallet and reached out his arm to me.

"It is time. Will you come with me, sweet Mari?"

I wanted nothing more than to hide my head and remain ignorant of what was about to happen. I wished no memories of this day's end. But I could tell that ben Adamah wanted me to come. How could I refuse? I leapt to his shoulder and settled there, pressed against his neck, in full view of any who chose to look.

He walked out across the terrace and down to the beach, past the piles of stinking snail shells, beneath the walls of Aqhat's workshops, to the place where the snail fishermen kept pools among the rocks to hold their catch. Ben Adamah's shadow rippled along the empty sand, running along the base of the compound walls as we passed. I could even see my own shadow, a small lump on his shoulder.

At last he stopped beyond the pools, where a rocky outcrop hid us from the house and compound. The house cats had gathered to wait for us there, the Grandmothers behind them, with Aqhat and Tirzah to one side. None of the other cats was there . . . except, to my surprise, the kitten peering out from behind Tirzah's neck. This was not a public meeting.

"The time has come to choose," the son of Earth said softly. "You all understand your choice. Let no one seek to force the heart of another."

The sun dazzled my eyes, pouring its last brilliance over ben Adamah, light to light. As his words whispered into silence, a flock of gulls rose from the rocks, silhouetted for a moment against the glare of the horizon. They tumbled and spun around us, shrieking with coarse screams like the cries of maddened cats, weaving and spinning in a measured dance. With each fierce cry, I saw a gull dive toward the water—and a cat slink away into the dunes: as if the birds wove an aery tapestry reflecting the cats' choices below. Cats were flattening their bodies into the sand beneath the swooping gulls, hissing and snarling in confusion. Almost against my will, I looked into the eyes of the yellow male I had fought outside my window. But in the instant that I caught his gaze, the rage and ferocity in his orange eyes blurred into fear, self-awareness into brutish cunning, and he crept off into the gathering dusk, no more than a mindless hunger in the night.

I realized then that the gulls had stopped screaming, and were settling back onto the rocks. The sky was glowing like copper, fading into night even as I watched. Perhaps half of the original house cats remained crouched on the sand, fearful and uncertain. The son of Earth made an odd warbling noise in his throat, almost like a mother cat calling her kittens, and reached his hand out in blessing over those who remained.

"Come, children of the Mother," he said gently, "let us go home!"

Cat tails and purple snails

The fate of Aqhat's cats shook me to the very roots of the soul ben Adamah had nurtured in me. He'd once given me a choice similar to the one he offered those lost cats. Panicked by the pain of self-awareness and the anguish that came with love and loss, I'd been almost mad with terror, and he'd offered me a way out, a way back into the simplicity of an ordinary cat's life. In that moment of choice I'd looked into my own eyes and seen them grow blank, like those of Aqhat's cat, no longer remembering the son of Earth or the love we'd shared. And I was more appalled by the threat of that loss than by anything I might suffer at his side. I had chosen light, and the pain of love.

Still, even if I'd chosen the solace of forgetfulness, I don't believe the son of Earth would have let me wander into the darkness without his kiss burning on my brow. I wouldn't have fallen into the void I glimpsed in that yellow cat's eyes. How could even a simple beast touched by the light of ben Adamah's love shrivel into such nothingness?

11

I Am Who I Am

Wind on Water speaks

Peace walked the halls of Aqhat's house that night. The cats ran back to the house with the humans, frisking about their feet like kittens. They ate chopped food from their bowls and settled into exhausted sleep with hardly a murmur. They even accepted Purple Shadow. And like the cats, the humans also slept soundly.

In the morning the son of Earth joined Maryam and the twelve for breakfast, and went with them on a long walk along the beach. Several of his human followers seemed confused and in need of reassurance after his venture into shepherding cats.

I didn't see how my presence would contribute anything, so instead of accompanying ben Adamah, I helped Aeliana move into Tirzah's house.

"I like the rooms on the roof, Aeliana," I purred. "Why don't you pick one of them? You can see all around, and there's a nice breeze."

We were standing in the courtyard, with Tirzah looking on but offering no opinion. She'd left Aeliana's choice of room entirely up to her.

"Yes, but the nice breeze smells like rotten snails, and the rooms only have three walls."

"They have hanging screens," I pointed out.

"Screens aren't walls," she replied, and walked away.

In the end she chose a small room under the stairs to the roof, against the wall of Aqhat's house. One tiny window let in a trickle of light, and the room smelled suspiciously like a wool closet. I shrugged. Her choice was the closest thing Tirzah could offer to the secluded room in Eli's house. With Aeliana's room decided, the two women set to sweeping and scrubbing, so I left them to it.

The autumn sun beat down warmly on Tirzah's roof. I settled into the corner where the roof's low wall met the roof itself. I could almost feel myself melting into a puddle of sunlight, what with the sun pouring down from above and sun-warmed clay baking me from below. Just as I was falling asleep, I felt Purple Shadow curl up beside me.

When I awoke, the kitten was gone, and I could hear rustling in Tirzah's weaving room. I stretched long and deliberately, sauntered toward the open door . . . and paused. Purple sat in the shadows in front of the tall loom, studying its heights as if planning an assault. But before I could intervene, I sensed Tirzah coming up behind me. She laid a restraining hand on my shoulder and smiled and shook her head. Aeliana was climbing the stairs to join us, warned by Tirzah's gesture to walk softly.

Puzzled by their silence, I turned back toward Purple. She was pacing slowly beside the hanging weights, stopping now and then to pat them with her paw, apparently untangling twisted threads. This was strange behavior for a kitten! Tirzah and Aeliana watched quietly, but I could sense Tirzah's fascination. Once the weights hung in their proper order, swinging and tapping together gently, Purple leapt up onto one of the wooden uprights and clawed her way to the crossbar. Still Tirzah made no move to stop her.

Purple seemed to consider her position for a moment, and then turned toward the bar. Tiny as she was, she could just fit inside the space where the crossbar held the warp threads apart. She crept along the kitten-sized tunnel, between the threads that hung behind the bar and those that crossed over top of it. The clay weights at the bottom jittered and clicked as she moved. Now and then she paused as if examining the threads of this strange cave that was no cave.

Emerging at the far side of the crossbar, she launched herself up the frame to the loom's top, sparing only a glance for the shuttle with its loose thread. Once on top of the finished fabric that was rolled around the top bar, she paused briefly to lick her fur into place before returning to her study of the loom—still unaware of our presence. Balancing herself on the edge of the roll, she leaned down to look at the narrow band of weaving below it. Her movements uncertain, she inched her paws down toward the hanging cloth, hind claws digging into the roll. I saw it coming; the world being what it is, it was unavoidable. Purple lost her grip (after all, she was hanging upside down by now), and caught herself in an amazing somersault that left her clinging to the roll's bottom by a few straining claws of one front paw. Almost too quickly for me to see, she curled her hind legs up, hooked the claws of all four feet into the fabric, and started digging her way back to the roll's top.

Now Tirzah stepped in: I could almost feel her wince as Purple's claws snagged and pulled at the unfinished weaving. Catching the kitten up in her hands like a ball of fleece, Tirzah carefully detached her from the threads and carried her out to the low roof wall, where she sat down in the sun, Purple in her lap.

"Now, Purple kitten," she smiled, scratching the kitten's ears (but also holding her firmly to prevent her escape), "will you tell us what you were doing?"

Purple turned innocent eyes on Tirzah. "I just wanted to understand," she replied.

"Understand, little Shadow?" Tirzah asked.

"How it works, Tirzah! How the threads fit together. I think I understand, but I fell off before I finished," she added in a small voice.

"What were you trying to see?" Tirzah asked. I could sense her mind reaching, trying to grasp the kitten's meaning.

"How the threads that go across push up between the hanging ones."

Tirzah and Aeliana looked at each other in consternation, but all Tirzah said was, "Come, then, Purple, and I'll hold you so you can look."

Tirzah carried the kitten back to the loom on her shoulder, just at the level where the last rows of the weft thread had been pushed into place the day before. Aeliana and I followed. The bottom thread had started to sag slightly, and Purple stretched out her paw toward it. Tirzah leaned in close enough to the loom for the kitten to reach it, watching her intently.

Purple pushed her paw against the thread until it touched the row above.

"There!" she purred. "I thought it worked like that."

By the time the son of Earth returned from the shore, I wasn't the only one waiting for him. A slowly growing crowd of people had been gathering outside the garden gate throughout the morning. I wasn't surprised. Aqhat's household might not have paid much attention to a Jewish cat trainer, but Tirzah's healing was a different matter. Even though I'd heard Aqhat warning his servants not to talk about ben Adamah's presence, who could blame them? What family didn't have at least one dying elder, or one sickly child? Surely the healer could lay his hands on just this one . . . and so the news spread.

Those who knew ben Adamah by sight hurried out to meet him as soon as he turned the corner of the garden wall, and the others followed close behind. He smiled and took time to lay his hands on each one, and then came inside, pausing for me to leap to his shoulder from the wall. He'd hoped that there'd be time for him to help Aeliana settle in before people noticed his presence, but events had overtaken us. I guessed we'd be leaving soon, lest gossip about a young woman who'd arrived at Ebed Ubasti's workshop with the Jewish healer became part of the story that filtered back to Sepphoris.

The son of Earth took the indirect, but private, route through the house to Aqhat's workshop. We found our host in a large room filled with cloth: stacks, shelves, boxes, bags, and piles of cloth—dyed and plain, embroidered bands and large rolls. As soon as the door closed behind us, my eyes began to burn from the strange fumes in the air; I tried burying my head in ben Adamah's mantle, but it didn't help. Aqhat was standing in the room's center, writing on a roll of papyrus and calling out orders to the workmen hoisting bags of cloth onto a wagon for shipment on an outgoing merchant vessel. But when he saw us, he stopped and ushered us past a heavy tapestry into his own workspace, chatting pleasantly as he released the tapestry to fall closed behind us. I blinked and looked around. The fumes were slightly less worrisome here.

Shelves full of colorful cloth lined two walls, mixed in with smaller spaces for parchment rolls—like those I remembered from Lazarus' tower. Patterned carpets softened the floor, and tapestries covered the walls where the shelves didn't. Ornate brass lamps swung from the ceiling. A large wooden desk stood in one corner with several chairs, but Aqhat showed us to a low table surrounded by large cushions. A young man entered with a tray of fruit, cheese and watered wine and served us deftly before withdrawing. At last Aqhat spread his hands wide and smiled at both of us.

"How can I be of service to you, my friends?"

The son of Earth lost no time in pleasantries.

"Aqhat, I must make arrangements to leave sooner than I had hoped," he replied. "Word of Tirzah's healing has spread, and with each hour that passes, it spreads further. I don't wish to call attention to Aeliana's arrival, and if I remain here as your guest, her presence will become part of the tale. I want her to begin her new life without any shadow of the past, to walk forward in her own strength, which is considerable, even though she doesn't realize it yet."

Aqhat looked at ben Adamah shrewdly, as if weighing the many things he hadn't said aloud, and then nodded his head.

"Perhaps I might arrange for you and your followers to visit a wealthy wine merchant in the city who suffers terribly from gout," he smiled. "Surely he'd be delighted to welcome you—as his own dear friend, no doubt, with never a mention of the eccentric cat worshipper who hosted you first."

The son of Earth laughed, and shook his head in amusement. "It's a good plan, Aqhat, and you're a clever man. I thank you. I'll be sorry to leave you so soon.

"But before I go, my friend, I have one last request of you, more demanding than the first."

"You have only to ask, Rabbi."

"I ask you to accept the role of guardian for Aeliana. You know the law. Should she have need of legal standing, as a widow alone she would have few recourses. You could guarantee that such a thing never happened."

I looked up in surprise. A guardian? A grown woman with a guardian?

But Aqhat beamed with pleasure. "I'd be honored! I've seen little of her since your arrival, but if ever a young woman's goodness was transparent as Phoenician glass, it is Aeliana's. I'll see to the details tomorrow.

"May I ask you a favor in return?" Aqhat inquired.

"Whatever is within my power to do for you, I will," ben Adamah said quietly.

"Tell me who you are," Aqhat answered.

A long silence filled the room.

"Who are you, that healing burns in your hands like light, and power flows through you like the ocean tides?" Aqhat pursued. "You hold the lives of the goddess' sacred cats in your hands, and bend their wills to your own. Who are you, that you can take the crippling weight of years away and restore a blind woman's sight? This I would know, Rabbi Yeshua ben Yosef."

The son of Earth paused, and then caught Aqhat's gaze in his own, holding it for long and long, until Aqhat began to shake with a sudden palsy. Ben Adamah released him then and grasped his hands with his own.

"I am who I am, my friend," he replied. "I am who you see. I am my father's son, and I come to offer your suffering world words of healing and love, calling them to turn again, and remember—like your cats, Aqhat—to remember that they are the beloved children of the One who created them, and that they are neither lost nor alone."

"My Lord!" Aqhat gasped.

"You may call me so, my friend. But I would rather you looked at me and understood my father's love—or my mother's, if your heart yearns for her. Look at me, see how I love her suffering children, and understand the depths of her love. Feel my joy as you reach out to know me, and know the joy she feels when you turn to her. See how I love her children, and love them in your turn. The One is love, Aqhat. Mother or father, grandmother or grandfather, all love is one, as he is One."

Aqhat had curled forward onto his knees. His hands reached out toward ben Adamah. Tears streamed down his face, trickling into his beard and dripping onto his silk robes. But in his face I saw the same light that burned in ben Adamah's own, and I knew that Aqhat had found his answer.

Cat tails and purple snails

Aeliana was unique among the humans the son of Earth healed. Most of the people he touched vanished back into their own worlds with hardly a backward glance, at least as far as I knew. A few, like Maryam, found their lives transformed, and became disciples. But Aeliana was neither a follower nor an anonymous sufferer. Ben Adamah stepped into her life a second time after Eli's call, as if there were a thread that bound their paths together.

Perhaps the answer lay in the name he'd given her that first day: *Eliana*, "God has answered your prayer." That name spoke of ben Adamah's certainty that the One had guided his steps to her. But why did the Mother send him to her, rather than to some other suffering human? And why did her path intersect his a second time? Was her life of special significance? Or did he simply reach out again because he could? Did the threads of light he wove back into her spirit bind them both? When he bound her shattered bones with ragged strips cut from his own robe, did the One weave her fate into his? And what about the new name he gave her, "God is weaving"? What exactly did that mean?

Humans have a foolish saying about curiosity and cats, but I don't think we're so different from humans. How can anyone learn if she doesn't ask?

Still, pointless questions don't sit well with a cat's digestion. Life simply *is*. Any cat will tell you so. Why waste energy chasing sunbeams when you can bask in the sun and just be? Besides, even if I asked the son of Earth, he'd probably only smile and shake his head. The Mother keeps her own counsel.

I do know one thing: Ben Adamah's love had permeated the very walls of Aqhat's home. We might be leaving, but the One burned brightly in the three humans who remained behind, and in one clever kitten as well.

12

Man of No Particular Virtue

Wind on Water speaks

When the young maidservant admitted us, we saw Tirzah standing in one of the open rooms on the roof, weaving at the large loom with Aeliana. Like perfectly balanced dancers, the two women swayed and bent together, passing the shuttle back and forth through the hanging threads, beating it tightly into the woolen fabric rolled up on the loom's top as they went. Purple Shadow lay sprawled on top of the loom, legs hanging down on either side of the rolled cloth. I could sense that Aeliana had found peace at this familiar task—perhaps even more so through sharing with a woman whose delight in her work was at least as great as Aeliana's own. They both looked down into the courtyard and greeted us with broad smiles.

"Son of Earth," Tirzah almost laughed aloud, "be welcome in my home! We'll come down and join you."

"No, Tirzah, we'll come up," he replied, and started up the stairs. "I enjoy watching you weave together. You remind me of larks, dipping and mounting up into the sky, weaving patterns in the evening light."

I saw Aeliana blush as he spoke, but she returned to her weaving and soon lost herself in the rhythm. Time passed, and the thread on the shuttle thinned and then dropped away to hang loose on the loom. Rather than twisting in a new length of thread to continue their work, the two women looked at each other, laughed for the pure pleasure of their craft, and walked out to join us on the roof's edge. Tirzah called to the serving girl to bring bread and wine, and we sat down together in the late afternoon sun. When Purple realized she'd been left alone, she scrambled off the loom, trotted out to join us, and settled in Aeliana's lap.

We sat in comfortable silence for a long time, although I noticed Tirzah glancing sharply at ben Adamah now and again. At last the son of Earth spoke.

"Aeliana, I must speak with you. Will you and Tirzah walk with me along the shore? No, it's nothing to be afraid of," he smiled as she shrank into herself.

I could see her eyes filling with fear, in spite of his reassurance, but she nodded just the same and followed us out into Aqhat's courtyard and through the garden to the beach. Purple climbed her shoulder and burrowed under her hair. Tirzah walked close beside Aeliana, their arms linked. A flash of Tirzah as I'd first seen her overlaid her image for a moment and I purred softly. Ben Adamah smiled into my thoughts in return.

Fog was creeping in over the shore, and the sun's light felt pale, almost without warmth, where it touched my fur. The great ocean was quiet. I could almost persuade myself that it was a lake, its far shore hidden in the mist. I shivered and curled more tightly into my sling, chilled in spite of the afternoon's warmth.

Aeliana walked with her head down, looking neither at the sea nor at the son of Earth. I sensed the despair in her silence: another blow was about to fall, and she had no power to prevent it. But Tirzah greeted the shore with delight, and embraced ben Adamah's presence with joy. When we finally outpaced the stink of dead shellfish, the son of Earth led us to a wave-worn reef jutting out of the sand where we sat down, Aeliana by ben Adamah and Tirzah at her side.

"Tirakemah," the son of Earth murmured, taking her hand in his.

Aeliana didn't reply.

"Tirakemah," he said again, this time his voice heavy with love and entreaty.

I knew she wouldn't ignore him. No one who loved him could. I remembered how it had felt when I'd tried: as if my beating heart were being torn from my body . . . as if endless darkness awaited my refusal . . . as if I would lose even the memory of the sun's warmth . . . no, she would answer.

She turned her head to meet his eyes. "Yes, Lord?" she whispered.

The son of Earth caught her gaze and held it, drawing her into his peace. She sighed softly, and at last she smiled.

"Tirakemah," he said for the third time, holding her eyes with his own. "Tomorrow I must leave, and you must stay."

I felt her heart stumble at his words, but he held her spirit close, and she neither pulled away nor spoke aloud.

"I had hoped to stay with you longer," he continued, "but it cannot be."

She nodded with a sharp jerk of her head. Still he held her gaze, although I could feel her struggling to withdraw.

"Do you remember that I told you I would never leave you?"

Again the abrupt nod.

"I spoke truly, Tirakemah, because I can do no other. For as long as the sun rises in the morning sky, you will live in my heart, as I will live in yours. I will not abandon you, no matter how deep the darkness may feel. If you need me, call. You may not see me in the flesh, as you see me now, but my spirit will be with you. My love, my comfort, my guidance . . . all these are yours wherever your path takes you. Only open your heart and know that I am there.

"I am as close to you as the breath that soothes your soul to sleep. Can you separate music from melody? Words from verse? Warmth from fire? No more can you sever my love from you. I am the Beloved, and you are safe within the circle of my arms.

"Do you understand, child?" he whispered, and I felt him relax his gaze.

She dropped her eyes and shuddered briefly, but then she looked him full in the face and managed a small smile.

"I won't see you again, will I?" she husked. "You're really leaving this time."

"No one truly knows the future but the One alone, daughter. I'll return and walk this beach with you again if I can, but already I feel the clouds gathering. Still, no matter what happens, I shall be with you always, even to the end of days."

Aeliana's face crumpled, and I barely had time to climb to ben Adamah's shoulder before she threw herself on his breast, sobbing bitterly. Purple crept out and licked whatever she could reach of Aeliana's face. The son of Earth stroked the cascade of her hair that fell loose down her back. Tirzah leaned close against them. The sea hissed against the sand, and the air grew chill as the sun sank lower. At last Aeliana straightened and dried her tears. Purple butted her head against her chin.

"You will remember, won't you, Tirakemah?" he asked. "You are worried and full of fears, but when once you gather the courage to face those fears, they will vanish in the light like the trailing wisps of a spent storm. I say to you what I said to Aqhat's cats: 'I offer you my peace.' My peace I give you, daughter. It is yours if you will accept it. My blessing on your days, beloved of my father! May you walk in joy!"

As he spoke these last words, I saw his gaze embrace them both. Then he rose to his feet and held his hands out, raising each of them to stand beside him. For a moment he looked out over the setting sun, and then together they turned back toward Acco.

The mist had drawn in by the time we reached Aqhat's house, and the stench of dye and dead snails was so heavy it felt like rotting vines tangling themselves in my senses as we made our way toward the house. But once Aqhat's door closed behind us, the air cleared. Lamps with scented oil flickered wherever we turned, and a fire blazed in the dining room . . . where we could see that Aqhat had organized a farewell feast for our last evening in his house.

I felt ben Adamah's inward sigh as Aqhat came hurrying toward us. The day had been long and difficult, and his heart was crying out for solitude, but he greeted our host with a smile, allowing himself to be led to a couch, where servants brought bowls of scented water to wash his hands and feet. I settled on the floor beneath his couch, out of the way of watery accidents.

Much to her distress, Aeliana was also summoned to the meal. Surprisingly, Aqhat seated her beside the son of Earth, in a place of honor. Tirzah took a moment to help bind Aeliana's loose hair before seating herself on Aeliana's other side. Maryam and the twelve reclined at the far end of the chamber, beyond a group of strangers I hadn't encountered before: three human females and one male, none old enough to be a wine merchant with gout, so I didn't waste any effort trying to guess who they might be. Not that Aqhat gave me the chance.

"Honored Rabbi, and friends," Aqhat spoke loudly into the room's babble, "I'm pleased to be able to introduce you to my family at last! Here are my three wonderful daughters, Alba, Elissa, and Donatiya, and Donatiya's husband, Ahumm. They've been away in Sidon visiting Ahumm's family, and have only just returned."

I watched curiously as the four humans rose from their seats and approached the son of Earth with polite smiles of greeting, but their delight at Tirzah's amazing recovery was sincere, their joy unfeigned . . . except for the husband, Ahumm (a strange name to my ears, like a slow yawn). But then he hadn't lived his whole life with Tirzah, growing up with her as family rather than servant. He was also the only one in the room wearing the gaudy traditional robes of Phoenicia—brilliantly colored and richly trimmed with woven and embroidered borders, robes oddly out of place among Aqhat's family's restrained Roman garments, and the plain mantles of the Galileans.

But what concerned me most was the way his eyes kept straying toward Aeliana—and the flicker of heat I saw kindling in their depths. I remembered my own shock when I'd first noticed how lovely she was: beautiful beyond the wont of mortal women, I'd said to myself. How might a man of no particular virtue respond to that beauty? A man inclined toward greed, I mused, as I studied his face and lightly touched his thoughts.

I turned a worried gaze toward ben Adamah, and felt the same concern. But even more clearly than his thoughts, I sensed Tirzah's flaring outrage: clear recognition of this human male's lust, and a mother's protective fury on behalf of both Aeliana . . . and Donatiya, a young woman she'd long loved as her own. But now Aqhat's daughters were turning to Aeliana and welcoming her. If they found her appearance unsettling, they disguised it well. Alba, the youngest, seemed almost giddy with pleasure at Aeliana's arrival. Donatiya showed no signs of jealousy. Like Aeliana, she kept her eyes cast down and said little beyond the necessary pleasantries, although her vagueness might be excused by what I could see was the imminent birth of her child. Elissa was polite, but distant. None of the three possessed Aeliana's startling beauty, but they'd be attractive enough when not eclipsed by her brilliance.

I sighed and rubbed my head against ben Adamah's ankle. He'd promised Aeliana she'd be safe here. Could he be certain now? Aqhat might be a kind and virtuous man in his own way, but he didn't always notice the world around him. The son of Earth dropped a hand to my back as he seated himself again. I could feel his thoughts running with mine.

Cat tails and purple snails

Over time I'd begun to wonder if the son of Earth hid himself from others' view more often than I'd realized. How likely was it, after this day's healings, that he could have walked along a busy shore among fishermen and laborers without being noticed? Or, for that matter, walked through the gates of Acco at the head of a throng of cats? I'd noticed long since that he could thread his way through a crowd without causing even a ripple, but I'd never thought much about it. The question uppermost in my mind this night was why he didn't make use of this skill more often?

I sighed and flicked my tail. Not my concern. Perhaps it was about not abusing his extraordinary gifts. After all, did a mother hide herself away from her kits?

13

A Cautionary Tale

Wind on Water speaks

*T*irzah was expecting us when the son of Earth knocked softly on her door after the rest of the house had settled into silence.

"Come in, ben Adamah," she murmured with a distracted smile. "Eliana and I have been sitting on the roof waiting. I knew you'd come."

We climbed the stairs to the roof, where Tirzah offered us blankets against the chill. A steady breeze had sprung up from the shore, and the air was sweet, if cool. Ben Adamah refused, but Aeliana was already curled up with one of Tirzah's own weavings in the corner of the wall where I'd napped only the day before. I noticed she was sharing a cup of warm goat's milk with Purple. A small lamp glowed in the midst of our circle, more for the women's comfort than for light. The waxing new moon and the stars lit the shore brightly, at least to my eyes.

"Have you and Aeliana spoken?" the son of Earth asked Tirzah. Aeliana looked up curiously, and the kitten paused to wash the milk off her whiskers.

"No, ben Adamah. I didn't know what to say. I was waiting for you."

The son of Earth grew silent, saying nothing for many long beats of my heart. I settled beside him on the wall, since he was sitting with his elbows on his knees, offering me no lap. At last he straightened and looked up at the stars for a moment.

I didn't envy him his task. This new situation had all the seeds of a disaster as bad as the one that had driven Aeliana from Sepphoris.

"Aeliana," he said at last, "did you notice anything odd about Ahumm, Donatiya's husband, tonight?"

Aeliana looked up with surprise.

"No, Teacher, not really. His manner was strange, but he's a gentile and a man of Sidon. How could he not seem strange?"

"I'm going to tell you something you won't want to hear, child, but you must: it's important. Will you listen?"

She nodded, suddenly frozen like a bird before a snake. Mother of Cats! Had events not drawn enough of her heart's blood for one day?

"First, Tirzah and I both want you to know that you bear no blame in this, any more than the caper tree is to blame for the beauty of its blossoms. Do you hear me?"

Aeliana nodded hesitantly, and the son of Earth moved off the wall so that he could sit cross-legged opposite her.

"Tirzah and I both watched tonight as Ahumm looked on you with lust—not love, daughter, but the kind of desire that corrodes and corrupts."

Aeliana shrank even further into her blanket, if that were possible. Her eyes grew wide with fear before they glazed over, like the windows of an empty house. Tirzah moved close to her and drew her into her arms, murmuring reassurance and rocking her like a child.

"Tirakemah," ben Adamah said sternly. "You must listen to my words. You agreed to hear me."

Slowly her eyes refocused, although she looked out from under her brows like a beaten animal.

"This is my advice, child. You must share a room with Tirzah rather than shutting yourself off in your own room. Do you agree, Tirzah?"

The older woman nodded emphatically.

"Tirzah, you will need to bring a maidservant you trust into your house and give her the room that would have been Aeliana's, so that two women in addition to Aeliana will always be here in the night. Do you understand?"

Aeliana seemed to be encouraged by the son of Earth's practical approach to this new disaster. She relaxed slightly and sat a little straighter.

"Never leave Tirzah's house alone, Aeliana. I don't care how foolish it might seem to you. Always stay close to other women, women you trust—or to Aqhat. Never speak to Ahumm, never go near him, never, ever allow yourself to be alone with him. If you sense him approaching, flee. Run if you have to. I suspect you are a fleet runner," he smiled.

She smiled at that, but quickly grew solemn again.

"Make friends of Alba and Elissa as soon as you can. I know Alba is eager to know you. But avoid Donatiya—not because she wishes you harm, but because I suspect Ahumm would use her to trap you.

"When you've been here longer, you'll make other friends, friends you can trust. You'll know who they are. I believe Ahumm is the only viper lurking here, and you may find that like most snakes he's more frightened of you than you are of him. Still, as the master's son-in-law, he has power, power you must never give him the opportunity to turn against you.

"So your task is to be beyond reproach, in public and in private. Never allow yourself to be alone. Tirzah will do her best to watch over you, but you will be your own best protection. If people ask why you behave this way, simply tell them that you are a woman alone, and if you don't guard your good name, who will?

"I'm speaking carefully about these things, Aeliana, because I want you to hear and remember. Do you hear? Will you remember?"

"Yes, lord," she whispered.

He smiled and leaned forward to kiss her brow.

"I'll delay my departure at least until midday tomorrow so I can be sure of a chance to speak with Ahumm."

The son of Earth rose then, cocking his head slightly as he glanced down into the garden. For the briefest moment I saw him as an eagle glancing over outspread wings, scanning the earth for prey.

"It's been a long time since I troubled to tutor a snake," he sighed. "And although his bright robes remind me of an overlarge caterpillar, I have little hope of his transformation."

Ahumm's respect for the son of Earth might be reluctant, but it was real. Aqhat had lost no time telling his family about Tirzah's healing and the healings outside his gates—not to mention the miracle of the cats. So when we arrived at Aqhat's workshop to share the midday meal with Aqhat and Ahumm, the young man was deferential, if not exactly humble.

He was taller than his father-in-law, and heavier; I guessed he'd been eating well in Sidon. He waited until we were seated at the low table to remove his peaked hat, and then almost seemed to regret the concession. I didn't like the man, but then I already knew that. He ate with huge appetite and worse manners. Surely Aeliana could outrun this slug any day!

The son of Earth waited until Ahumm was well into his meal and feeling comfortable before speaking.

"May I share a story with you as we eat, my friend?" he asked Aqhat. "It's an old story, but perhaps one you've never heard."

"By all means, Rabbi!" Aqhat beamed. "We'd be delighted!"

"Once, in a land not so different from this one, there was a wealthy merchant," ben Adamah began, and Aqhat smiled. "This merchant had several ships that carried his goods across the seas, but in one thing he was unique: he always took a hand in the design and building of his ships, and they became like his children to him. He loved their lines, and the way they flew lightly across the waves. He always took great care in choosing his captains, consulting the mariners' trade guilds for any whisper of scandal, even examining the candidates' families. Each captain was as carefully chosen as if he were marrying one of the merchant's own daughters."

"Yes, yes," nodded Aqhat, "I can imagine that such a thing might be."

"On one of his long voyages," ben Adamah continued, "the merchant saw a ship lovely beyond his dreams, pure of line, fleet as the wind. Her decks were smooth and glowing. She was as sound as any ship could be. And she was for sale, for a pittance, because her owner and builder had fallen on hard times.

"The merchant jumped at the chance to buy her, and sailed her home himself. He towed his adopted child into his shipyard and cleaned every inch of her, painting and buffing until she shone like a gemstone.

"But before he could send her out on her maiden voyage, one of his most trusted captains—master of the flagship of his small fleet—conceived a lust for this lovely ship. Like a cancer the craving grew in his breast, until one moonless night he turned his back on his vows to the merchant and to his own ship, and stole the ship, ravishing her away from the merchant. Then after he tired of her, he cast her aside for the wreckers."

I could see that neither of our hosts was enjoying the story anymore. Aqhat wore a puzzled frown, but Ahumm was breaking out in what looked to me like cold sweat. He'd stopped eating as well.

"Can you imagine," ben Adamah asked lightly, pinning Ahumm with his gaze, "the anger that merchant felt when he discovered his captain's betrayal? His ship was lost to him, but he pursued the renegade captain with all the power of his wealth and standing, until at last a royal galley returned the fugitive to him for sentencing.

"'Death is too good for you,' the merchant exclaimed. 'You coveted beauty and power; I grant you filth and impotence. You sought to ravish and destroy; today I deliver you into the hands of the destroyers.'

"And so it was.

"In time the merchant's flagship was entrusted to a truer captain, who honored her as she deserved. And to the merchant's unending delight, he finally located his lost ship—not destroyed by the wreckers, but salvaged by one who had seen in her the beauty of her youth, and kept her for himself. So in the end she was returned to the merchant, and rather than throwing the enterprising pirate into prison, he hired him as her captain."

"But the moral, Rabbi? What can the moral of this tale be?" Aqhat nearly wailed.

"Why, the dangers of coveting what is not yours, my friend, and of breaking faith, and stealing. Any of us would do well to heed such a cautionary tale! This man chose to ravish what his neighbor loved, and paid a high price. Even here, among your cats, the Mother of Cats gave me power to consign her children to darkness if they continued in their perversity. And though I may leave you, do you suppose any cat who returns to those evil ways can escape the fate she laid on them?"

The son of Earth sat back for a moment and let his words settle into silence. I crouched sphinxlike on the cushions behind him, my eyes slits of feline glee, watching Ahumm squirm.

"And you, Ahumm, did *you* find my story instructive?" ben Adamah asked at last.

"Indeed, Teacher, it was very illuminating," he replied, all but choking on the words.

"I am pleased that you have ears to hear, husband of Donatiya."

Aqhat just looked confused.

cat tales and purple snails

No one could ever mistake the son of Earth for a soft peddler of pious proverbs, or an innocent easily duped . . . at least not twice. Much as I depended on his unfailing love, as a cat I watched him stalk human prey with delight. He took less time than the hovering eagle to read a human soul, and his reactions were just as swift. Where love and nurture had the slightest hope of effect, his patience was boundless. But where humans like Ahumm crossed his path—souls so complacent and self-absorbed that nothing but their own desires penetrated their minds—his words struck like eagle's talons, terrifying his target with sudden visions of their descent into nothingness. Yet even with these, he never stopped trying, unless, as with Shabtit, he sensed that nothing was left but devouring evil cloaked in human flesh.

Perhaps Ahumm would be one of the fortunate ones.

Part Two: Weaving

Weaving involves two sets of strings: a fixed set, the warp, and a second set, the weft, interlaced into the warp. But the flexibility of string makes interlacing terribly difficult without a way to hold some of the strings in place—a frame to provide tension. Discovering how to provide tension made true weaving possible.

paraphrased from E. J. W. Barber,
Prehistoric Textiles

14

Hidden in the Light

Purple Gleaming in Shadow speaks

Aeliana clutched me tightly against her breast as she watched the son of Earth disappear through the garden gate toward the city. I squirmed to loosen her grip, but only succeeded in drawing her attention, and her kisses, and getting doused with tears. No one seemed to realize that I was feeling miserable too. My first and only friend had left with ben Adamah, curled in the sling beneath his robe, watching the road ahead as they walked on to their new adventure. Meanwhile, I was going nowhere, except back into the house I'd despised since my birth.

But I had to admit, Aqhat's house wasn't all bad. With the bullies gone, the other cats had been decent enough, and usually left me alone. Aeliana needed looking after, too: the son of Earth had made that clear. And I liked being near Tirzah. Sharing a room with her was a little like being with the son of Earth. They both had a glow like sunlight that warmed me all the way to my bones. Of course, ben Adamah had mostly kept his fire banked down . . . I'd seen what it could do when it burned hot.

I didn't feel his absence like Aeliana did, but I think I understood her grief. Whenever I'd been with him I'd felt as if I were everything I'd ever dreamed of being—and still changing into someone I couldn't even imagine. I was going to miss that, although I'd begun to notice that when I thought about him, those feelings came back, almost as if he were still here.

And then there was the loom! I smiled in spite of Aeliana's stranglehold. What was it about the loom? I tried to make sense of it, but I couldn't quite grasp it. The threads reminded me of water currents along the shore, moving around the rocks in eddies and swirls and layers . . . or seagulls dipping and diving, weaving patterns in the air . . . or maybe memories, mixed and twisted, tangled together in my mind. If only I could get my paws into the weave, maybe pushing the threads around would make sense of the tangled thoughts in my head.

Ignorant kitten! What nonsense is this? I hissed to myself.

I squirmed down from Aeliana's arms and wandered through the house to Aqhat's kitchen. What I needed was a nap in the afternoon sun. I'd discovered that if I climbed up onto the roof of the kitchen arbor, I could make my way across the roof tiles to the wall that joined Tirzah's house to Aqhat's, and leap from there to her flat roof. Otherwise I'd have to ask some human to open the door for me, and even a kitten has her dignity.

I was crouched on the roof's edge, surveying the shore from Tirzah's roof, when the knock came. Startled, I stared down over my shoulder at the closed door. Full dark was gathering under the trees and along the base of the garden wall: it was late for visitors. Since Tirzah had already sent the girl Vita to her bed, she approached the door herself, cracking it hesitantly and lifting a small clay lamp into the darkness, its faint bloom of light hardly brighter than a firefly's glow. Aeliana hovered in the courtyard behind her, as if poised to flee up the stairs.

But it was Aqhat who stood there, holding his many-flamed lamp high to light his face. I could sense an unusual nervousness in him even from my perch on the roof.

"Aqhat!" Tirzah cried in surprise, stepping back to allow him entry. "Come in, and be welcome!"

"Thank you, Tirzah. I apologize for disturbing you at such a late hour, but I came to ask if you and Aeliana might join me in my sitting room. My mind is in turmoil. It would ease my heart if we could speak together about these last few days. Who else is there but we three? And the cats, of course."

"We will be honored to come, old friend," Tirzah smiled, reaching out toward Aeliana, summoning her to follow. The three of them vanished through the door, closing it behind them. I followed over the roof.

Muttenbaal, Aqhat's head housekeeper, was waiting in the sitting room with a tray of food and hot spiced drinks. After seeing to the humans' comfort and feeding, she disappeared, although I could hear her moving around in the kitchen. I leapt onto Aeliana's lap to wait for whatever Aqhat might have to say. But before he'd even taken the first sip from his cup, a delegation of household cats strolled through the open door, settling on chairs and carpets around the room. One large golden female climbed onto Aqhat's lap. He smiled and shifted his food to make room for her.

"This is Eye of the Mother," he almost purred. "She came to me after the others . . . left, and told me she would be pleased to share her thoughts with me if I wished. We're becoming good friends."

I could sense his dizzy delight in the golden cat's regard. She seemed content as well. I was happy for them, although the feral kitten in me still found all this human-cat bonding peculiar.

At last Aqhat set his cup down on the small table beside him and sighed deeply.

"My life has been turned upside down and wrong side out," he began, lifting his hands up into the air and letting them fall again. "The man called ben Adamah has pulled all my beautiful carpets out from under my feet and left me to walk on drifting sand. I don't know where to turn, except toward him. But where is he? He's gone from my house, soon to leave the city. Yet my place is here, he said, with all of you, not following him on his travels."

He looked around the room at his listeners, human and cat alike, and sighed again.

"Can you imagine waking up one day and finding that the sky had turned red, and the water yellow? That the ceilings of your house were now floors? That fire made you shiver and cold made you sweat? That doors were solid and walls insubstantial as mist? And worst of all, that my goddess was no goddess at all, but a fading Earth spirit, powerless to help or harm?

"This is my new world, my friends, and I am a stranger in it."

He reached out to pick up a golden statue of a cat-headed woman, stroking it as tenderly as if it were alive.

"A wandering Galilean rabbi steps into my life with fire in his words and healing in his hands and reshapes my life as if I were no more than a lump of clay on a potter's wheel. He tells me that there is only One god above all others, who loves me like a father, and a mother, and who seeks my love in return. My beautiful feline children are exiled from their home, some never to return. Yet I find myself blessed with the fullness of my deepest desires: a speaking cat of the Mother who makes her home beside me, and the Creator's presence in my heart, real beyond any possible doubt. My spirit soars on wings of fire, yet my flesh cringes away in terror.

"Tell me, how can I survive this tempest?"

No one answered for many long heartbeats. To my surprise, it was Aeliana who spoke in the end.

"Perhaps the Teacher meets us in different places, Master," she began slowly. "He came to me when I was lost in the dark, despairing of ever finding my way back. My parents had been burned alive, and

I'd lost myself entirely. He brought the world back to me, and with it healing and light. More, he promised that whenever I felt the shadows draw close, if I called out to him he'd drive them away. He said he'd never leave me, that I'd never be alone, if I could just trust him, that I need only turn and look within to find him there.

"Do you suppose it might be the same for you? My world isn't turned on its head, but I wonder if learning to trust isn't as hard for me as walking on ceilings is for you? He calls me. He draws me on, always toward him and toward the One, but I think his path often lies through the darkest shadows in my soul."

Aqhat nodded and sank into his own thoughts, clearly unconvinced.

Another voice began to speak, although for a moment I couldn't have said whose it was. Then with a plummeting sense of horror I understood: the voice was my own, and I was offering my useless thoughts aloud—without even choosing to!

"Wind on Water told me," my voice went on, "that the humans of Rekem who knew ben Adamah as a child—and the cats descended from his Egyptian cat Miw—still meet together at every turning of the moon to remember him and celebrate the love of the One."

Everyone stared at me, even the cats. I cringed into the folds of Aeliana's robe, wishing I could disappear.

At last Tirzah spoke, her voice slow and thoughtful, "Thank you, Purple Gleaming in Shadow." I could feel her smile even from under Aeliana's robe. "What an inspired idea! I wouldn't be surprised if Mari didn't share this with you just so that you could tell us. A special time together may be exactly what we need."

I summoned all my courage and opened my eyes. No one was laughing at me. The stars hadn't fallen from the sky. I sighed and set about giving my fur a careful grooming, cocking an ear toward Tirzah's thoughts.

"I'm thinking about what you said, Aqhat," she continued. "How can the Creator's world change, old friend? The One created all that is: his spirit abides in his creation, and it is good. We're the ones who change. Like blind kittens, we grow into understanding. Our eyes open slowly, adjusting to the light around us. As long as we live, we're still learning to see. When I first saw the great ocean, it was chaos and terror to me until I understood what I was seeing. Without wisdom, sight is nothing. Haven't we all seen strange trees in the night and thought them fearsome beasts?

"Among my people the prophets say that a human being can't look full upon the face of the Lord God and live. No more could human flesh stand in the heart of the sun and survive, and the sun is only a shadow of the One's presence. But the son of Earth has reached out to us, saying, 'Take my hand, children of the One, and follow me! Feel the warmth of my love and know the splendor of the One. Gaze into my eyes and see the glory of his face. My father calls you home! Come to me, and I will lead you into the fullness of his light!'

"You spoke the truth, Eliana, when you said his path lies through the darkest shadows in your soul, because our darkness hides his light. If we follow him, we must recognize our darkness for the illusion it is and walk through it to the light. Aqhat, the goddess who is no goddess stood between you and what is true; would you rather hold to the lie? The confusion we feel is only our new vision adjusting to the One's glory. He *is* always with us. I suspect he always has been. Yet without ben Adamah's guiding hand, we don't see clearly. We shrink back into our darkness and away from his light as if it were only the troublesome glare of summer sun on the waves. Thus we have always done.

"Do you see, old friend? Do you understand, Eliana?"

I stirred in Aeliana's lap as a flicker of light rippled through a corner of the darkened room. The other cats rose to their feet also, even Aqhat's companion, looking in the same direction. I still can't say whether the image I saw was in my own mind or in the room, or if the voice that spoke to me touched my ears or spoke directly to my heart. I don't suppose it matters. But we all knew that the son of Earth stood among us.

"Beloved of my father," ben Adamah said, "I am with you always, in your hearts, and in your midst whenever you gather together. The love of the One binds us together. Remember, love each other as I have loved you, for love is the beating heart of the law and the end of all wisdom."

Then he was gone from our sight.

Muttenbaal came to refresh the humans' food, and to bring appropriate food for cats, and finally retired to her bed. My humans sat on. The other cats drifted away soon after eating, but I've noticed that humans have trouble letting go of things that give them pleasure. If it's a thing, they always want more. If it's an experience, they keep trying to stretch it out . . . or bring it back . . . or talk it into dust.

But even they finally saw that they could take it no further. Aqhat was the first to change the subject.

"Aeliana," he said, "ben Adamah told me that you don't wish to share your past with anyone here, and I don't question this. It's for you to choose."

I could feel Aeliana shrinking away from him, bracing herself.

"But," he continued, "we must tell people something. If you wish to avoid attention, weaving a mystery around yourself is a very bad way to begin."

Aeliana said nothing, but I felt her fingers tightening on my fur.

"I agree, Aqhat," Tirzah added, "but part of Eliana's silence is her reluctance to lie. She's been hoping people would just lose interest and forget about her."

Aeliana glanced up at Tirzah with relief, and then down at her lap again.

"Ah," Aqhat smiled. "Well, I'm sorry to spoil your strategy, child, but people won't *ever* lose interest if they scent a secret; especially when the mysterious one is as clever and lovely as you!"

He reached over to pat her hand. I was impressed that Aeliana didn't flinch away; she wanted to.

"Perhaps you could think of your time here as a drama. As if you were playing a role at the theatre. It would be a kind of pretend, not lying."

Aeliana looked at him blankly.

"Tirzah?" Aqhat asked, obviously confused by Aeliana's lack of response.

"We don't have many theatres in the Galilee, Aqhat. She doesn't quite understand."

"You played games of pretend as a child, didn't you?" Aqhat asked, his voice sounding a little strained.

"Yes, Master, of course, but mostly I worked with my family."

"Listen, child," Tirzah interrupted, "when you weave, doesn't your mind ever wander? Don't you imagine other places, other people, even other lives that you might have led?"

Aeliana nodded, the familiar ideas relaxing her wariness. Aqhat breathed a sigh of relief. How could he know that when Aeliana felt threatened her fears snarled her thoughts like tangled mats of uncombed fleece?

"Think of the story you must tell here as a weaving-dream, a story you once told yourself," Tirzah urged. "We'll work out the details of your story-life, and then you can live forward from there, as if it were true. When you're with new people, your dream story will drop down like an embroidered tapestry between Acco and your true past. If you wish to speak of your past as it really happened, we'll always be here to listen . . . as will ben Adamah. Can you do this?"

"Of course she can!" Aqhat boomed cheerfully. "She's a bright girl."

I had a feeling that he was exhausted with too much unaccustomed thinking. The comforting refuge of his bed was looming large in his thoughts.

"Here's my idea," he beamed, holding his hands out like Muttenbaal offering food. "You and Tirzah can comb the snags out later. You're a young widow from somewhere far away. It would be better if you weren't Jewish, since Jews aren't popular in Acco. Your parents are dead, and you had no children—or maybe they died. Now you're a widow with a small amount of money left from your husband that you've invested in an apprenticeship with me, because of your skills with weaving. A widow has more status than an unmarried girl, you know. People would gossip about a maiden leaving her people and going off on her own. Widows can do what they like.

"So, there! That's settled," he announced, rising from his chair with a yawn. "I'll say goodnight now, and meet you on the shore in the morning."

Cat tales and purple snails

The son of Earth *was* like light, just as Tirzah said, although I'd have described it as warmth. Maybe that's what light felt like mixed with the love he spoke of: like light and heat together, in a warm puddle of sunshine.

No, that wouldn't work, either. It left out the more alarming ways his light showed itself—like how he shone that night near the beach, or the glow he pulled from the waves, or the lightning that flashed through the room when he healed Tirzah. It didn't explain the brilliant light I sometimes felt in my own mind when he spoke to me, either. I suppose you *could* describe all those different things as light. But even so, I had a feeling Tirzah had meant something else again, something I didn't quite understand. Still, I'm a very young cat. As Tirzah said, what is sight without wisdom? Maybe I'll understand as I grow older.

15

Snail Bait

Purple Gleaming in Shadow speaks

I was just settling into the warm hollow Aeliana had left behind in our bed when Tirzah scooped me up and carried me out to the courtyard. I struggled to open my eyes on the too-bright day. We'd had a long stressful night, and a prowl on the beach had made mine even longer than theirs.

"You're going to start earning your keep today, lazy kitten," she smiled, holding me up so that I could look into her eyes.

I'd never really looked at them before, maybe because when I'd first met her, their milky whiteness had unnerved me. But they were deep green now, shot through with streaks of gold—unless the gold was only reflected sunlight. And they were laughing at me.

"Earn my keep?" I scowled. "Why should I earn my keep?"

"You're a member of this household now, young one, not a little savage running loose on the shore!" she chuckled. "Eliana needs to learn what we do here, so you must learn with her."

"*I?*" I squeaked in disbelief.

"It was ben Adamah's wish that you stay by her side, to help keep her safe. Not only can you sense a human approaching before Eliana can, but with a little practice, you'll learn to hear human thoughts and understand whether they intend good or ill."

My eyes must have grown huge at those words, because she laughed out loud, placed me on the ground, and spoke clearly into my thoughts.

"Yes, Purple Shadow, and this is your first lesson. Can you hear me speaking?"

"Of course, Tirzah, you know I can."

"Good. We can agree on that. Tell me now, can you hear my thoughts if I don't speak them *to* you?"

She stopped talking to me and turned her back. I heard something like the soft murmur of the sea sighing along the edge of dreams.

"Keep trying!" she whispered into my mind.

I crouched down on the ground and listened hard. A mouse rustled in the pantry . . . birds fluttered in the garden . . . flames hissed in the oven . . . the maidservant ladled goat's milk out of a pail . . . *and Tirzah was wondering how strong the dye fumes would be today*!

"I heard you!" I cried, jumping to my feet and tearing around to face her. "I heard you wondering about dye fumes!"

"Well done, little Purple!" Her lips curved in a smile, and she held out her hands for me to jump up. "I knew Ben Adamah and I couldn't both be wrong about you!"

"Ben Adamah told you I could do that?"

"He did indeed, small one. He said, 'Purple Gleaming in Shadow will be as clever as Miw, the cat I loved as a child, who was daughter of the Great Cat Who Is Bast.'

"Enough for now," she added brusquely. "Breakfast is on the table, and Eliana is waiting for us."

"But . . ."

"Practice listening, Purple Shadow, and more will come to you every day. Today we go to the shore."

As clever as the daughter of the Great Cat Who Is Bast, I whispered to myself as I settled on the bench next to Aeliana. Then the smell of fresh milk and cheese distracted me from visions of future glory, and I turned to more immediate pleasures.

I knew from growing up on the shore that the dyers started work with the sun. But in spite of Tirzah's question about dye fumes, we walked past the already stinking dye yard and made our way to the pools carved into the rocky shore where fishermen stored their catch of sea snails. Two fishing boats had been drawn up on the sand nearby. I could see their humans squatting in the sand, sipping hot drinks by a small fire. Aqhat stood beside them, pointing toward the open sea.

"Ah, here they are!" he cried, smiling at Aeliana and Tirzah. "Are you ready to begin?"

Begin what? I wondered.

Aeliana hung back as if unsure what to do. If she was unsure, I definitely wasn't interested. But just as I was crouching to spring off her shoulder and away, Tirzah grabbed me. Again.

"Oh no, Purple, we're all going. You too."

Going? In those little boats? On the ocean? No. Absolutely not. I refuse.

I squirmed in her grip, scratching and biting at her hands . . . and found myself suddenly dangling from her hand by the scruff of my neck like a blind newborn. Paralyzed. Limp. Helpless.

"Do you give up?" she smiled into my face. "Are you ready to be a good kitty?"

Good kitty? I glowered. I couldn't do much else.

"If you don't promise to behave nicely, I'll have a fisherman shut you into one of the bait jars," she said sweetly.

I said nothing.

"Well?" she asked, after several unpleasant heartbeats.

How long could she hold me like this? Already I was feeling a little stretched. Maybe waiting her out wasn't a great idea.

"Alright," I muttered at last. "I promise."

She released her death-grip on my neck, but still held me tightly.

"Your promise carries your honor as a speaking cat of the Mother," she said sternly, holding me up to her eyelevel. "See that you remember that."

I hung unmoving in her hands, resigned. Aeliana and Aqhat were following our discussion with interest.

"Ready now?" he laughed, and gestured for us to join him by the boats.

Tirzah kept a firm grip on me, probably wisely. Aqhat was making meaningless introductions to the strange fishermen. I ignored him. I didn't want to know their names. I just wanted to get away from them. They were the sort of men who trapped cats for snail bait and hawked them on the docks; I could see it in the way they looked at me. I shut my eyes and endured.

But I couldn't ignore the way the boat rocked beneath us as Tirzah climbed in. Better to keep my eyes open. At least I could see disaster coming when it struck. What I saw was a jumble of empty buckets on our boat's bottom, along with a pile of clay jars strung on long knotted ropes with some kind of stinking flesh in them. *Probably dead cat.*

Tirzah and Aeliana and I sat in the middle of one boat, with a fisherman at either end rowing us out into the water. To my surprise, Aqhat remained on the shore, watching us briefly before turning away. Four men were rowing the other boat, so it moved swiftly around the rocks toward the distant reef, its small dragonhead skimming smoothly across the water. We followed more slowly.

The sea was still quiet inside the reef's wall, and I was grateful. I even managed a twinge of curiosity when the boat ahead of us pulled close to the reef and the men stopped rowing. All four stripped off their short tunics down to their breechcloths. Two men gathered long coils of rope with heavy stones attached and dropped them over the boat's sides. Then carrying small net bags and a coil of rope attached to the boat's end the other two men slipped into the water.

I'd expected it, but it was still a shock, seeing an intelligent creature (however unappealing) disappear into the depths of the sea. Then Tirzah's voice distracted me from my shock.

"They'd be diving naked if we hadn't come with them," Tirzah whispered to Aeliana. "Aqhat asked them to keep their loins covered, even though the cloth makes them slower and clumsier in the water."

Aeliana's face may have paled at Tirzah's remark, but the sudden splash of our own boat's ropes hitting the water distracted me, and I wasn't sure.

"What are they doing down there?" Aeliana asked after a moment.

At least she didn't seem worried by the boat. I hunkered down in Tirzah's lap and tried to relax.

"They're pulling themselves down to the sea floor on those weighted ropes," Tirzah replied. "Once they reach the bottom they swim around picking up any purple snails they find loose in the sand, and then they hook the full traps to the rope they carried down with them so the men in the boat can pull them in. After they come up again, they'll drop new jars with fresh bait to catch more snails. Wait, you'll see."

I noticed that the humans in the other boat were filling the empty pails with seawater and setting them back in the boat. Then they started hauling on the rope the divers had carried down; one by one, full bait jars appeared over the boat's edge, water streaming from what must be holes in the bottoms. But before emptying their catch into the pails, the men peered into each pot. Once one of them yelled, and hastily dropped a pot onto the boat's bottom. Carefully keeping his distance, he flicked snails from the pot's mouth with a long-handled spoon, until he seemed satisfied that all the snails had been removed. He paused for a moment—with the other man looking on—took a deep breath, grasped a long knife, and stabbed violently and repeatedly at whatever remained in the pot. When he finally stopped, both men laughed, clapping each other's backs as if some fearsome feat had been accomplished, and dumped the pot's mangled contents back into the sea. Then they returned to the other pots. I turned to ask Tirzah what had happened, but she and Aeliana were looking away, apparently fascinated by a large fisher bird on the reef.

Time was passing. I began to worry that the divers weren't going to make it back up. What if everyone had to jump into the water to try to pull them out? But the men in the other boat seemed unconcerned. They were still busy dumping the jars' contents into the pails of seawater when Aeliana spoke my fears aloud.

"They've been down an awfully long time, haven't they?"

Tirzah smiled and patted her arm. "Don't worry child, these divers can hold their breath much longer than we could. They've been doing it since they were children, and their fathers and grandfathers before them. They'll come up soon."

And they did—not with the explosive panic of laboring lungs, but quietly, like river rats emerging from a hidden burrow. The two men who'd remained in the boat took the snail nets from the divers and helped them climb back in. The divers sat down to rest while the others added the nets' contents to the pails and retrieved the anchor ropes. Then all but one picked up oars and rowed on; the last man carefully dropped the rope of freshly baited pots into the water as the boat started moving away. At our next stop, they switched tasks, the divers staying in the boat and other pair diving. This time Aeliana,

Tirzah, and I all leaned out over the boat's edge—balanced by the two oarsmen leaning the other way—to watch the divers at their work.

To my surprise, I enjoyed it. The sun had risen high enough to strike down through the water now. The blue depths were clear, untroubled by currents or drifting sand. My back was warm, and the boat rocked gently, like an olive branch in a breeze. Although the men dove to a bottom so far down that many humans could have stood on each other's shoulders without reaching the surface, we could see them clearly. They skimmed the sandy bottom like strange froggy fish, hooking full jars to the boat's rope, and swimming back and forth, plucking loose snails from their beds.

The divers dove less than a paw's count of times before returning to the shore with their catch. They delivered us safely to Aqhat, who was waiting for us on the shore, and then emptied the snails into the holding pools and picked up two other divers to begin their real day's work. As I watched, they laughed and pointed at us—or at least at Aeliana (it seemed to me)—making quite a show of discarding their loincloths. They did look more efficient without them.

"So, Aeliana," Aqhat beamed, "did you enjoy your diving lesson? I make sure that everyone who works with us understands the whole process, from diving for the snails to shipping out the finished cloth."

"It was fascinating, Master," she said softly, glancing uneasily at the departing divers. "Will the snails live in these pools for a long time?"

I jumped up onto the rim of one of the round pools to see how the captive snails spent their days, but the water was murky, and the bottom hard to see.

"No, not long," Aqhat replied. "We only keep them in the pools until we have enough to make a good batch of dye. If they stay there too long they start to die—and kill each other. You're lucky, Aeliana, because we'll be clearing the pools tomorrow. You'll get to see us start the dye!"

Aqhat smiled all around as if he'd just promised us a priceless treasure. I looked askance at the piles of stinking snail shells further along the beach. I knew what awaited us; I'd watched humans drilling and cracking snail shells. It was nasty, smelly work, and the humans' hands would be raw and bleeding at the end of the day—apart from being stained purple. Even a cat knew that only slaves shelled the purples. Humans with purple hands might as well wear tattoos on their foreheads proclaiming them slaves from the dye beaches, whether they wished to declare it or not.

I switched my tail in irritation at the next day's plans and started back toward the house. Another early morning. At least this one wouldn't be spent in a boat. I ran ahead of Aeliana, glancing up at Tirzah as I passed.

She winked at me.

Cat tales and purple snails

The closeness of so many humans made me dizzy at times. I'd always lived on the outer edges of the human world, watching from a distance, never venturing close. For one thing, it wasn't safe. Ebed Ubasti's love for cats was unusual. Although some wealthy families adopted cats as lap-animals, and all humans respected us as rat-killers, to most we were of no more significance than the birds in the trees—less than the fish in the sea. Few humans actually ate cats, but all of us had heard the rumors that poor men trapped cats for bait. We tried not to think about it, but it was a menacing shadow brooding over our days.

16

Threads

Purple Gleaming in Shadow speaks

*W*e'd almost reached Aqhat's terrace when the first scream shattered the morning's calm. Ululating wails of agony beat on my ears as if the sufferer were right behind us, but when I looked, I saw the humans turning and pointing along the shore, far out in the water, where a cluster of diving boats had gathered.

"Scorpion fish!" I heard Aqhat hiss under his breath, and then he was running toward the beach, shouting orders to the women working in the dyeing compound.

Several women pulled flaming driftwood out of the fires and threw them into a kettle. Aqhat grabbed the pot and jogged along the shore toward the point where the boats were heading. Other humans followed him with armloads of dry wood and jugs of water. Tirzah hurried behind them, delaying only long enough to grab a scrap of undyed linen from a pile in the dye-yard.

"Eliana!" she called over her shoulder, "Bring more water!"

Aeliana looked around in confusion. Finally noticing a freshwater well sunk into the dye-yard, she filled a large water jar, and ran after Tirzah. I followed more slowly, unsure of my welcome.

By the time I reached the boats, the women had a kettle of water steaming over a hot fire. The boats were just reaching the shore. It seemed to me that the poor man's shrieks were growing more panicked with every breath.

Divers gathered around the boat that carried the thrashing man; I could see him now; he was barely more than a lad. They wrestled him out of the boat, laying him close to the fire and kneeling around him, leaning all their weight on his flailing limbs to hold him down. I looked for blood, but saw none, only writhing human flesh.

Tirzah dipped the linen in the hot water (now billowing with steam like a vat of dye) and handed it to Aqhat. With only a moment's hesitation, he placed the cloth on the boy's hand and dabbed gently. Never have I heard human or beast scream so! Tirzah and Aeliana together were pouring the hot water from the kettle into a shallow bowl. Tirzah handed it to Aqhat, who removed the cloth from fingers so swollen that they looked more like a paw than a human hand. Aqhat tested the temperature of the water with his own hand, and then with the other fishermen's help, he plunged the boy's hand into the bowl. The young diver's eyes rolled up until I could see only white, and he fainted. Thankfully, his screams faded with him, although I found the silence almost more troubling than the young man's cries, holding as it did the promise of his agonized return to consciousness.

More women were arriving now with fresh wood and more water.

"Tirzah?" I whispered.

She sighed deeply, and offered me a small smile. "It's a scorpion-fish sting, little Purple," she sighed into my thoughts. "It was hiding around the traps with the snails, and it stung the poor boy when he reached out to hook the rope to the jars so they could pull it up. Men can die from these stings, but heat kills the poison. So we must do this, even though the pain of the sting itself is already so terrible that it can drive men mad."

I remembered the divers looking carefully into the full bait pots—and their violent reaction to something they'd found there. *Scorpion fish!*

At that thought the boy started screaming again.

Alba and Elissa were waiting for us on the terrace when we finally returned to the house. The injured diver had been carried home on a litter, the linen knotted between his teeth to help him bite back his screams. His pain had finally begun to lessen, although Tirzah said it would be late night before it stopped. They all agreed that the sting wasn't likely to prove fatal, and diving families knew better than anyone how to deal with such stings. Our part was done.

"The noon meal is ready, Papa," Alba murmured, laying her hand on his arm. "The servants put cold food on the table so you could eat whenever you came in. Would you like us to serve you?"

"Sweet child," Aqhat said tiredly, and cupped her face with his hand. "That would be kind of you. I know we're all hungry."

We followed his daughters to the dining room, and to my surprise, they served us all, even me. Aqhat drank considerably more than his usual frugal serving of watered wine.

Maybe it was my imagination, but it seemed to me that Alba was only masking her high spirits with downcast looks, assuming a token respect for the morning's tragedy. After she decided that enough time had passed, her enthusiasm exploded out again, like new wine from a too-tight wineskin. I was grateful Aeliana had greater restraint.

Alba never seemed to run out of words, even when she had nothing to say. I'd decided that most of her conversation was like a cat's purr: a sign of contentment and pleasure in the moment, rather than something that required response, or even attention. Once I'd figured that out, we got along better. I suspect Aeliana had come to a similar conclusion, although I think she may have found Alba's constant chatter soothing.

Elissa was older and quieter. From what I'd heard among the cats, she spent most of her time helping her father with his business. Aeliana's arrival made scarcely a ripple in her calm manner; she welcomed her warmly, as if she'd always been part of the family, and then withdrew into her own concerns.

Alba declared her older sisters boring, although Donatiya had become so only recently. Apparently since her marriage she'd grown quiet and withdrawn; Alba blamed Ahumm, whom she was convinced was an eel magicked into the shape of a man as part of some dire black sorcery. Alba liked to talk about magic.

Once we'd finished our meal, Alba turned to Aeliana, and spoke eagerly. "Before that poor boy was stung, we'd planned to go into the city after lunch. It's still not too late, you know. Wouldn't you like to come with us? Papa said you hadn't seen Acco yet."

She paused then, noticing Aeliana's hesitation.

Aeliana glanced at Tirzah, who smiled and turned to Alba. "Who else is going, child?"

"Batnoam is coming with us to look at that merchant ship that just docked, and Muttenbaal's coming too since she needs something for tonight's dinner. Elissa needs scrolls and ink. Donatiya said she's too tired, and Ahumm said he's had enough of markets for the whole winter, but that'll still be five of us. Do come, Aeliana!

"And, Tirzah, you must come, too! Think how long it's been since you went to the market! All your old friends—all your old enemies!" she laughed. "You must both come! It'll be a such a relief for you after this terrible morning!"

Tirzah shrugged, and Aeliana smiled at Alba. "I'd love to, as long as you'll tell me if I do something stupid. Everything feels so strange to me here, I might as well be in Rome."

So it was decided. If I hadn't been so tired I'd've been chasing my tail with excitement. I suspected Aeliana and Tirzah must be tired as well, but neither Aeliana nor I had ever been inside the city walls, and Tirzah was happy to see Aeliana exploring her new world.

Alba hurried us off to her room to find a robe for Aeliana after informing her that she looked just *too* much like a country cousin. But once in Alba's bedchamber, Aeliana's eyes grew wide, and she backed away from the closet, shaking her head over the filmy silks and almost transparent mantles Alba offered her.

"Alba," she whispered, "don't you feel like a *hetairai* in those clothes? Decent women don't wear such things in my village!"

"Oh, you sound like my aunts!" Alba pouted. "All the fashionable women in Rome dress like this. They call it the 'new woman'!"

She smiled into her mirror and held a heavy gold earring up to her ear. But Aeliana stood her ground, shaking her head stubbornly, while Alba went through her wardrobe like a typhoon, discarding robe after robe, flinging silks and jewelry everywhere, until she was finally satisfied with herself. Tirzah managed to discourage her more startling choices. I'm sure I heard her muttering something like, *This girl needs a mother!*

I asked Alba if she'd make me a sling like Wind on Water's with one of her scarves, but once she got over the shock of conversing with a cat, she informed me that women in Acco didn't wear slings around their necks like goatherds. I was Aeliana's cat, wasn't I? I could ride on her shoulder.

Acco's gates faced the hill where the old city had once stood. Many human lifetimes ago (so I'd heard) the sea had sunk away and turned the old city's harbor into mud, so all the humans had packed up their possessions and followed the sea to the new shore. The empty hill still towered above the new city, with the ruins of the old buildings—

among them the Lady's temple—sticking up like the ribs of a wrecked ship. Hardly anyone lived there anymore. The road turned away from the hill now, toward the gates. Stone walls rose high and solid around the new city built by the sea, leaving the old hill outside, like a human graveyard.

"We don't really need walls anymore," Alba was telling Aeliana. "They're just left over from the old days. Now we have *thousands* of Roman soldiers here to protect us if there's any trouble! Wait 'til you see!" She grabbed Aeliana's hand and did a small dance.

I figured many humans must agree with her, judging from the sprawl of buildings going up outside the gates. Nevertheless, the walls remained, at least in most places, and soldiers still stood guard at the gates. The stone gate towers loomed high above us, almost as tall as the hill beyond, blocking out the sky as we hurried through the dark tunnel leading into the city.

Chaos lurked inside the gate: humans milling everywhere, like waves crashing together from different directions, swirling human tides overflowing the streets and eddying against the buildings. I shrank back against Aeliana's neck, pressing myself under the coiled hair beneath her mantle. This was no place for a kitten of the open seashore! Then I felt Tirzah's calming touch in my mind and breathed a little easier. I wasn't alone anymore. I was safe. Ben Adamah had changed all that. I gathered enough courage to peer around Aeliana's neck.

A broad plaza paved with stone stretched out around us, huge buildings with tall pillars jammed together all along its sides. Here and there a small alley broke their solid front. I couldn't see what difference Aeliana's clothes could make here: these humans wore every possible style of clothing ever known to humankind, or at least so it seemed to my dazzled eyes. Fortunately for me, Aeliana had stopped just inside the gates, confused by all the strange sights, and Alba was happily explaining everything that crossed our path. Without Alba's patter, I think I might have buried my head in Aeliana's hair and disappeared into the nowhere place for the rest of the day.

"Look, Aeliana, here's the street to the market, just ahead! It's lined with shops all the way from here to the market itself . . . but I never bother shopping along the street. The very *best* shops are all up at the forum. Come on, I'll show you!"

I tried to make sense of what I was seeing. Tall trees with chopped-off branches lined the wide stone street, with roofs added on above their stubby limbs. On the ground small merchants' and craftsmen's tents jostled for space beside the road, and here and there corridors opened into the huge buildings behind them. But as soon as we left the plaza I realized that the trees were actually stone columns, shaped by human hands to rise like trees—larger versions of the pillars in Aqhat's house. How was I ever going to make sense of such things?

Because, small Shadow, you are growing in me, and in wisdom, the voice, unmistakable, answered.

"This road goes all the way to the temples on the seawall," Alba was saying, "but we're not going that far."

I tried to gather my (growing) wits to listen.

"We'll get to the market long before that . . . Oh, look, you can just see it, Aeliana!" Alba cried, grabbing her hand and squeezing it excitedly. "There's the market, way down the road ahead of us! See the roofs? And you can see the theatre over there, and the baths, and the . . ."

"Enough, child!" laughed Tirzah. "Let Eliana catch her breath!"

I tried to look ahead, but without success. The road just vanished into a jumble of roofs and columns and porches, each more confusing than the next. Then without warning, catching us unawares among the babble of other foreign sounds, a mass of marching legionaries overtook us, crowding us off to the side of the street, burying the rest of the city's commotion in the clamor of stomping feet, jangling weapons, and hoarse breathing. I tried to burrow deeper under Aeliana's robe, but even as I did, I felt her shrinking down inside herself, and backing around one of the massive columns toward a low-hanging display of tanner's belts and sandals.

"Did you see that centurion?" Alba breathed, clutching Aeliana's hand tightly and preventing her escape. "He looks like a god, doesn't he? He could have modeled for the mosaics in the nymphaeum . . . you'll see them, I'll show you some day. I always hope he'll be on duty when we come to town, but it doesn't happen very often: there are lots of centurions. Can you believe our luck?"

She turned back to watch the soldiers without waiting for Aeliana's reply. I could sense Aeliana dimly trying to sort out Alba's words, gathering her scattered thoughts, and staring at her companion as if she'd suddenly started baaing like a half-witted sheep. But Tirzah drew her away before she could say anything, and whispered in her ear.

"Alba doesn't understand, child. She's never known soldiers as anything but saviors and protectors. The gentiles of Acco welcomed the Romans when they came. Their empire has brought wealth to the city, along with wide streets, flowing water—and slaves. She doesn't know what it's like to see legionnaires descending on you like Babylonian hordes, swords flashing, filling the streets with blood."

She suddenly stopped, remembering where she was.

"Alba can't help who she is, Eliana. Don't let it poison your friendship."

Then she patted Aeliana's hand, smiled into her eyes, and moved back toward Alba just as the crowd cut off our last glimpse of the retreating Roman helmets.

The market was amazing. I'm sure it was. But all I remember was a riot of colors, shrill voices crying out in a confusion of strange languages, the reek of strange foods, people jostling us on all sides . . . and now and then male humans stumbling over their own feet when they got a close look at Aeliana. For her part, Aeliana liked the market even less than I. I could feel her exhaustion and anxiety pushing her past all bearable limits, into some place I couldn't reach, where everything but her own darkness disappeared. Fortunately, Tirzah noticed too, and made our excuses to Alba. She steered us away efficiently, her own stubborn strength supporting Aeliana through the crowds like a sleepwalker, finally leading her stumbling through Aqhat's garden gate and into the small room they shared.

"Here, child, lie down," Tirzah urged, helping Aeliana onto her bed. Then bringing a cloth and a bowl of cool water, she bathed Aeliana's face and hands, murmuring softly until Aeliana's breathing slowed, and her eyes cleared.

"It gets so dark sometimes," Aeliana whispered. "The smoke is so thick, and I can't find my way . . ."

"There, child, I should have realized how confusing the city market would be to you, especially after this morning," Tirzah crooned. *And how terrifying it would be to find yourself caught up in a crowd again,* I heard her add to herself.

"I'm sorry, Tirzah," Aeliana sighed. "I ruined your afternoon."

"Oh, no fear of that, Eliana!" she laughed. "I only went to please Alba. Penniless old women with creaking bones don't find markets nearly as enticing as young women with coins in their purses!"

Aeliana smiled, her eyes drooping in spite of herself. In another moment she was asleep. Tirzah sighed, dragged herself across the room and collapsed on her own bed. I leapt up and settled on her breast.

"Did you really see the Romans attacking, Tirzah?" I asked.

"Oh, kitten, I don't want to think about that!" she groaned. "It's all in the past now. Like Eliana, I was hardly more than a child. I've spent many hard years learning to live with those awful memories, just as Eliana struggles with her memories now. Don't ask me to call them back."

In answer, I licked her hand and purred softly. Soon all three of us slept.

Lying on Tirzah's breast, I dreamed of a huge loom, but instead of leaning against the wall like Tirzah's, it lay stretched out on the ground, pounded into the earth by tall poles with crossbars. The warp threads were stretched tight and straight, but weft threads wove through them crazily, first at one angle and then another, creating strange and confusing patterns. The warp threads were deep brown, nearly black, like the undyed wool of a black sheep, but the weft threads were all different colors, pulsing with living light, as if each possessed its own personality. They might have been people, those threads: ben Adamah, perhaps, and Aeliana, Tirzah, and more I couldn't name. The colors danced against the black warp like flames on a night sea, leaping this way and that, making glittering images in the darkness.

In my dream, I suddenly leapt onto the weaving. I could feel it bounce under my paws, like a small tree branch. Then, without thinking, I started digging at the patterns I saw forming there, hooking the threads up with my claws, trying to unravel the story it was telling, to change it in some way I didn't understand. But the more I fought the pattern, the more determinedly it spread, and the more frenzied and desperate my digging grew, until the dream suddenly snapped apart, unraveling like hissing snakes, and I felt myself lifted out of sleep by Tirzah's gentle hands. Together we sat on the edge of her bed. She held me close against her breast, her silent tears mingling with my own grief, both flowing from the same dream that hung in the air like an unspoken curse.

What Aeliana may have been dreaming I couldn't say.

Cat tales and purple snails

After that, I rarely thought of my humans without those colors coming to my mind. The son of Earth burned like one of Aqhat's rubies. Tirzah glowed gold like ripening barley. Aeliana shone with a clear blue, intense as an autumn sky. Aqhat and his family glimmered in shades of brown, like undyed wool. As time passed, I often dreamed of the loom, and although the patterns changed, the colors never did.

17

A Tangled Skein

Purple Gleaming in Shadow speaks

The rising sun spun our spindly shadows almost out to where the small waves broke at the bottom of the beach. The tide lay close to its lowest ebb, exposing the top of the reef like a rocky ridge. The sand felt cold under my paws as I trotted unhappily beside Aeliana. From what I could see, she'd recovered from her visit to the marketplace, but she and Tirzah were carrying heavy metal pots with tools the purple harvesters would need for their work, and neither was inclined to carry me as well. After yesterday I knew that my presence was required; there was no point in trying to evade Aeliana's lessons, or mine.

Above the holding pools a large stone outcrop rose out of the sand, much of it shaped and smoothed by human hands. Two broad stone platforms with shallow drains along their length had been carved from the stone, each ending where it met the bedrock sloping down to the high tide line. Around these stone platforms a shelter had been built. Quarried blocks reached as high as Aeliana's waist on three sides, rising higher at the corners to support the low stone roof. The fourth side stood open to the sea.

Several chattering women (with purple hands) sat waiting on the nearby rocks as we approached, while an oddly assorted group of humans, from young children to old men, waded around the holding pools, plucking purples off the sides and bottom and dropping them into a line of waiting buckets filled with sea water. Now that we were away from the dye yard, the chill breeze blowing off the water smelled only of salt and the wide sea; I knew that would change as the day progressed.

I could hear Aqhat's voice as he approached rapidly from behind us. Did the man never simply walk? He seemed stuck at a trot, or even a canter, like a donkey whose rider was always goading him to go faster. Who could be goading Aqhat, I wondered?

"Good morning, Aeliana, Tirzah, and Purple kitten," he laughed. "Shall we begin?"

The women had stopped gossiping at Aqhat's approach, and now drifted toward the shelter. Aqhat called out introductions as he trotted ahead of us into the building.

"Aeliana, if you would put your pot here," he smiled, pointing to the downslope end of one platform, and Tirzah, yours here," pointing to the second table.

They put their heavy lidded pots down and stood back.

"Now," Aqhat smiled, removing one of the lids and reaching into the pot, "these awls go up at the head of the tables. And these smooth rocks" (he reached down to the floor in one corner) "go with them. These bigger rocks," he said, moving to another corner and picking up a rougher stone, "go in the middle of the tables."

He reached into the pot once more and drew out sharp slivers of obsidian. "These stay down here at this end near the pots . . . and these," he turned to pull several large baskets off hooks on the low walls, "go down on the sand at the end of the tables."

He waved them on to carry out his instructions and finally sent them to the distant water line with pails to get enough seawater to fill the two pots half-full. He set the pots he'd been carrying off to one side for later. I wandered off toward what remained of the original outcrop and found a sandy hollow where the morning sun was already warming the stone nicely. The slave women quietly took their positions around the tables, several along each side, watching Aqhat warily. Tirzah and Aeliana had just returned with their pails when two young boys arrived at the shed carrying buckets almost as big as themselves, sloshing with seawater and snails from the pools. One woman from each table took a bucket from a child and set it at the top end of her table.

"Now," boomed Aqhat in his best lecturing manner, "We're ready to begin. What you'll see first, Aeliana," he explained, gesturing to the buckets with snails, "is how we make holes in the shells in the exact right place to weaken them so they'll break. The women at the end here will begin now, and you can watch. Then after they drill the holes, they pass the shells to their sisters, who will smash the shells *just so*, exposing the purple gland. Then they pass the crushed shells on to the end, where the last workers will scrape the gland away from the rest of the snail and place it in the pot—which must always stay covered now, except when the glands are slipped in, because too much light ruins the dye. The rest of the snail and its shell we throw into one of these baskets to carry to the midden."

He stopped and beamed at everyone. "Have a pleasant morning, ladies, and I'll return around noon.

"Oh, Aeliana," he added, turning back, "I'd advise you not to handle the purple glands themselves, or even the crushed shells, or you'll stain your hands. Not that it isn't a lovely color, but it lasts for weeks and weeks. Anything else you'd like to help with, please do."

He trotted back toward the workshop.

Tirzah quirked her eyebrows at the other women, everyone laughed, and the work began, as did the stench. Mucous oozed out of the shells and onto the women's hands, changing color like some nightmare rainbow, from pale yellow to green and blue and finally violet. Tirzah and I knew what to expect, but Aeliana gagged and reeled back, fleeing the hut with her mantle over nose and mouth. I hadn't chosen a perch upwind of the hut for nothing.

All the women laughed, including Tirzah, who beckoned Aeliana back. She returned reluctantly, and didn't try to escape again. Still, I could feel her discomfort, surely greater than simple distaste for an unpleasant odor. Remembering Tirzah's lesson, I tried to listen to her thoughts more closely.

To my surprise, I sensed more fear and rage than thought. Every one of the purple workers' tasks seemed to strike Aeliana like a blow. Even plucking the shells from the buckets inspired creeping dread. She flinched like a beast from the hot brand each time an awl pierced a shell's whorl, and when a stone shattered a shell, I felt it echo in her mind like the crushing of her own bones. When the broken shells were passed to the last women in the line for the reeking gland to be cut out she invariably closed her eyes and struggled against dizziness that left *me* reeling even at a distance. Flashes of fire and hate-filled faces flickered in and out of her mind. I knew I should understand the images crowding my thoughts, but they refused to come clear. I was missing something important here.

Finally Aeliana pulled her mantle away from her face and bent over to speak to a slave woman hammering an awl into a shell. "Why do you put the little shells aside?" she asked abruptly. Her voice was edgy, cracking with emotion. "Do you do something different with them?"

The woman glanced at Tirzah, who answered for her. "No, they're too small to cut the dye out, so we just throw them on the midden heap with the crushed shells. Some dyers throw them in a pot and cook the whole shell, but Aqhat says color made that way isn't worth the trouble."

"But they're still alive!" Aeliana shrilled, her voice rising unsteadily. "They're just babies! They don't deserve to die! Can't you put them back? Let them grow up?"

I sat up and looked at Aeliana oddly. *Babies*? How could anyone in her right mind care what happened to one of these disgusting creatures, regardless of its age? I felt her thoughts roiling with unexpected emotion, unbalanced, out of place in the moment.

"The snails can't survive in shallow water where the tide runs in and out, child," Tirzah replied, her voice gentle. "And the divers aren't going to take them back out in their boats to dump them where they came from. Anyway, they'd probably just crawl into the bait pots again. What would you have us do?"

Aeliana paused for moment, and then murmured, "I'll take them. You can save them for me in a bucket of water and I'll carry them out before the tide comes in and throw them as far toward the reef as I can. It's better than letting them die on a trash heap."

I'd never seen the expression that crossed the faces of human slaves when confronted with the *delicate* sensibilities of their owners before, but I saw it now. It was partly a blank, glassy stare, but mixed in where even a cat might notice it, was contempt, and something close to hate. All the women wore the same look, all but one, who raised her eyes to look at Aeliana with compassion, and sadness. I know Tirzah noticed their regard, because she picked up the bowls of tiny snails and herded Aeliana out of the shed. I watched curiously as Aeliana eventually strode down the beach with her bucket, waded out into the waves, and threw one tiny shell after another across the water toward the reef.

"They really are rather nasty creatures, Eliana," Tirzah remarked when she returned with her empty bucket. "They're predators, you know. They drill holes in other shellfish and eat their flesh out through the holes."

Aeliana only glowered in response. At least rescuing the "babies" seemed to have taken the edge off her distress.

All in all, it was a disgusting morning. The breeze dropped, and the stink spread. The mounds of dead snails in the baskets grew higher and higher, until the drone of biting flies and feeding wasps drowned out even the rhythm of the surf. What the women handling the snails must be suffering I couldn't imagine. Imagination isn't one of a cat's more obvious gifts.

By the time Aqhat finally came to fetch us for lunch, children were sloshing buckets of seawater along the tabletops to clean off the worst of the slime. Servants who arrived with Aqhat picked up the purple kettles, bearing them reverently to a storage building like the priceless treasures they were. Older men carried the fly- and wasp-infested baskets of dead snails toward the distant midden heap. The slave women would have to return to their noisome task after lunch; we wouldn't.

I watched as the men reached the midden heap with their first heaping baskets, saddened, but not surprised by the assortment of creatures that came running toward them as they dumped their loads. Sea gulls and other scavenger birds, cats, rats, dogs—even humans—fought for the snail flesh thrown away by the dyers. Food, fresh food, wasn't a thing to be wasted, no matter its source, or odor. I found myself hoping that the women from the shelling shed didn't have to dine on their own garbage.

Aeliana had moved away from the shed and was watching from a distance. Her erratic emotions had been replaced by a blank wall . . . of fog? stone? closely-woven wool? One was as likely as another. As soon as she saw Aqhat approaching the shed, she waded out into the water to wash as much of her skin as modesty allowed before returning to the house. Like me, she'd probably be imagining the stink clinging to her body many days from now, even after numerous baths.

"Tirzah?" I mumbled between mouthfuls of grit as I bit at a stubborn itch between my paw pads.

She was resting after lunch before returning to the afternoon's tasks, while I groomed myself on her belly. Aeliana was curled into a tight knot on her own bed.

"Yes, little Purple."

"Why is Aeliana so upset?"

Tirzah sighed. "Ben Adamah told you what happened to her, didn't he?"

"Yes, Wind on Water did, but what does that have to do with the city market, and snails? And she seems even more anxious since the son of Earth left."

I abandoned my bath and settled to watch Tirzah's face as she considered my question.

"You realize that she doesn't remember what happened to her, don't you?"

I blinked in agreement.

"Well," she began, and then paused. "Human minds can be very complicated," she said at last. Another pause. "It's as if there were two armies fighting for Eliana's mind: one wanting her to remember, and the other reinforcing the walls that keep the memories hidden. It's hard for a human to feel comfortable when parts of herself are at war. Eliana feels off balance."

Tirzah paused again. "You're an observant little cat," she continued thoughtfully. "Picture the loom you find so fascinating. Imagine a finished weaving hanging there, waiting to be tied off. Can you do that?"

I blinked again.

"Now imagine that somehow the weft threads are pulled out completely, leaving nothing but the warp. Where once there was a pattern, a useful image, a length of fabric, now there's only an empty framework, waiting for patterns to be woven into it. Eliana's memories of her near-death are like the unstrung weft threads of a weaving: they've fallen out of the pattern and lie in shadow, tangled and out of sight. Only a whisper of their shape remains, like the afterimage of a brilliant light. This whisper disturbs her mind by its very presence, because she can't understand what it is, or why it's there. And in the meantime the loom knows itself bereft, empty where it should be full."

"But why would someone tear the pattern away? Where have the threads gone? And who will weave them back?" I demanded.

"Ah, those are difficult questions, little one. Be patient for a moment while I see if the One will speak answers to my mind."

It was more than a moment before Tirzah opened her eyes again, and when she did I was certain that she was looking at something my eyes couldn't see.

"Eliana herself stripped her memories away," she sighed, "although she doesn't remember that, either. She couldn't bear the torment of their presence in her mind. Perhaps this is a good thing. Maybe she needs time to gather her strength before she can look at them; she's still very young. So like a jumbled mess of loose thread, they wait in the darkness beneath her mind's loom for her to take them up again.

"Spinners and weavers roll their thread into skeins and set them carefully aside for good reason: thorns and thistles blow across the floors in human houses. Eliana is just discovering that brambles also blow through our minds; those loose memories can be snagged and rucked up into the light when she least expects it, like today, when she watched the snails being harvested, or yesterday, being jostled by the crowds. Both those times were similar enough to the terrible memories of what happened to her that they hooked them and pulled them up close to her waking mind. The pain and terror of these glimpses is agony to her, and she'll do whatever she can to avoid them, until the time is right.

"The son of Earth hoped that he might help heal the wounds in her mind, but whenever he reached out to her, she shied away from his touch. He forces his healing on no one, so that opportunity has come and gone. Still, though she may have feared his healing, he was a light in her darkness, and she grieves for his loss.

"Yet Ben Adamah said that the One is a weaver, and I believe this is so. Eliana is safe in his hands. The One will know when the thread of her spirit is spun strong enough to bear the weight of those memories without breaking, and his love will guide her hands to the loom. On that day she will come into her own."

cat tales and purple snails

Another loom. Another weaving. All as different from each other as the night sky from the noonday sun, yet still the same. Looms wove fabric: patterns, coverings, shelter, work for human hands and beauty for human pleasure. But my dream loom was never intended for wool. If anything, it wove lives, and not always in patterns that seemed good to me. What did it mean? Why had it entered my dreams? I might be curious about looms, but I knew almost nothing of weaving. Where did such strange ideas take shape? Why did I feel such a desperate need to do something no cat could hope to accomplish?

Because, small Shadow, the voice echoed in my memory, *you are growing in me, and in wisdom.*

How could I argue with He Who Brings Light to the Earth?

18

Fabric of Hope

Purple Gleaming in Shadow speaks

The reeking pots of priceless snail slime had to sit covered in a dark building for three days before the color would be intense enough to use in the next stage of the dyeing process, so for now we were spared any more of Aqhat's lessons in purple dye. He took pity on us that afternoon, and instead of sending us out to the dye yard to study less costly dyeing techniques, he invited us into the house to look at his own collection of weavings.

I may find looms and weaving fascinating—and for a cat that's a bizarre enough taste—but the human mania for *collecting* makes me yawn . . . and yawn . . . and, finally, nap. Aqhat's prized tapestries were no exception. I did stay awake on a cushioned sofa long enough to notice that Aeliana's knowledge of fine fabrics and dishes left him almost speechless, and for Aqhat, that was rare. I heard snippets of conversation here and there, between one nap and another: "My grandparents were weavers and merchants, and my mother taught me a lot . . . my father's family made ceramic ware, amphorae and lamps mostly, but my mother loved red slipware, and she even had a Phoenician glass bowl . . . Eli used to say that he preferred wool from Cappadocia and linen from Alexandria when he could find them . . . and the twill from Raetia . . ." After that I slept soundly.

As a result of Aeliana's surprising expertise, Aqhat invited her to dine at his table that night, along with his daughters and Ahumm, to help entertain three visiting merchants from the north.

Tirzah ran around our little house like a demented cuckoo, pulling robes out of the trunks that Aeliana had brought with her from Cana, trying to decide what would be most fitting for a young woman in Aeliana's uncertain position. In the end she chose a dark blue wool robe with a woven border of yellow flowers. Aeliana smiled at her choice.

"I wove that as a gift for Rachel, but when I wasn't looking she slipped it into my trunk before I left. I suppose it's foolish of me not to wear it."

So I watched as Tirzah arranged the robe's folds around Aeliana's shoulders. I thought she looked very elegant, with her hair coiled on her head, and a slim band binding it in place. And very beautiful. Tirzah escorted her to the dining room and left her in Alba's care (who looked like a puffy cloud of scarlet silk and tinkling gold). I hadn't been invited, but I came anyway, and hid under the table until I could see where Aeliana would be sitting.

Aqhat and Ahumm were standing at the room's far end with Elissa and three strange men when Alba and Aeliana entered. From my perch under the table, I could see the men clearly. Each of them, Aqhat as well, wheeled in unison like a column of Roman soldiers to stare at Aeliana. A deep flush whipped across Ahumm's face, followed by a scowl. The three merchants stood mute. Aqhat recovered first.

"Ah, gentleman, here is my youngest daughter, Alba, and her friend Aeliana, who enjoys the protection of my house while she works as an apprentice weaver here. She is a recent widow from a village north of Sidon. You should see her at her work, gentlemen! Her shuttles fly like swallows, and her needles dart like dragonflies!"

Perhaps you may wish to take some of her fine work home to your wives, eh?"

I thought the men looked as if they'd like very much to watch Aeliana doing anything at all. I felt the hackles rising on my neck, especially when I looked at Ahumm. *Practice*, Tirzah had said. So I stared at Ahumm and listened, listened as hard as I could . . . and cringed away at the rage and cruelty boiling up from inside him, all aimed at Aeliana. No wonder Wind on Water had feared for her safety! Yet, I could also tell that he was pushing those feelings down hard, like a presser in a fuller's yard. *May he not lose his grip!* I muttered to myself.

No anger darkened the other men's thoughts, although the tallest of the three visitors seemed oddly disturbed. Sweat was popping out on his beardless face, and his mind spun like a wobbling spindle. Even in his thoughts I could sense such a thundering heartbeat that I marveled I didn't actually hear it with my ears. *Males,* I muttered with scorn, and turned my attention back to Aqhat, who was guiding his guests to their places. I realized then that I knew none of their names; I'd been thinking my own thoughts and missed his introductions. I'd have to pay better attention.

Fortunately for Aeliana, Ahumm was seated near Aqhat, between his wife Donatiya and one of the merchants. As befitted her relative insignificance, Aeliana sat near the table's foot, beside the tall merchant, who seemed to be the least important of the three strangers. I crept across to her couch and leapt up beside her, unnoticed in the shadows. She laid a trembling hand on my fur and took a deep breath.

"Your dinner companion feels like a nice enough human," I purred into her thoughts. "I think he'd lay himself down on the floor like a carpet for you to walk on if you asked him," I added.

I sensed her smile in response. *Good!* She needed to relax and impress Aqhat tonight. Tirzah had been very clear about that.

I listened as conversations started up around the table while the humans waited for their food to be served. Only Aeliana stared down at her hands, saying nothing and avoiding her neighbor's gaze.

"'Aeliana,'" the man said hesitantly, still struggling to get his pounding pulse under control, "means 'sun-bright maiden,' I believe, lovely as the dawn rising from the womb of the Mother of Mountains."

Aeliana glanced up at him quickly, but then ducked her head and flushed deeply. Beautiful human female that she was, how could she be surprised by such comments from human males?

"'Mother of Mountains'?" she murmured. I could feel the effort it cost her to respond.

"You've not heard of her?" he asked with mock amazement. "No," he continued, when she shook her head, "few people know her name anymore. Today she is called 'Cybele,' and sometimes 'Demeter,' but she is always the Mother."

Ah, I purred to myself, *this human honors the Mother of Cats!*

"In the mountains where my people came from, the Goddess was known as Mother of Mountains, she who gave birth to all the Earth. In past times we carved images of her enthroned between her beloved lions. [*Ha!* I smiled] In the flat lands she has other names, but her lions often remain by her side."

I didn't understand why, but the more this agreeable human talked about the Mother, the more uncomfortable Aeliana became.

"There are mountains in Miletos, sir?" she managed at last. "I thought it was a seaport."

"No, lady, my family comes from the mountains far to the east in Anatolia. We've only lived in Miletos since my grandfather's time. We came down from the mountains with our flocks to escape the constant fighting. For longer than anyone can remember, one army after another has sought to control our mountain passes, and much blood has been shed."

I had the sense that Aeliana was enjoying this conversation as little as a cat struggling against the lash of a torrential rainstorm.

"And *your* name, sir," . . . *Surely she was gritting her teeth now!* . . . "Chariton. It means kindness, or mercy?"

"Indeed it does, lady, and I fear I have far too much of both in my nature to be the merchant my father hoped I'd be."

He smiled with mock sadness, shaking his head as if in regret.

"I should be more like our good Philokrates, seated there by Master Aqhat at the head of the table. He, as his name suggests, pursues power diligently! Do you suppose, Aeliana," and he bent his head toward her, as if sharing a confidence, "that the names our families choose for us do indeed shape our fates? That we become what we are named?"

I felt Aeliana drawing into herself like a snail. Something in Chariton's last remark had distressed her. I wondered what her birth name had meant.

"Aeliana!" I hissed, "He's just being polite! Even I can see he doesn't mean to offend you! You mustn't pull away. Remember what Tirzah said: if you can't do anything else, at least be pleasant enough to help Aqhat sell his goods!"

Aeliana straightened her shoulders and managed a smile aimed somewhere near the merchant's breastbone. It was better than not looking at him at all, I supposed.

"My father's name meant 'a cluster of grapes cut from the vine,'" she finally murmured, shrugging, "and he died before his time. Perhaps you're right."

Now *that* was a conversation-stopper.

Chariton floundered briefly, running a nervous hand through his thick black hair, but I could feel him gathering his thoughts to pick up the tattered shreds of their conversation as best he could.

"Do you hope to become a dyer of purple cloth yourself, lady?"

Aeliana laughed aloud, caught off guard by the question's absurdity.

"No, Chariton of Miletos, if it were mine to choose, I would never be a dyer of purple. I love weaving and embroidery. Master Aqhat has been instructing me in the harvest of the snails and the preparation of the dye, but I find it distasteful. Surely there are enough merchants eager to make their fortunes with royal purple for a simple widow to choose another path!"

Now this was more like it! Aeliana's response had fire, and the merchant was intrigued.

"But, lady," he answered slowly, his curiosity plain, "I assumed that any woman bold enough to leave her home and apprentice herself to a famous weaving master must have a powerful desire to succeed in the marketplace. Why apprentice yourself to a merchant of purple when you have no interest in its secrets?"

"Sir, my one desire was to leave my old life behind and start anew as a weaver of fine fabrics. Aqhat was a friend of my family, so I came to him." She frowned briefly. "I may become a merchant as well as a weaver one day, but I'll be happy to leave the purple to others. I don't wish to make my way in the world by battening on the pain of other creatures, no matter how unappealing they might be. At least sheep regrow their fleece.

"And you, sir, do you trade in purple?"

"I do, or at least my father does. The Aegean Sea is rich in the pebble-purple snails, and we raise many fine sheep for their wool . . . although I swear by all the gods that I've never laid a hand on a snail to do it harm."

Aeliana laughed in spite of herself, and actually glanced at Chariton's face. I sat back and considered my friend. Who was this suddenly forthright young female? What invisible corner had she turned in the last few moments? Where was the fearful child who had huddled in her bed after our brief visit to the marketplace only the day before?

Listen, small Shadow, and you shall have your answer! I heard *his* voice speaking to me, and felt myself resting in ben Adamah's hands. My sudden elation bore me toward Aeliana and Chariton, a soft pressure like a caress on my fur urging me to reach out, to listen more carefully.

At first I heard only the familiar pulse of Aeliana's thoughts, but then I realized I was hearing a different rhythm as well, running along beside hers, above and below, deeper and thicker, mingling and twining . . . not words, but . . . a pattern! They were weaving together, like two weavers at a loom, one handing the shuttle to the other, weaving the threads together, beating the weft into new cloth! Only they were weaving a fabric of words, feelings, hopes, and fears, all unaware of how their movements complemented each other, of how easily they created this thing of beauty out of threads of air.

Oh! I almost hissed aloud in surprise. *It's a mating dance!*

Cat tales and purple snails

Not until we'd left the dining room that night, and I sat on Aeliana's lap listening to her talk with Tirzah, did I realize that she and Chariton had been speaking in a different language from the one I was accustomed to hearing among my humans. When I recalled the sounds that had touched my ears I could almost taste their difference, but I also realized that what I had *heard*—what I always heard—was not human speech, but human thought. I'm not sure how that can be, or why, but it is so. My head grew pinched and tight with trying to understand, and I soon gave up. Maybe when I grew older . . .

19

Weavers and Dyers of Wool

Purple Gleaming in Shadow speaks

"You're very quiet, Eliana," Tirzah smiled. "You haven't said a word about how the dinner went. Perhaps I should ask Purple Shadow."

I smirked, but said nothing. We were sitting in Tirzah's small living room, the two humans sipping sweet drinks. Aeliana had hung out her blue robe to air in the courtyard before packing it away again, and was wearing ben Adamah's old mantle wrapped around her sleeping shift. The fire burned low in the tiny hearth, and the night was quiet.

"The men were very friendly," Aeliana murmured, "except for Ahumm. He looked like a thundercloud."

We all considered that, but no one said anything. What was there to say?

"I liked the man who sat beside me," she smiled hesitantly. "His name is Chariton, and he comes from a city on the coast of the Aegean Sea, near Ephesus, called Miletos. His family are weavers and dyers of wool."

Tirzah looked puzzled. "But, child, what is he doing here at this time of year, he or his companions? The sailing season is past; no ships have left Acco for more than two weeks now. The sea won't be safe to sail any distance for another four months. Surely they don't mean to go all that way by donkey!"

"Oh, Tirzah," Aeliana laughed, "Chariton is much too tall to ride a donkey! No, one of the other two men, the one called Zosimos, got sick with a fever in Damascus, and the rest of their company went back to Miletos without them on one of the last ships. Chariton and Philokrates stayed with Zosimos to care for him. They're planning to explore and meet new merchants, but Zosimos is still weak, and the journey from Damascus overtaxed him, so they'll be staying around Acco for a week or two, maybe longer. They may go home overland in short stages, but that will depend on what new markets they find here."

"And you'd like him to stay a while, Eliana? You'd enjoy speaking with him again?"

"Perhaps," she whispered, and ducked her head to hide the blush. "He was very pleasant, even if he is a pagan and worships the great Goddess."

"Well, that's good," Tirzah smiled, looking down at her lap as she swirled her drink around in its cup. "Because Muttenbaal told me that Aqhat is hoping to bring them back tomorrow to tour the workshop."

Aeliana slept poorly that night (I always notice, since my rest depends on the quietness of her sleep). Then she woke early to bathe herself and prepare for the day . . . and took an uncommonly long time dressing. I followed all this with interest. I wasn't old enough to birth kittens myself, but I'd observed the older cats in their careful dance. Still, humans probably did things differently. I wondered when Aeliana's urge to produce kits of her own would drive her out in search of this handsome human male. Surely it would be soon, judging from the males' reactions to *her*. I considered asking, but Tirzah and Vita woke up then, and breakfast distracted me.

Elissa came knocking at Tirzah's door even before the humans had cleared the breakfast food off the table, summoning Aeliana to the weaving workshop to greet the guests. Aeliana emerged from her room wearing yet *another* change of clothes, this time a soft linen tunic with a wool over-mantle. I found that I enjoyed watching what humans wore, now that I'd begun to understand weaving. Aeliana had told me that most of her clothes were hand-me-downs from Rachel, the wealthy merchant's wife who'd cared for her in the Galilee. Without them, she'd be dressed in rags, she said. I suspected the tall merchant might not care.

Chariton's face lit up like a cat's at a winter sunrise when Aeliana entered Aqhat's office. A moment later he saw me peering out from under her hair and paused in surprise, but then smiled broadly.

"Good morning, Aeliana," he murmured when we drew closer. "I see you've brought your lion along!"

Aeliana flushed, and I did my best to squirm invitingly, the way humans seem to find appealing in a cat, and to my endless chagrin, I fell off her shoulder, only catching myself by clutching at her mantle on my way down. But before the wool could snag, the human male had caught me in his large hands and lifted me up to meet his eyes.

They were nice eyes, but strangely colored, like the sky on a bright morning. And they seemed to see *me* more clearly than humans usually did: he didn't examine me as a beast, but almost as another human . . . the way Aeliana, or Tirzah, or ben Adamah, looked at me.

Animal speaker? I barely breathed in my mind.

Speaking cat of the Mother? he whispered back.

Both Aeliana and Aqhat were watching us with surprise. Aqhat might not understand much, but he caught the gist of our meeting. The others continued their conversations, oblivious.

"Come, everyone," Aqhat called, clapping his hands together. "Let's move on into the weaving rooms—and, Chariton," he added in an undertone, "later we must sit down and talk together."

Looms! Wherever I looked, looms! In one room women wove borders and patterns on tiny looms and tablets, in another, looms like Tirzah's leaned against the walls, only huge . . . wide enough for three or four grown cats to lie end to end across the rolled fabric! Some were so tall that the women weaving had to use steps to reach the tops. Groups of women worked together at each one, laughing and even singing together. I could hardly absorb what I saw in one room before Aqhat was herding us into another. Rooms with flax, rooms with cotton, rooms with wool, and even silk. Then at last we came to the room where the new two-beam looms had been set up.

With a cry of delight, Aeliana moved closer to watch the women at their work. Unlike the older weighted looms, the warp threads were attached to a bottom beam as well as the top, and the weft threads were beaten down, not up, allowing the weavers to sit while they worked.

But Chariton wasn't looking at the new looms. Gesturing to an older loom, unattended in a corner, with a length of partially woven wool stretched on it, Chariton turned to Aqhat and asked, "May I try my hand?"

"You, sir?" Aqhat's eyebrows shot up in surprise.

"Indeed, Master, weaving has long been a skill among the men of my family . . . but not spinning, you understand." He grinned at Aeliana. "Our women draw the line there."

He walked toward the loom, holding his hand out to Aeliana.

"Will you weave with me, lady?"

Aeliana shrank back, away from all the staring eyes, but Aqhat waved her on.

"Go ahead, my dear. What a novelty, to see a man and woman weaving together! I can dine out on this for weeks! Please, begin."

I leapt off Aeliana's shoulder and trotted over to the loom, climbing rapidly up one side to perch on the top. I ignored the twitters and pointing fingers. Let them laugh. What did I care about these strange humans? I wanted to be in the middle of this!

Aeliana moved hesitantly toward the loom. Once there, she studied the simple weave, and then turned to remove her mantle and hang it from a peg on the wall. She looked a question at Chariton, who shrugged and smiled. Taking up a place on the loom's near side, she plucked the shuttle from its resting place, while he walked to the far side. Then taking a deep breath, she began.

Back and forth the shuttle flew, one or the other of the humans beating the weft up into the finished cloth as the cross-weaves accumulated. Their fingers flew faster and faster, weightless, winged, the rhythm complex and instinctive: as ben Adamah had said of Tirzah and Aeliana, like larks wheeling in the sky at sunset. Except that I sensed that beyond their obvious skill, these two were weaving yet more subtle patterns into the fabric they'd begun the night before.

Then abruptly, they stopped, almost knocking me from my perch with surprise. As if at some secret signal, they backed away from the loom, breathing quickly, their faces full of laughter.

Aeliana was the first to remember where she was. She flushed, looked down at her hands, and stepped away to retrieve her mantle. Aqhat was cheering loudly, and the other humans were laughing and exclaiming, all except for Ahumm, who had joined the group late and now stood scowling at Aeliana. Chariton watched her too, but with a softness in his eyes that belied the intensity of his stare.

"Well, Chariton, if you lack for employment this winter, I'll hire you anytime!" Aqhat laughed. "Here in Canaan we think of weaving as woman's work, but I'm always happy to try something new. How else could I have grown my business, right Elissa?"

Elissa smiled in agreement.

"But let's stop for now, since lunch will be served shortly," Aqhat continued. "Wander around and explore as you will for the next little while, and someone will find you when the table is laid.

"Chariton, Aeliana, will you join me in my office before we go in to eat?"

So Aeliana, Chariton and I followed Aqhat into his office. I'd heard about this room from Wind on Water, but I'd never seen it before, since cats weren't allowed in the workshops unless invited by humans. It held no surprises, except for Eye of the Mother, who was already there, sleeping on a golden cushion the same rich color as her fur. She opened her eyes briefly when we entered, found us uninteresting, and resumed her nap.

"How do you come to be so familiar with cats?" Aqhat asked Chariton as the tapestry closed behind us. His eagerness showed clearly in his eyes as he waited for Chariton's answer.

Chariton smiled and studied Aqhat's face.

"The great temple at Ephesus has cats," he answered at last. "People say the Egyptians brought them to our coast years ago, when the goddesses Bastet and Artemis were first hailed as one goddess. How could one serve the mighty Bast without her cats? But times have changed, and the cats mostly run wild now, although the priests and priestesses still care for many of them." He shrugged.

"And *your* gift, Chariton?" Aqhat pressed. "You *are* an animal speaker are you not?"

Chariton smiled and inclined his head. I could see that this was something he didn't care to discuss.

"Ah," Aqhat sighed, "you are fortunate. I have only the tiniest taste of this gift. In her kindness, Eye of the Mother has adopted me, much as she might an orphaned kitten."

Humph, I thought. I *know a lot of orphaned kittens she never looked at twice.*

"The gift has run long in my family," Chariton admitted. "In times past, we would use it to speak with the gods."

With the gods? I puzzled. *How with the gods?* I thought Aeliana looked disturbed at this remark.

"My family has *no* such gift," she said decisively. "With me it started with ben Adamah, when he and Mari guided me here."

"Ben Adamah?" Chariton echoed.

"Oh, Chariton," Aqhat exclaimed, "we *must* tell you about Yeshua ben Yosef! The cats all call him ben Adamah, or the son of Earth, but he's a Galilean healer and holy man . . ."

At that moment a servant boy pulled the tapestries aside and summoned us to lunch.

Aqhat ushered us out, gripping the merchant's shoulder briefly, while he announced to the world at large, "What I want to know, my friend, is whether you're planning to steal my young apprentice away from me before she ever begins her studies, eh?"

I felt Aeliana's heart lurch in her breast, and a terrified shadow within her flee into deeper darkness.

That night I dreamed of the dark loom again, but this time the threads hung limp, their colors dull. At first sight, I stopped abruptly, considering the difference, wondering if this might be a good thing. Perhaps the pattern I disliked was changing, the invisible weaver preparing to rearrange her threads. But then I saw the broken threads, dangling frayed below the fabric, threads of drab cloudy blue, their vibrance drained away like rain running through dirty streets—Aeliana's threads. This could *not* be a good thing.

I leapt onto the fabric. It didn't bounce as before, but hung slack and loose beneath my weight. I tried reaching down under the weave to pull the broken threads back up into the pattern, but how could I twist them back together? How could a cat's paws spin thread? I sat up on my haunches, trying to snag and hold the ends with my claws, even licking and chewing on them, but they fell away before they ever touched, never offering me the slightest chance to repair them.

Climbing off the loom, I sat down to study it from a distance. Already it had an abandoned feel, as if hope and life had fled. Its earlier pattern might have terrified me with hints of chaos and pain to come, but at least it had been alive! I crouched down beside the loom and tried to think. I must not be as clever as Tirzah said, because no thoughts came. Only darkness, and heavy breathless air, disturbed by neither sound nor scent. Nothingness.

Ben Adamah! I wailed, and woke to the early morning sounds of the garden outside Tirzah's house.

Cat tales and purple snails

I never used to dream, not dreams like these anyway. I would dream of my mother's warmth, my dead brothers and sisters, tasty treats my mother brought home, even the taste of the milk from her breast. But when the son of Earth entered my life, everything changed.

Once my world had been like a warm den, with comfortable limits and orderly rules. There was fear, and danger, but they made sense in a manageable way. Day followed night, and one sunny day was much like the last. But when ben Adamah came, the roof of my den was torn away like a tent, leaving me cowering beneath the vast dome of heaven. Gone was the comfort of predictability. Endless horizons of possibility mocked me on every side. In some incomprehensible way, what I did from moment to moment suddenly *mattered*. Even in my dreams.

20

Like A Fortress

Purple Gleaming in Shadow speaks

Aeliana refused to join Aqhat and the visiting merchants in their morning excursion with the divers, claiming "women's" problems. I wasn't sure what those were, but I was fairly certain that she didn't have any. The longer she lay curled up in her bed, the more I sensed the nothingness of my dream gathering around her in the waking world. I could read no thoughts in her mind, only walls.

"Tirzah?" I called at last, climbing slowly up the stairs to her weaving room. "We need to do something for Aeliana. I feel like she's fallen down a deep well. I can't reach her."

"Yes, Purple Shadow, I agree," she sighed, letting her hands drop from their work. She turned away from the loom, and together we walked out onto the sunlit roof.

"Something must have happened yesterday. Tell me about your morning with the merchants."

So I described our tour, Aeliana's weaving with Chariton, our words with Aqhat, and my sense that what he'd said had frightened her. In retelling the tale of our luncheon, I realized that by then Aeliana had already disappeared inside herself. She was mastering the curious human art of social masks at an impressive rate. The merchants had left for an appointment in the city immediately after the meal, and Aeliana had returned to the workshop with Alba. I'd gone my own way. Neither Tirzah nor I had really spoken to her after that.

"Foolish man," Tirzah sighed. "Aqhat has a heart as large as Leviathan, but the wit of a mongrel hound."

I considered that intriguing image for a moment.

"You're right, Purple," she concluded. "We must do something, but I don't know what."

"I dreamed about the loom again last night, Tirzah."

"Tell me, little one," she said, her gaze sharpening.

When I'd finished, she said, "And the last thing you did in this dream was to call out for ben Adamah?"

I blinked.

"Perhaps we should do the same," she mused. "Did he not say we might call him if we needed him, and that Aeliana should also? I don't believe she's calling him, Purple, so that leaves us."

How do you call someone who isn't there? It was one thing to think about him and get a feeling that he was near. It was something else again to set out to *call* him to come. I tried as hard as I could. So did Tirzah. But nothing happened. The sun shone, the dye vats fumed, and seagulls screamed over our heads.

Then, just as Tirzah was about to go down to the courtyard to help Vita prepare the noon meal, Aeliana emerged from our sleeping room and started up the stairs to the roof.

She still wore her night shift, and most of her long hair had escaped from its evening braid. Her eyes were heavy and swollen, as if sleep had rolled over her like a storm tide. She rubbed her hands roughly over her face and looked at us.

"I had such odd dreams this morning," she murmured. "When I remember them, they're clear as an autumn day, yet so different from the world I know that I might have been walking along the bottom of the sea."

"Can you tell us, child?" Tirzah prodded gently. "When I explain a puzzling dream to someone else, it often opens itself to me in the telling."

Aeliana walked to the far side of the roof and stared at the distant city walls for so long that I thought she wasn't going to answer.

"I'll try," she said at last, her voice hoarse and troubled.

She walked slowly back to the wall's edge where we were sitting and dropped down beside us.

"First I dreamed that I was sitting at Aqhat's table with Chariton," she began. "I kept pushing him away, treating him unkindly, doing everything I could think of to discourage him short of saying, 'Go away!' In my dream I knew he cared for me, and that he hoped I might care for him, but I wouldn't even consider it. It was asking too much of me. I shut myself up like a fortress and slammed my gates in his face.

"So he left. Sadly, and in great grief, but he left, just as I'd asked him to. Somehow I could see him in my dream, riding a horse through the city gates and along the road to Tyre. When I saw that he was really gone, I fell to my knees struggling for air, like a fish gasping on dry land, unable to draw breath. I wheezed and heaved until I was sure my lungs would burst. He'd gone away, and stolen the very breath of life in his going. Yet he'd done no more than I asked."

She paused then, rocking a little in place. Neither Tirzah nor I dared speak lest we startle her into silence.

"The dream changed then," she said, "and maybe other dreams came in between, but at last Chariton appeared again, right in front of me now, running toward me with his hands reaching out to me, tears streaming down his face, his eyes anguished and blazing with pain. He looked as if his whole world were shattering. His eyes burned so! I woke up terrified, calling his name. Yet the voice that rang in my ears as the dream dissolved around me wasn't my own, but ben Adamah's. He said . . ."

She stopped, unable to speak for the tears choking her throat.

"He said," she tried again, "'Tirakemah, be careful. You sleep when you should wake. You flee what you should embrace. How can a weaver weave if the thread says, "I will not!" and unravels at his touch?'"

Then she slipped to the floor, drew her knees up against her chest, wrapped her arms around them like a desolate child, and wept.

After a miserable interval I crept along the wall and pushed my nose against the back of her neck.

"Ai!" she cried in a strangled voice. "That's cold!"

I pushed again, and again, until she turned and drew me into her arms.

"Did your dream come more clear to you when you described it to us?" Tirzah had decided to treat Aeliana's welcoming me as an encouraging sign.

"What it said makes no sense," Aeliana replied, her voice muffled by my fur. "How could Chariton's happiness, and even his life, lie in my hands? What right does he have to lay such a burden on me?"

"That depends on what you've promised him, child, and how strong the bonds may be that already bind you to each other."

"Tirzah, I only met him two days ago! I've promised him nothing."

"What does time matter, Eliana? Who knows when the One first set your feet on the road that led you here? And Purple Shadow tells me that the two of you moved deeply through each other's depths yesterday, even though no words were spoken. She's learning how to listen for such things, you know. Was she mistaken?"

Aeliana said nothing.

"What is it you fear, child?" Tirzah whispered.

Aeliana still hadn't answered by the time Vita called up the stairs that lunch was ready, but Tirzah waved her away. When at last Aeliana broke her silence, her words came out in a wild lament.

"I don't know!" she wailed. "I don't know what I fear!"

"That's a poor reason to break another's heart," Tirzah murmured, and moved over to put her arm around Aeliana. "What if you heeded ben Adamah's voice, and at least tried not to flee, tried to crack the door open to see what the future offers before saying, 'No, I won't!' Could you do that? After all, doesn't your dream warn you that your happiness is at risk along with Chariton's?"

"But Tirzah, are you saying that the son of Earth *wants* me to take Chariton as a husband? He's a pagan and a worshipper of the Goddess, and I'm a Jew!"

"That is a hard question, child, but did ben Adamah not tell you to feel free to go among the nations? Did he not choose a name for you that suited a gentile and a Greek? I wonder if this day wasn't in his mind all along. After all, who is left to disapprove among your people? Eli and his kind wife, perhaps, but they agreed to send you here, with their blessing, already knowing Aqhat and his city. Whose censure do you fear if the son of Earth has set his benediction on your path? All he asked of you was to hold the One in your heart: he offered no advice concerning husbands, Jew or Greek."

Aeliana had nothing to say in reply.

That evening Aqhat himself came to Tirzah's door to ask after Aeliana's health. She greeted him herself, white-faced and hollow-eyed, but calm, and assured him that she would be well in the morning.

"Oh, my child, I'm so happy!" he exclaimed, patting her shoulder awkwardly as he balanced Eye of the Mother on his other arm. "I've planned an excursion for us tomorrow! We're going up the hill into the old city, where the Lady's ruined temple lies. Chariton didn't say outright that he wouldn't come, but there are so many ways to say something without speaking the words, aren't there? I'll wager a pot of purple dye that he'll find some excuse to stay behind if you're not with us, and if he refuses, how likely are the others to come?"

Aqhat paused to catch his breath and Tirzah turned to him with a puzzled smile.

"But Aqhat, I thought you were planning to show Aeliana how we begin the dyeing process with the new batch of purple dye tomorrow? It's the third day."

"Oh there'll always be another day to learn purple dye, Tirzah! My dyers know their art. They don't need me there. This is far more important, believe me. Imagine the profits to be made if I could set up contracts with Chariton's father: the most respected cloth merchant in the eastern Aegean!

"So, everything's arranged, then!" he beamed. "I'll send someone to summon you when our guests arrive in the morning. Muttenbaal will pack a lunch for us, and servants will follow to see to the details. Alba will be there, and Elissa, and perhaps Ahumm. The cats will come, of course, and we'll have a grand adventure!"

Eye of the Mother gave him a withering look and slitted her eyes. I'd be very surprised to find her on Aqhat's arm in the morning.

"What shall I wear?" Aeliana managed to rasp out as Tirzah closed the door behind Aqhat. She sounded exhausted. "Tirzah, how will I get through the day?"

Her voice sounded as if she were struggling beneath the weight of the fallen temple itself.

"Hush child, you'll be fine. We'll both be fine. If my old bones can manage it, so can you. Just wear something practical—and perhaps ben Adamah's mantle over all . . . Yes, that's what you should do. It'll give you confidence, and something to talk about with our guests as well. Your embroidery is exquisite, you know, and it'll offer them a chance to see your handiwork."

So the sun set on chaos in our little house, with Aeliana agonizing over every possible detail and unlikely catastrophe. She hardly slept at all, although Tirzah's sleep was untroubled. If I slept, I don't remember it.

Cat tales and purple snails

Being part of an "us" isn't easy for a cat. We're loners at heart. That's the way the Mother of Cats made us. A mother cat loves her kittens, but what they do with their lives once they're weaned is of little concern to her. Oh, there's a kind of distant regard, and maybe even some affection. Still, it's all pretty vague.

But now apparently I "had" a human. We were "bonded," or so I'd been told. I didn't remember choosing such a thing, but that didn't seem to matter. There it was. Done. Not that I regretted it. It just wasn't what I'd expected out of life.

Expectations. Tirzah says they're dangerous things. They dash the sweetness of the moment from your mouth and replace it with the dust of "might-have-beens." But is this something normal cats even think about?

Ben Adamah said I was as clever as one of the great temple cats of the Egyptian cat goddess Bast, so I suppose it must be so. But I wonder if I would have been happier as a simple wild cat of the seashore, bearing kittens in my season, and never thinking about much beyond my next meal.

Maybe I'm just tired. Even a cat gets peevish from lack of sleep.

21

Into the Hills

Purple Gleaming in Shadow speaks

The glare of the late morning sun on the fallen temple stones dazzled my eyes. If Aqhat hadn't insisted that we were standing in the midst of what had once been a temple, I wouldn't've known it. We'd climbed up into the sky! Nothing stood between me and the vast emptiness above: no trees, no walls . . . or at least no walls that stood higher than a human's legs. A sudden burst of wind would surely send me tumbling off into the air like beach wrack in a storm, except that I'd have a lot farther to fall. I burrowed under Aeliana's hair and dug my claws into ben Adamah's mantle.

"Look!" cried Alba. "There's a cat!"

Everyone turned to look where she was pointing. Sure enough, an ordinary cat sat on a stone block washing her face.

"Do you suppose it's a sacred cat, Papa?" she asked in softer tones, almost whispering: as if cats weren't as normal a part of her life as sleeping and waking.

"I'm certain of it, daughter," Aqhat smiled. "This temple is where all the cats of Acco had their beginning. Don't you agree, Chariton?"

But before the merchant could answer, the cat interrupted her
bath and trotted toward him. Once she reached him, she rubbed
insistently against his robe, and then stood up on her hind feet to
reach as far up his body with her paws as her length would allow. He
hummed to her in return and dropped down beside her, bending his
head to touch hers. She leaned against him, rubbing and butting his
head with her own. In the end he picked her up and set her on his
shoulder.

Aqhat, Tirzah, and Aeliana were watching him strangely. The
others just laughed.

"That's not the behavior of a normal temple cat, Chariton," Tirzah
mused softly, "or perhaps you're more than a simple animal speaker."

"Ah, little mother, you've seen through me," he replied with a wry
grin. "In the mountains of my homeland, before we moved to the city,
my grandmothers had always been dedicated to the Mother of
Mountains. Our family has always had a special link with beasts,
especially cats, since lions were sacred to her. They often guided our
seers in their trances, and helped them find their way home again from
the shadowlands, but this little lady is more sensitive than most.
Usually if I don't reach out to them, animals don't notice me."

"So you're one of those dedicated to this goddess?" Tirzah asked.

"No, not officially," he shrugged, "but it runs in my blood, and
some of my family still bear her gifts."

"You're a seer, then?" she pressed.

"Let's say I have dreams, little mother—like you," he grinned.

Tirzah frowned.

"I've made no effort to train myself in the Goddess' mysteries," he
continued, "and I don't wish to be one who intercedes between this
world and the paths of spirit. Servants of the mysteries too often find
themselves consumed, flesh and spirit, by their calling."

Then he turned away, removing the cat from his shoulder, and reached out to take Aeliana's hand in his.

"Come away, daughter of the Mother, and let us see what remains of this temple," he smiled, and led us away toward the center of the ruin.

I could tell that Aeliana wanted to wrest her hand away and flee, back to Tirzah's house if possible, but she was held by her promise to Aqhat. So she allowed herself to be pulled along in this strange human's wake.

Unlike Aeliana, I found his revelations fascinating, especially after the strange cat's behavior. His meeting with her seemed to have opened him to me as well. When I looked at him now I saw ancient caverns in his soul, lit with fire, and musky with the scent of spilled blood, going back through uncounted lives of humans and beasts. Strange shapes and stranger voices filled my mind and pulled me toward dreams . . . until Tirzah's voice intruded like a clanging gong in my mind.

"Purple Shadow, come here to me," she said sternly, approaching us at a brisk walk. "Wake and sit on my lap."

Then she was plucking me off Aeliana's shoulder, shooting a concerned look at my human, and carrying me off to a massive stone block, where she seated herself carefully after peering around it for snakes.

"Listen to them, Purple, and tell me what you hear," she urged me. So I reached out, and to my surprise, I could hear them both clearly. I listened, and Tirzah listened through me.

"My words alarmed you, lady," Chariton said. He didn't ask it as a question. He stated a fact.

"Yes."

Aeliana stood silent for many beats of my heart and then spoke again.

"I must tell you one of *my* secrets, Chariton. I'm not a Phoenician woman from beyond Sidon, but a Jew from the Galilee. The mysteries you spoke of are forbidden to my people, and they frighten me."

"I knew this already, lady. And you have no cause for fear."

"You knew? How did you know?"

"A thousand small things," he smiled, "and a few dreams. It matters little to me. I see your face, and the spirit leaping in your eyes, and I know all I need to know."

"You're a sorcerer!"

"No, lady, a sorcerer is a twisted soul who calls up spirits and small godlings to work his will. My people follow the Goddess. We are her servants, and keepers of the Earth."

"Son of Earth . . ." Aeliana whispered, "that's what the cats call the man whose mantle I wear, and who brought me safe to Aqhat's house."

"Tell me about this man, Aeliana. Aqhat mentioned him as well."

Aeliana shrugged helplessly, as if to say, *Tell you? How can I tell you?* But she tried nonetheless.

"His name is Yeshua ben Yosef, and he's a prophet and healer from the Galilee. He . . . he found me . . . he . . . he . . ."

Fire and pain flooded her thoughts. Her mind struggled, staggered, and gave up. She started again.

"He took care of me after my parents died in a fire. He brought me to stay in the home of his friends. I recovered, and they sent me to Aqhat because of my skill at the loom."

She grew silent then, and I could feel her thoughts opening out, uncertain, touching the fallen stones around her.

"Many people died here," she whispered. "The men who pulled these stones down were filled with hate. I can feel it."

"I'm not surprised that you feel it, Aeliana. People say that a Jewish army destroyed this temple, seeking to force the people of Acco to worship the god of Israel. Servants and worshippers of the Goddess died in great numbers. Their blood still cries out to those with ears to hear.

"But come," Chariton urged, "come away from this sad ruin and sit with me by the quarry, where the Earth speaks of little but her own scars."

He guided her to a slab of unfinished stone at the top of a cliff overlooking the river plain. Several poor houses huddled together further along the hilltop, apparently cobbled together with stones salvaged from ruined buildings. In the distance and off to one side, Aqhat's compound straggled along the shore beside the glittering sea. Almost too faint to be heard, seagulls screamed above the fishing boats. Aqhat's voice rose and fell among the temple's fallen columns. The human tensions drained away. The day felt oddly peaceful.

Chariton smiled deep into Aeliana's eyes. I felt his gaze reaching out to her, and hers meeting his in return, each coming and going, like the shuttle in their loom.

"Why do the cats call this healer the son of Earth?" he asked gently.

"I'm not sure," she said. "They just do. The cat who travels with him called him that already."

"Is he an animal speaker?" he asked.

"Oh, yes," Aeliana smiled. "He did amazing things with Aqhat's cats. And he rescued my kitten."

She went on to tell him about ben Adamah's visit with Aqhat.

"What did he say to you about himself, lady?"

Aeliana wrinkled her brow in an effort to gather her thoughts.

"He said there is One god above all others who is both a mother and a father, and that he has come to tell us that the One loves us as his own children and wishes us to love him in return."

She paused and then spoke again.

"He said that the One is a weaver, and that he weaves our lives on his great loom, for good and not ill if we let him. But he forces no one. He only asks. Oh, and ben Adamah said he would always be with me, that even if he weren't here in person, I could call him and he would hear. I see him in my dreams sometimes, and once I saw him in a waking vision."

"I wish I could have met your prophet, lady. Do you know where he went when he left here?"

"Why . . ." Aeliana stopped with a surprised look on her face. "He might still be in Acco! He left Aqhat's house to stay with a merchant in the city, an old man with gout. It's only been a few days, not even a week! We must ask Aqhat!"

"There's time enough, Aeliana. For now I want to talk with you. Tell me why you fear the Goddess and her mysteries. Didn't your friend ben Adamah tell you the One is both mother and father?"

"Oh, but that's different!" she said, and then stopped.

"Why is it different?" he smiled.

"Well, the goddess . . . has prostitutes, and men . . . um . . . harm themselves when they serve her. And she's cruel, isn't she? Ben Adamah describes the One as a very different kind of Mother, with no dark mysteries, not even sacrifices. He said the One created the universe and loves it like a mother or father loves a child.

"I'm not explaining this very well," she sighed. "I'm no rabbi. But isn't the goddess you serve cruel, Chariton, like the one I've heard about? And you offer blood sacrifices, don't you?"

"Even Jews offer sacrifices, lady," he smiled. "Isn't this prophet a Jew?"

"Yes, of course . . . but I don't think he likes priests much. I'm not sure why. We don't talk about it. He mostly talks about me when we're together." She stopped and blushed as the sense of her words rang in her ears.

"Do you love this man?" Chariton asked.

"Oh, yes," Aeliana beamed, and then, almost leaping to her feet in dismay, "Oh, no, not like that!"

"Good!" Chariton laughed.

They were silent for a time, and then Aeliana spoke again.

"You didn't answer me, about your goddess. How *do* you worship her?"

Chariton leaned back on his arms and stretched his legs out in the sunlight.

"We don't live in the mountains of my ancestors anymore. My family lives among strangers, just as you do. I've visited their temples, but the Mother I've always known in my heart isn't there. So I walk into the hills, with the sheep and goats, among the olive groves and orchards, and I find her there. Sometimes I lie down and sleep in the meadows, and she comes to me. Or her animals come. I look into their eyes and I'm drawn into a fecund darkness, where the ages of Earth vanish and I'm one with the deep fires of creation. Today I find myself wondering if your friend knows this place too."

Now Aeliana did jump to her feet, with a laugh. "Come, Chariton, let's go ask Aqhat! If ben Adamah is still in the city, you might be able to meet him today if we hurry! And Chariton?"

"Yes, Aeliana?"

"If you go to see him, would you take my kitten with you so she can tell me about it?"

"With pleasure, lady," he bowed.

Cat tales and purple snails

The One had a loom? Aeliana had told us what ben Adamah had said about the weaver, but I just thought he'd been using images she'd understand. My dream, and Tirzah's, since she'd dreamed it too—what did it mean? Had we dreamed of the One's loom? All those beautiful lights, the disturbing patterns, the broken threads: what were they saying? The loom's broken threads had sent me to Tirzah for help, and help had come: Aeliana had dreamed a dream, and heard ben Adamah's voice.

I was getting more and more tangled in these mysteries . . . my fascination with looms just kept growing . . . and Ben Adamah seemed to be everywhere. So. Did the stubborn itch I felt in my paws mean that I really could make a difference in the patterns?

My questions were kinking my mind like a matted fleece full of thistles!

22

No Time for Evasions

Purple Gleaming in Shadow speaks

*T*he sun was sinking low as Chariton left Aqhat's house that evening
(with me on his shoulder) and set out for the city. The son of Earth
hadn't gone far at all. He'd left the house of the now gout-free
Phoenician merchant the day after arriving there, and had gone to stay
with a friend of Eli's, an elderly scholar of Jewish law. His host was out
for the evening, so rather than invite strangers into his host's home,
he'd agreed to meet us at the forum, on the steps of the library,
adjoining the public meeting hall. Even at night vendors in the
marketplace were hawking their wares by torchlight, and people were
coursing through the streets. With more than a legion of Roman
soldiers camping in and around the city, street crime was rare.

The disciples had been right about Acco's hostility toward Jews.
The people of Acco were delighted to receive ben Adamah's healing,
but they turned a deaf ear to his words. Even cats made better
listeners. We discovered that he'd be leaving for Tyre the following
day. Our timing seemed blessed by the Mother.

Chariton knew from my excited purring, or maybe from his own
gift of seeing, which of the men standing near the library steps was the
son of Earth. Or perhaps he sensed Aeliana's hand in the finely woven

mantle he wore. I wouldn't have been surprised if ben Adamah himself had sensed our approach as soon as we'd stepped out Aqhat's door. Anyway, the two humans walked up to each other like old friends, grasping arms and exchanging smiles with no sense of restraint.
I purred my happiness at seeing Wind on Water again, and her hum in response was almost as sweet to me as her touch. But we were witnesses to human business tonight and not free to visit as we chose.

At Chariton's suggestion, we walked together around the end of the temple precinct, past the old cemeteries that overlapped the city wall, and out onto the road that followed the seawall. The vast temples loomed at our backs, and the vanished sun's glow hung over the shining sea like a copper basin.

The increasing darkness made this strange errand more bearable to me than it would have been in daylight, but I hadn't anticipated anything like the silent forests of stone that stretched beneath the temple roofs, or the massive seawall and its dizzying height above the even more terrifying waves that boomed against its base, sometimes sending salt spray high enough to bead my whiskers. I wasn't liking this seawall, and I could tell Wind on Water wasn't either. I burrowed under the folds of Chariton's mantle as best I could. After all, I didn't need to see the two humans to hear their words.

"I wanted to meet where we might speak freely, Lord," Chariton said as they gazed over the wall. "I hope this place doesn't offend you, under the eaves of the temples as it is."

"Have no fear, my friend," the son of Earth smiled. "I'd be a poor prophet indeed if people's foolishness offended me. There are no gods in this echoing emptiness, only mislaid hopes and dreams."

"Who are you, Lord?" Chariton asked suddenly, and bluntly.

"Your question is an easy one to ask, Chariton of Miletos, but not so simply answered. Perhaps you should decide for yourself."

"It was worth trying!" Chariton laughed. "You might have answered me."

"I'll ask you the same, Chariton: 'Who are you?'"

"I, Lord? I'm a man who seeks the face of the Goddess, and who hopes one day to ask for the maiden Aeliana in marriage, she who lives in the house of Aqhat."

I sat up at that remark.

"I've felt your spirit leaning toward hers, and hers toward you, my friend," ben Adamah replied. "She is a beloved daughter of the One, but deeply wounded in body and spirit."

Chariton was silent, his thoughts too turbulent for me to follow.

"I've sensed her scars, Lord, and her fear. Will you tell me how I might help her find healing?"

"You don't ask for the tale of her days?" ben Adamah asked softly.

"If she chooses not to tell me, I have no right to know," Chariton replied.

I could almost feel ben Adamah's smile.

"She cannot tell you, my friend, because she has chosen to forget the reason for her fears. Her tragedy was greater than her mind could bear, innocent and unsuspecting child that she was. I *will* tell you, as Aqhat told you, that she is indeed a widow, and not a maiden. But as to how she might find healing . . . that lies in her hands. I was unable to help her, because she wasn't yet ready to remember."

I sensed his shrug, and Wind on Water's sadness.

"When she releases her memories into the light, then her healing can begin."

"But, Lord, surely there is something I can do!" Chariton almost groaned. "She calls to me across a misty sea like the fabled sirens, and I will surely die if I cannot come to her!"

"Should I remind you that it was the men who *did* come to the sirens who died, my friend? Courting Aeliana will be no easy task."

"Tell me there is something I can do! Surely the gifts of my clan mothers count for something in this! Can I not walk into her dreams and bend her heart toward mine?"

"Would you do this thing, man of the goddess?" ben Adamah's voice snapped like a lash. "Would you step into her mind and violate her will, making her a prisoner of your passions? Is she no more to you than a possession to be gained by sharp dealing?"

I felt Chariton reel beneath the son of Earth's anger, and then collapse to his knees before him. I raised my head from beneath his mantle. Jumping down off Chariton's shoulder seemed like a good idea just then, except that in doing it I might inadvertently draw ben Adamah's wrath. I dug in my claws and flattened myself against my companion's shoulder.

"Mercy, Lord!" Chariton was crying, his hand outstretched as if to ward off a blow. "I spoke in desperate longing, without thought! Never would I ride rough across her will, nor quench her glowing spirit! Even among my people, such interference is forbidden, condemned as black sorcery. Forgive me, Lord! As you can surely see my heart, you know that I speak truth."

Tears were streaming down Chariton's face as he spoke, and his words came out in gasps. I wondered if all northerners were so passionate. It was all I could do not to leap free to escape the painful intensity of his emotions.

"Peace, my son," the son of Earth smiled, gripping the reaching hand and drawing Chariton to his feet. "I know your regret is sincere. But I say to you, look within, and see how close you tread to the edge of the pit! You mean well, but where will you find the strength and wisdom to hold you to your path? Is your goddess one who blesses men with wisdom? Does she burn with the glory of the One's face, or does she dwell in darkness, drinking your spirit along with your worship?

"The abyss of temptation yawning before you is the darkness of a love that is no love, a hunger that pursues the loved one as a lion stalks its prey, until the neck snaps, the hot blood spurts, and hunger is assuaged."

"Lord, your words do not comfort me!" Chariton cried.

"I do not wish them to," the son of Earth replied. "You would have been better off consumed at birth by the dark fires of your mountain goddess than you will be if you harm this child."

"I will never harm her!" Chariton ground the words out as if he were crushing stones. "Show me this One you speak of! How can I know him? What sacrifice can I offer to honor him?"

The son of Earth looked long and steadily at Chariton's desperate face.

"The only sacrifice the One asks of his children is the love of their hearts, freely and humbly given, Chariton. Can you offer that?"

"How can I love what I have never known, Lord?"

Ben Adamah's eyes softened. In spite of his fierce words, I sensed that he cared greatly for this human from the north.

"Do you love the golden light on the mountain peaks at evening, Chariton? Their soft blush at morning? Does your memory float on fragile wings of delight at the sharp scent of mountain pines? Does your heart reach out to the silver flash of fish as they swim in the waters of your bay? Is the warm touch of a new-shorn sheep's flank a blessing to your soul? When you look into Aeliana's eyes, do untold wonders stir there?

"Trust me, my friend, you know the One, for hers is the vision that brought all these things to birth. Her love upholds them in their beauty and wonder, and her grace will bring all things to completion in their time, even your love for Aeliana.

"You must look to the One if you would find the wisdom, and love, to call Aeliana out of the mists. If you can open yourself to the

One, you will have the strength to hold her secure in days to come, but you must be patient. If you truly love her, she will know it. If she loves you, her love will drive her to seek healing. You can weave a safe arbor around her, where one day new life may spring from the close-furled seeds of her heart."

"Lord, you must help me!" Chariton gasped, falling to his knees again. "How can I do this alone?"

"Have I not called you 'friend'?" ben Adamah smiled. "I have come to show the lost and suffering people of the Earth how the One loves them. Look to me, Chariton, and find him looking back at you."

"But Lord, I don't know you, either. You are a stranger to me."

Ben Adamah sighed, and shook his head. "You have many excuses for a man so desperate! Why do you struggle so? The time for evasions is past. All that remains to you is opening to the One's love. You have already made your choice, Chariton. Have the courage to act upon it!"

With those words, everything shifted. Light rolled across my vision, flashing and streaming like the curling edge of a burning leaf, now afire with sparks like the delicate hues of a rainbow, now sunlight piercing like needles through dense foliage. A curving horizon of whirling colors rushed away at great speed. For a moment I imagined myself inside a flashing bead of dew expanding until it enclosed the whole universe. Above me, the glowing arc of heaven soared up and away, joining the horizon in its mad increase. The air trembled with the shimmering stars of a clear night weaving themselves into an intricate dance, their patterns hovering for the slightest pause before exploding into greater, ever more resounding rhythms. Light was music and music, light—music that was too unearthly for mere ears to perceive, yet intoxicating in its harmonies; indescribable colors defying eyes of flesh to behold them, yet dazzling my eyes with their vibrance.

Faster and more dizzying the lights swirled and the music soared, until, slowly, they fell back together, merging, shielding their brilliance. Then they were gone. The night's darkness returned, and I was looking at Chariton's ear—but an ear transformed. If I looked closely, didn't I just glimpse the whirling colors of that infinite dance? "Infinite?" What did *infinite* mean? I was speaking thoughts I'd never had, ideas I'd never understood. Yet they existed, and I knew them. Who had changed here? Chariton, or me? Or both?

Oh.

Chariton had opened to the One . . . and I'd gone along for the ride. Now the dance of creation was awake in even the smallest piece of his being (like his ear) and perhaps in me as well, and the living cosmos was larger, and more alive, because of it.

Cat tales and purple snails

And you, small Shadow? I heard his words vibrating in my blood and bones as Chariton gathered himself together where he knelt on the stone. *Are you going to carry tales to Aeliana like a dutiful little witness?*

"Umm . . ." I replied.

"Let's leave the two of them to work this out by themselves." I could feel his smile.

"Yes, ben Adamah. I can hold my tongue."

"If you feel the need to gossip, call me. I'll help stem the tide."

"I'm not a baby, you know!" I grumbled.

"Yes, you are," he laughed, "but you're growing quickly."

"Son of Earth?"

"Yes, small Shadow?"

"What just happened?"

"Your eyes were opened, Purple Gleaming in Shadow."

Beneath our words I felt Wind on Water's deep purr.

23

I Am Changed

Purple Gleaming in Shadow speaks

*F*ull darkness lay upon the seawall and the waves below. Chariton was leaning on the damp stone, his arms resting on a low space on the wall. The son of Earth stood nearby, separated from him by a higher piece of wall, one of many that alternated with low places, like a line of jagged teeth. Wind on Water and I had both exchanged our humans' warmth for the shelter offered by a temple column, well away from the wall, across the narrow lane.

"I am changed," Chariton rasped.

"Yes," ben Adamah replied.

"The night looks different. It sounds different. My eyes are dimmed, and my ears."

I looked across the road with concern. Was the human wounded?

"No, my friend, not dimmed. Only different. You've stepped out from under the shadow of the small earthen gods where you've lived your whole life, and into the light of the One. Your eyes will adjust, as will your hearing. But unless you choose to return to the old gods, you will never see as you did.

"Gone is the pounding pulse of the caverns of sacrifice, and the blood ties that linked your blood to the lesser beasts. No more will the lust of the hunt overwhelm your mind. Nor will your soul dissolve into the dark mysteries of the Mother of Mountains, or make spirit journeys in her service. Your dark goddess has long hungered after the worship of humankind and the illusion of power their worship brings. She denies her fealty to the One and beguiles human devotion without yielding it to her Creator. Blinding her followers to the presence of the One Mother, she offers them a self-serving travesty of the One's love. What you glimpsed of the One as you worshipped her dark shadow was your own soul's light seeking its true Creator."

"Have I lost all the gifts that made me a man of spirit?"

"If you have, would it matter to you? How would you use them, suitor of Aeliana?"

Chariton opened his mouth to speak, but then closed it again, and ben Adamah continued.

"You said that among your people using power to influence the will of another is forbidden, black sorcery. Is this so?"

Chariton nodded.

"How, then, did you use your gifts? To influence beasts or weather, move fate in your favor, manipulate spirits with your offerings and rituals? What is this but influencing the will, and wellbeing, of others, to achieve your own desires?

"So, I say, 'yes,' you have lost these gifts. You cannot manipulate the One nor bind him to your desires. And he will not tolerate your manipulating others, because in doing so you abuse them and set yourself up as a little god. The children of the One are free, unless in their own foolishness they forge shackles on their own ankles."

"Am I defenseless, then, in the face of all the world's perils?"

"You have always been defenseless, my friend, had you only known it. Your goddess cares no more for your safety than for the legions of creeping things in the dirt, unless it serves her purpose."

"But what point is there in your god if he makes me no stronger than other men?"

"Here we come to the heart of your confusion, Chariton, although you don't realize it. Who serves whom? Does the servant serve the master, or the master the servant? Does the child obey the parent, or the parent the child? The One does not exist for your pleasure or convenience. But unlike the small, greedy gods, neither do you exist for his. The One loves you, Chariton, and would fill you with his wisdom and love until you are so full of light that you can converse with him like a son grown to the fullness of his manhood converses with his earthly father."

"Surely a human being cannot converse with the Creator as an equal, ben Adamah! We are flesh, mortal, doomed to die into the Earth. One touch of his hand would reduce us to ash."

The son of Earth paused, looking intently into Chariton's face. Even in the darkness I sensed that his eyes saw even more clearly than mine.

"I come to tell the children of the One how he loves them, to touch them in a way they can see and understand; but as I live among you, as one of you, I also bring your frail flesh into the One's wholeness. Your fear, your weakness, and your pain—all the ills of the flesh—abide now in the cleansing fires of his heart. He *knows* you in a way that has never been before. The One has always loved his children: now he suffers *with* you as well. And in his suffering, he reaches out to sustain you in your own.

"This is the 'point' of your Creator, Chariton: he brings you into your full humanity with his light and wisdom, he gives you strength upon your way, he loves you with a love beyond all human understanding, and he promises never to abandon you. And that is only the beginning. All children of the Mother have their own paths. In her own time she gives them the gifts necessary to walk those paths.

All she asks is openness to her love, and you have already offered her this. I can make you no clever prophecies, for like all else in life, her gifts come without warning, although they never come as a violation of your will.

"I should warn you also, Chariton, that the One promises neither safety nor length of days, except in the eternal joy of his presence."

Wind on Water's voice broke into my thoughts. "I'm hungry, Purple. Let's go catch some temple rats. There're sure to be plenty, with the docks so close."

I looked at the two humans doubtfully.

"Oh, they'll be talking all night. I know the signs. Besides, the son of Earth always calls me if I'm not back when he leaves, and he knows you're with me."

I was watching Wind on Water stalk a wily rat in a zigzag course across the temple court when the reeking bag came down over my head. I hadn't heard a thing.

"Gotcha, you nasty little vermin!" a rough voice chortled.

I was tumbled into the bag like a rat in a trap, or snail bait in a bag, only to land on a stinking pile of dead fish.

"Oh, ick!" I yelped, trying to twitch my body away from their noisome touch, climbing the rough weave of the bag in my panic.

"Wind on Water!" I screamed. "Ben Adamah! Chariton! Help me!"

"Shut up, you hairy little rat, or I'll smash your greasy brains out on the wall," my kidnapper hissed.

I shut up, but increased my silent shrieks for my friends.

Even more than the rotting fish, the bag stank of terror, and all the unsavory bodily reactions that came with it. *Cat* terror in particular. I could smell nothing beyond my revolting prison. The human was walking rapidly now, carrying me further away from rescue with each step. Then without warning, he screamed, half stumbled, and swung my sack around like a cudgel.

"I'm here, Purple," Wind on Water announced calmly.

Then the man shrieked again, and swung the bag once more. I was getting dizzy, and not only from the swinging: I was well and truly mired in the putrid fish offal sliming the bottom of the sack.

Wind on Water must be creeping in close to the villain in the dark to maul his ankles and then streaking away before he could catch her. It was slowing him down, if nothing else. And his screams should make him easy for my friends to locate. I couldn't understand the words he was spewing at Wind on Water—they weren't translatable into cat thoughts—but his rage was unmistakable. Then he spoke words I understood.

"Do that again, you demon's whelp," he roared, "and I'll wring your precious kitten's neck."

That I understood, although I almost wished I hadn't. I curled into a slimy ball and lay still. Maybe he was bluffing, but if dead fish suited his purposes, dead cat probably would as well.

"You have something that doesn't belong to you." The son of Earth's calm voice cut through the vile bag as if he were inside the sack with me.

"Get out of my way, Jew!" my captor growled.

"How can I be in your way, man, if you don't know where you're going?" ben Adamah replied calmly. "But if you don't turn around soon, I fear you'll find yourself in a fowler's bag as well."

I could feel the brute hesitate. His aura of uncertainty was almost as strong as the bag's odor.

"A certain centurion has had men out searching for you ever since you stole his child's dog, and I believe I heard the guard approaching just before you started screaming. A thief's luck always runs out in the end. You know that. Isn't it time you took thought for your future? I promise you, if you don't, you won't have one.

"Now," his voiced dropped into tones that permitted no argument, "give me the bag and run."

I felt the stifling bag sailing through the air, but there was no mistaking the feel of being caught and held in ben Adamah's hands. Then he was opening the sack and pulling me out. I lay exhausted, panting like a trapped bird. Heavy footsteps echoed through the temple courts, vanishing rapidly into the distance.

"I don't think you're quite ready to be a temple cat, small Shadow," the son of Earth smiled, and stroked my stinking fur, cradling me briefly against my breast, disgusting as I was.

Then he set me down beside Wind on Water, who gallantly attacked my filthy fur with her tongue. Chariton approached us slowly from the shadows.

"That man might have killed you, Lord," he said wonderingly. "You risked your life for a *kitten*?"

I looked up from my bath long enough to glower at him.

"Such a man offers me no threat, Chariton. Apart from the strength of his body, he is weak and full of fear. His life is a torment, and he only strikes out against those weaker still. I spoke true when I warned him that his pursuers were closing in.

"But now the hour is late, my friend, and I must return to greet my host. Will you see our small captive home safely before you go to your rest?"

"It is the least I can do for you, and for Aeliana," he sighed. "By the gods, I'm tired!"

Apparently he noticed ben Adamah's glance, because he looked abashed, although he said nothing.

"You have no need for oaths, Chariton. Who are the many gods but drifting mist? And how can a creature swear by his own creator? Better not to swear at all," he smiled.

"My blessings on you, man of Anatolia, and beloved child of the One. Walk your path with courage, with your eyes ever on her face. Be patient. Clarity will come, and with it, joy. Mother or father, the One never abandons her children. I will always be with you to comfort you: only look within to find me."

He held his hand toward Chariton as if in blessing: "My peace I leave with you," he smiled.

Then he stretched out his arm to Wind on Water, and started to walk away. With a last nudge at my chin she leapt up to join him.

I swarmed up Chariton's robes, snagging the threads deliberately, and settled on his shoulder, pushing my ripe fur close against his face.

Risked your life for a kitten, indeed.

Cat tales and purple snails

I'd fallen from the dizzying heights of a vision of living light to the reeking pit of a stinking poacher's sack, in the span of a few moments. Surely there was a lesson there: the unpredictability of life? death waiting around every corner? miracles likewise?

I wondered if I'd be smelling this sour stink in my fur until I shed it out in the spring. Tirzah had sent me out to sleep by the hearth when Chariton had finally brought me home, and although she swore I was clean after dunking me like a bundle of fleece into a variety of nasty steaming pots, I knew the truth. I stank.

Were miracles always a trade-off? You caught a glimpse of someplace achingly beautiful, only to discover that where you usually lived was even worse than you'd realized? Was a gift of wonder always followed by its complete opposite? Were miracles inevitably stalked by devastation? Surely if the Mother of Cats gave you visions of delight, they should trickle down into the ordinary moments of your day, leaking their light into your darkness. Maybe it was a matter of practice, blending the two together. Tirzah seemed to have gotten the knack of it pretty well.

But how often could a kitten explain away her confusion with, *Maybe when I'm older?*

Now would be a good time to discover the answer.

Part 3: Setting the Dye

True Royal Purple looked like congealed blood, blackish at first glance, but deep violet and rich in color on closer examination. When you consider the dangers of diving for the doomed murex, the battle with biting flies, maggots and wasps, and the incredible stench throughout the whole endless dyeing process, you begin to realize how costly the royal purple obsession was in human lives.

> paraphrased from Deborah Ruscillo,
> "Reconstructing Royal Purple"

24

Coiling Darkness

Purple Gleaming in Shadow speaks

Chariton left with a northbound mule caravan shortly after the longest night, with promises to return as soon as he could find a ship sailing our way in the spring—which could be any time now. The day when the long nights would give way to longer days was almost upon us, and Aeliana's eyes often strayed to the horizon as she sat stitching on the roof. I was pleased that Chariton had taken ben Adamah's advice and adjusted his pace to hers. He'd managed to be *present* in a way few humans understood. Day after day, he was simply who he was: a man who loved a woman enough to drop all his defenses, and wait patiently for her to open to him.

I didn't doubt that she would open . . . some day. His very existence drew her like the sage blossom beckons the honeybee, yet the walls she'd raised to protect herself from her memories had also imprisoned her heart. Ben Adamah had promised that a day would come when her love for Chariton would overbalance her fears, but that day was not yet.

In every other way, Aeliana was opening to her new life with all the zeal of the greening landscape burgeoning around us. Her colorful tapestries and patterned fabrics were making a name for her in the marketplace and commanding princely prices; Aqhat was ecstatic. With Elissa's guidance, she'd also learned how to keep Aqhat's records, and her gift for dealing with customers astonished even herself. Her startling beauty certainly gave her an initial advantage, but her own shrewdness concluded the sales.

Only Ahumm found anything to criticize in her work. Donatiya's child had been born: a girl, to Ahumm's chagrin, so his place in the family enterprise was secure, yet when I touched his thoughts, I found only corrosive jealousy and violent fantasies of revenge. I tried to scour the images from my mind like mud from filthy paws, but, like most cats, my memory refused to release knowledge once gathered; willful forgetfulness seemed to be a human gift. Aeliana sensed his mood as well, and rarely relaxed her guard.

Alba had fallen in love, fortunately with the young merchant to whom Aqhat had betrothed her, and I often saw Elissa in smiling conversation with a widowed wine merchant who found endless excuses to stop by the workshop. Tirzah spent most of her time dreaming in the sun and working at her loom. For the moment, Aqhat's family and business seemed blessed with sunny days and gentle winds.

Confident in the skills of his family and employees, Aqhat took ship for Miletos to talk with Chariton's father about partnerships as soon as a captain could be found to risk the early spring seas. Tirzah and Aeliana settled down to work at their looms and wait for Chariton's return.

In my dreams, the One's loom (for so I'd decided to call it) bounced lightly beneath my paws as I walked across its ever more complex weave. New colors had appeared since I'd first dreamed of it so many moons ago. I thought I recognized Chariton in the deep blue-greens like ocean pools, and perhaps my own eyes in the green flecks peering out from the shadows. More troubling were the muddy snarls appearing without relation to the larger pattern, snarls that felt unpleasantly like Ahumm. But most disturbing was the darkness that had been there from the first, and now was spreading like a strangling vine wherever I looked.

Through the winter months I'd come to think of the loom almost as a living creature. There'd been times when I knew I'd felt the gentle rise and fall of a breathing breast while I sat quietly on its surface. Even more strange, if I crouched on the fabric and listened carefully, I heard a faint hum, not exactly a voice, more like . . . yearning . . . or the enticing summons of the hunt. When I followed, I'd find myself drawn to a place in the pattern where my paws sank into the weave, down among the layered threads—except that instead of a single mesh of woven fabric, my paws moved through a maze of threads stretching out in all directions, reaching down into depths that weren't there at all when I looked at the loom from the outside. How could I describe it? The unseen threads *sang* when my paws touched them, calling to be stretched or shunted aside or even severed and reattached, things I never could have done without the help of the weaving itself. I know: I'd tried. Together, the loom and I were *changing* the pattern of the threads, just as I'd always longed to do.

And not only did the threads sing; whenever I got a change right, they breathed out an enticing aroma, like the soothing scent of a cat snugly content and at peace. Yet I remembered being reduced to bone-shaking terror the first time I awakened from one of my dreams to find that same elusive scent drifting around Aeliana as she exclaimed over some new insight that had just popped into her head. My dream weaving must be the source, but I didn't *want* that responsibility! True, I wasn't manipulating her thoughts like Chariton had considered doing: I was more of an apprentice weaver for the One. *But an apprentice of the Mother? Me?* Still, what choice did I have? Dreams had their being in a realm where my wishes carried little weight. The Mother of Cats had chosen to touch the world through my paws. She'd have to take care of the rest.

After watching Aeliana respond to my dreams several times, I began to see how the changes I worked in the loom's pattern acted like tiny cracks in her defensive walls. Chinks of light and air filtered through them, perhaps preparing for the day when the walls might actually crumble. I began to relax, and before long I was even purring with the threads as they sang.

Although the loom never guided me to any threads but Aeliana's, I often sensed an echo pulsing from the crimson threads that felt like ben Adamah's. Maybe, I told myself, if I just touched them more closely, laid my ear against them, even worked my paws in among them, I could understand what they were saying! But I found my claws snagged and held in a dense web of reluctance whenever I tried. So I never knew for sure. Maybe I really was sensing his spirit in those echoes, even his feelings and the currents of his life. Or maybe it was wishful thinking. Still, I couldn't help noticing that the glowing ruby threads attracted the heaviest mass of the coiling darkness.

"I think he's here, Aeliana! I think Chariton's ship is here!" Alba shouted, slamming the door of the weaving room behind her. "Batnoam said that the ship coming into the harbor sailed out of Ephesus; he recognized the name! Come on, let's go to the dock and see!"

Even from my perch on top of the loom, I felt Aeliana's heart lurch and stumble into a furious pounding, but she only smiled and shook her head.

"I can't run to meet every ship that docks, Alba. And I'm at a delicate point in this weaving. I don't want to leave it until I finish this bit of patterning. My hands might forget what they're doing."

"Oh, Aeliana, sometimes you're as mean as an eel! How can you just sit there? Chariton'll get tired of waiting for you if you don't give him some encouragement, you know. Think how pleased he'd be to see you waiting for him on the dock! Anyway, I don't know why you don't just marry him and get it over with. Everyone can see how he loves you, and you're bound to give in sooner or later."

Aeliana ignored the sudden sinking in her belly at Alba's words, *he'll get tired of waiting for you*, and answered calmly.

"If he's come all this way to see me, he won't turn around and go home just because I'm not there to meet him at the dock, Alba. Why don't you go see and tell me about it?"

From the way Alba huffed out I could tell she wouldn't go to the docks alone, but as soon as she'd left the workshop, Aeliana fairly flew up the stairs to the roof of the stone tower where Aqhat watched the merchant vessels coming into the harbor. I followed at her heels. From the tower wall I could see a ship moving between the breakwater and the lighthouse, maneuvering toward the quay. It looked like any other ship to me, too far away to recognize its humans as anything more distinct than scurrying ants. The intensity of Aeliana's yearning ached for certainty, but none was granted. Anonymous seamen and scantily clad sailors swarmed over the deck, tiny figures disembarked, and the jostling crowd dispersed. No one turned to wave at us in our distant tower.

Aeliana drummed her fingers on the stone in frustration, and finally ran down the stairs to the courtyard outside Aqhat's office, but shrank back into the doorway's shadow as Ahumm suddenly strode through the compound gate. I leapt to her shoulder, peering around the corner with her until he disappeared through the tapestries into Aqhat's office. His nearness made up her mind: rather than returning to the now-empty weaving room, Aeliana slipped out of the workshop and through the kitchen courtyard to Tirzah's house. Once there, she climbed to the roof and looked hopefully toward the city. No familiar figure was walking toward us along the beach road.

Sitting down on the roof's edge, she stroked my fur absently. I said nothing; the less I interfered, the better.

"Eliana?" Tirzah's voice drifted out of the weaving room behind us. "I think Chariton may be arriving today, dear. I've had a feeling since this morning, and it keeps growing on me. Maybe you should put on a clean tunic just in case."

"I'll do it right now!" Aeliana cried, and hardly touched the stairs in her headlong rush to her room.

I stayed on the roof to watch for developments—which weren't long in coming. A cat's eyes aren't at their best in bright sunlight, but I sensed Chariton's thoughts as soon as he passed through the city gates. If possible, his feelings were even more chaotic than Aeliana's. I agreed with Alba: it was time they settled this thing. Human mating was so complicated! Not that I was an expert. I was still anxiously waiting for my first time of making; no female cat is really an adult until she births her first kits. Even though the Grandmothers told me it should come soon, I could hardly wait to leave the last shreds of my kittenhood behind. And then there was that tawny male who watched me with such a beguiling look in his eye whenever I passed by . . .

By the time Chariton reached the garden gate, Aeliana, Tirzah and I were there to greet him. Propriety allowed no more than a formal kiss of greeting between Aeliana and Chariton, but I could feel the shock of their touch running along their bodies like tiny licking flames. Chariton shivered ever so slightly, almost like a horse bitten by a fly. But their eyes glowed with the intensity of their regard as they separated and walked toward the house.

"So you're back again," Ahumm's sullen tones rumbled from the shadows inside the door.

Aeliana flinched at the sound of his voice, and Chariton glanced at her with surprise, but turned to greet Ahumm politely.

"Your honored father was anticipating my return, Ahumm. I'll be looking into the details of the partnership he and my father are hoping to work out. I look forward to your suggestions once I start to work."

Chariton bowed slightly, but Ahumm merely flicked his hand and turned on his heel as if to leave, his scarlet-banded robes tangling around his heavy body.

"One of the women can help you," he smirked, turning back toward Chariton as if in an afterthought. He actually leered at Aeliana. "Our little widow here has become quite expert at managing her business affairs."

Chariton's eyes grew hard and black like wave-washed sea pebbles, but he said nothing.

"I have business in the city that will keep me occupied for some time," Ahumm added. "I'm sure she'll supply your every need." Then he disappeared into the hallway.

"Come," Tirzah said softly, shaking her head at Chariton, and leading the way to her house.

"By all the gods!" Chariton exploded when the door closed behind us, "What ails that man? I've rarely been so insulted in all my life! And was I mistaken, or did he intend insult to Aeliana as well? Yet this is a man who hopes to win trade concessions from my family?"

Tirzah held up her hands to slow his angry outburst, shaking her head all the while to assure him of her own distress.

"Sit, my son, and I'll tell you a story, told to me by the Eldest Grandmother of cats. She believes Ahumm is twisted as Aqhat's cats were twisted. Born into a house whose elders treated him like a god, he grew into an adult with all the grace and wisdom of a sewer rat. He cares for nothing but his own pleasure, which runs to violence and mayhem. In his mind, his desires shape the whole creation. His foolish parents used their wealth to insure that nothing ever contradicted his conceit, not even his carefully chosen young bride. So he never learned wisdom, or kindness, and he doomed my poor Donatiya to a marriage made in Gehenna. Anyone unwise enough to defy his exalted self he ignores as a momentary defect in an otherwise untroubled blue sky: a speck in his divine eye. He scowls and blinks, and the irritation disappears. Should the speck persist, he swats it like a mosquito. That is, he did until the son of Earth came to visit."

She smiled and winked at Chariton, and he drew back in surprise.

"Fortunately for Eliana," she continued, "Ahumm never laid eyes on her until the same dinner where he met ben Adamah, and his intent was as obvious to the Teacher as an angry red boil on his nose. After that, everything changed. Ahumm's confidence in his power to possess whatever he coveted was shattered beyond recall. In addition to the exile of Aqhat's cats and my own healing, the unexpected force of ben Adamah's will made this clear to him in one humiliating confrontation on the day ben Adamah left."

Tirzah smiled as she recalled Wind on Water's account of that meeting, but the smile quickly faded.

"Ahumm had a choice then: he could have fallen to his knees and cried, 'I've been blind! Whatever gods may be, forgive me for my arrogance!' But instead, he withdrew deeper into his stinking darkness, cursed the whole world for the affront to his dignity, Aeliana in particular, and gnawed on his grievance, waiting for the moment when he could revenge himself on those who'd denied him his proper respect.

"And so our household's uneasy tension has strung out more tightly with each month that passes. The son of Earth took trouble before he left us to explain to Ahumm the dire consequences awaiting him if he harmed Aeliana in any way. So he glowers and leers from a distance, making insulting remarks when he thinks no one hears, and abusing Donatiya in his frustration. But he dares not harm Aeliana . . . at least not yet."

I decided that Chariton must have amazing self-control to keep his temper (and his seat) while Tirzah spoke, considering the rage that I felt boiling up inside him.

"He has never harmed you?" he asked, turning to Aeliana, touching her cheek lightly.

"No, never," she smiled, although unsteadily.

Ahumm's latest loathsomeness had unsettled her more than she wanted to admit, even to herself, but she didn't deceive Chariton. I could see the muscles in his jaw clench and unclench in fiercely controlled rhythm. Ahumm was a fool to make an enemy of this forceful male from the northern mountains.

"Please, let us offer you refreshment, Chariton!" Tirzah urged. "Vita will bring wine and bread and olives, and we can talk about more pleasant things. I make it a habit never to waste any more thought on Ahumm than I must."

Cat tales and purple snails

I couldn't decide which was worse: growing up around hostile toms who might rip my throat out on sight, or being caught between two human males who could easily trample me unawares while they stomped around the house flexing their muscles . . . and tempers.

Maybe the breeding males of every species were equally obnoxious. What puzzled me was where ben Adamah fit into that picture.

25

Heart's Blood

Purple Gleaming in Shadow speaks

I didn't enjoy the backwash of that evening's revelations. As he'd done on his previous visits, Chariton stayed with friends in the city, but now he spent most of his waking hours at Aqhat's house and workshop. I could feel the sullen aura of his rage billowing around him everywhere he went. When Ahumm was in the compound, Chariton was always near, circling like a hungry griffon tracking a tantalizing whiff of decay, the shadow of his vast wings feathering through Ahumm's thoughts and darkening his vision. Yet with every other creature, human or beast, Chariton's presence might have been the Mother's own hand hovering over us to shelter us from harm. As for Ahumm, he swaggered and sneered, and fled away to the city at the slightest excuse. I couldn't help wondering if Chariton's unnerving vigilance might be linked to the mountain goddess's darker gifts. I only listened in on Chariton's thoughts once, and withdrew hastily, for fear of scorching my whiskers. No doubt the son of Earth would've told me it was none of my business.

Chariton didn't miss a chance to come to Tirzah's house in the evenings to share in our talk about ben Adamah, and although the son of Earth didn't appear to us as he had before, I never left our gatherings without a sense of his comfort. Most nights, in Aqhat's absence, Alba and Elissa entertained Chariton and Aeliana at their table in the vain hope of distracting them from Ahumm's rudeness, and his ever more obvious abuse of Donatiya. The women of the house had closed ranks against him, but cautiously, so as not to make Donatiya's life even harder. Mostly they took turns watching over little Arisha, lest her father contrive a convenient disappearance (sacrifices of children to the old and bloody gods were still commonplace among Phoenician humans, and Ahumm was fond of complaining about the worthlessness of female infants.) Whenever they could manage it, even the servants took turns carrying the baby on their backs as they worked.

Time passed, and the days grew slightly longer. Probably no one but a cat would have noticed, so slow was the change, but the sun's warmth is the fire at the heart of feline wellbeing. I saw, too, that Chariton's protectiveness was penetrating Aeliana's defenses as no amount of loving patience had done. They began taking walks together on the beach for no better reason than the pleasure they took in each other's company. Tirzah insisted that we accompany them to lend their outings an air of respectability, but considering the distance she left between us, I didn't see much point.

Who could say how long this relative peace might have lasted if darkness hadn't overwhelmed us all? Tirzah and I received the first warnings in the darkest hours of a night soon after the balancing of day and night. Like our first dream of the One's loom, we dreamed together, except this time we walked side by side in the same dream. When we entered the loom's chamber, its light was dimmed, almost extinguished. Yet the surface had expanded until I imagined it must encompass the whole Earth, with ben Adamah's crimson threads glowing in every part, out to the furthest horizons. But with every beat of my heart, I felt his light fading.

Unnoticed at first, too faint even for a cat's eyes to track without effort, sullen glints slid along a tangle of seething coils. A dry rasping rustled through the darkness of a wasteland drained of hope. Dread rooted me in place as I watched the thousand thickening tendrils of the strangling vine grasping ben Adamah's threads with a choking web of . . . no, wait! Not vines . . . never vines! Vipers!

Their scales brushed together like dry leaves whispering in the first autumn chill. Focusing my eyes at last, I looked out across an endless field of wedge-shaped heads swaying in a terrible dance. Jaws gaping, fangs gleaming, countless heads reared and struck, sinking their fangs into the flickering scarlet threads. Venom coursed through the crimson cords in streams of starless night, into the heart of ben Adamah's light. With a faint shudder, the warm glow grew darker, like the deepest core of the heart's lifeblood, and then failed entirely. The other threads pulsed uncertainly in the gloom, but I could hardly see them for the pall of smothering shadow that settled over my dream.

"Ben Adamah!" I screamed as I struggled to wake and plant my paws on the solid earth, even to breathe in the reassuringly normal odor of rotting snails.

But no sooner did I wake than I heard Tirzah cry out from her bed, "Lord! My Lord!" as she struggled to sit, her eyes blazing with terror.

I leapt across the small room, pressing myself into her shivering arms, neither of us able to fight free of the horror stalking the night. How could we escape? Dreams of the One's loom were never just dreams. They partook of the Mother's very essence, mingling flesh and spirit, speaking truth in each overlapping realm at once.

Where could we seek comfort when dreams offered no escape from care, but only visions of greater agony yet to come? So we huddled together in silence through the interminable night, waiting for a sunrise that neither of us was sure would come.

The sun did rise, just as it rose every morning, serenely unaware of the terror that had visited us in the night. Likewise, Aeliana seemed oblivious to any darkness staining the new day. Wind on Water had spoken of my human's considerable gifts of spiritual perception, but so far I hadn't seen them. Maybe they, too, were hiding behind her walls.

This new day was to be a dyeing day, with both fabric and fleece awaiting the royal purple. The most recent batch of snail glands had sat decomposing in the darkness of the stone hut for three days now, and was ready to reenter the light. Aqhat never varied from this routine.

The familiar reek of ordinary dyes stung my eyes as we entered the dye yard. Aeliana and Tirzah went to change into the stained tunics they always wore for dyeing, binding their hair tightly beneath bands of linen to protect it from odor as well as accidental stains: royal purple might refuse to penetrate vegetable fibers like cotton and flax, but animal fibers—including human hair—it claimed for its own. Today Aeliana and Tirzah had tied additional bands of cloth across their mouths and noses to block out as much of the purple's stench as possible. Looking like caravaneers fleeing a desert sandstorm, they eventually emerged from the robing room and approached the dye mistress.

The men always disappeared on days when the purple dye was steeping: like childbirth, this was a woman's mystery they wanted no part of. Chariton was no exception. Only Aqhat made a point of overseeing the purple dye, so important was it to his profits, but today in his absence Tirzah took his place.

The dye mistress selected a key from the ring at her waist and unlocked the stone storage hut, swinging the door wide and scurrying backwards, her hands clasped over her face. She, Aeliana, Tirzah, and four slave women stood at a little distance away from the hut, waiting for the worst fumes to disperse. I sat on a wall on the far side of the yard.

Eventually the servants entered the dark hut, and emerged carrying four of the heavy lidded metal pots, the first four of the day. My humans weren't actually there to do the dying; Tirzah would be supervising, and Aeliana learning. Aeliana had watched before, but Aqhat insisted that she repeat the exercise over and over again; happily, Tirzah had never forced me to come closer than the wall where I sat today.

In the yard near me two huge tubs of seawater were already heating over a hot fire. Just before the water reached the boiling point, several young women with infants bound to their backs, followed by small giggling children, approached with pitchers of liquid. I knew from experience what they carried: fresh baby urine, a valuable ingredient in dyes. Tirzah had told us that wool soaked in it beforehand emerged from the dye vats with more brilliant color. The young women poured their children's contributions into the steaming water, accompanied by much clapping and laughter from the children. Then the pale woolen cloth was stirred into the water and urine, and the fire under the pots extinguished.

I sensed that Aeliana was suffering acutely on her side of the yard. When I'd been very young, my mother had told me that nothing in the world smelled worse than rotting sea snails, unless it was the snail slime shut up in pots for several days in the dye hut. The pots of dye had now been settled carefully onto four stone hearths. Unlike the vats of watered urine, no fires had been kindled beneath them. An oven squatted beside each hearth, with a chimney sloping up from the oven's flames to an opening below the pot of dye. Nothing ruined the priceless purple dye as disastrously as letting it boil, so dyers took great pains to control the heat.

I probably yearned for the comfort of Aeliana's closeness as much as I hoped to comfort her, but whatever my motives, I finally wandered across the dye yard to join her, rubbing against her ankles to announce my arrival. At least we could be together in our misery. She held out her hand, and I leapt up to her shoulder, grateful that she was watching the pots from several feet away. Even so, when the servant lifted the nearest lid, the smell struck me like a bubble of exploding swamp gas, and Aeliana staggered back: I buried my nose in my paws.

Things didn't improve, either. The scummy mass of purple maggots and rotted snail bits floating on the dye's surface was almost as nasty as the stink. But the slave women went about their task impassively, as if there were nothing distressing about it. What point would there have been in complaining? Whether they'd been aristocrats or farm wives in their former lives, marauding raiders had swept those lives away. This was their lot now, and slave owners rewarded biddable slaves.

Grasping woven sieves, the women skimmed the revolting mess off the liquid and dumped it into waiting bowls. By the time they finished their straining, the pots of purple were steaming hot. According to Tirzah, one of these large pans of purple dye could stain a whole mantle to the nearly black purplish-red color coveted by Roman nobility, and said to resemble the color of heart's blood. I wasn't sure why anyone, royal or not, would wish to wear a mantle the color of dense clotted blood, but any cat will tell you that there's no explaining human taste.

As if summoned by my thought, a violent shudder gripped me, and the night's dream slashed across my inner eye. I fluffed my fur against its sudden chill. *What overlap could possibly exist between royal purple dye and ben Adamah's threads on the Mother's loom?* I asked in bewildered surprise. But why even ask the question? I had no answers. I hunkered down lower on Aeliana's shoulder. I'd endure; it's what cats did.

Women from the water vats were crossing the yard now, staggering under the weight of steaming tubs loaded with wool soaked in baby urine. Carefully setting their burdens down near the hearths, they waited while several other women filled the sunken stone pits beside each hearth with hot seawater and then opened drains to let the water run out into a series of lower pits until it flowed down a gutter to the sea. When the pits were warm enough, or clean enough, to suit them, the women sealed the drains and poured the dye in, followed immediately by sodden woolen fabric, lowered gently into the dye. Using smooth sticks dyed nearly black from long use, they stirred the wool into the dye baths until it was thoroughly mixed and submerged. The dye would cool in the pits for several hours now, stirred from time to time to insure even color. The stink never grew any less, but at least heating the dye killed the maggots.

Aqhat only had four dye vats for purple dye in his yard, so while the wool steeped in the dye baths, we were free to entertain ourselves. Later the women would take the fabric out, squeeze the leftover dye back into the vats, and hang the purple fabric to dry. The leftover squeezings were used to dye cheap lavender wool for local markets before the pits were cleaned for the day's second dye lots.

Tirzah and Aeliana managed to walk (rather than run) from the dye vats to the robing room to remove their dyeing tunics. When they returned, we fled toward the beach beyond the shell middens, where the air was fresh. I ran ahead of them, racing with the waves that foamed up the beach. The sky might be clear and the spring sun warm, but I could tell that the waves were getting bigger, and the air had a stormy feel. I wondered if the second dye lot would have a chance to dry before the rains came.

Not that it mattered: once the noisome purple dye touched wool or silk, it was there to stay. Not even after many washings did it fade. I supposed that was part of its value. But the stink never left it, either. Aqhat had a special warehouse with open windows all around just for airing the dyed wool—for uncounted days, and sometimes moons. Even then, workers dipped the finished cloth in perfume before shipping it out. To me the cloth merely smelled like rotten snails with perfume mixed in, but maybe humans didn't notice. If they did notice, and still paid huge amounts of money to wear clothes made with it, they were stranger than I'd realized.

cat tales and purple snails

Now that I'd been forced to watch the gathering and processing of the pebble-purple snails, I was having mixed feelings about my name. When the Grandmothers had first chosen it, I'd been vastly proud of it, especially after they'd explained its meaning.

But after endless moons of stench, rotten flesh, flies, wasps, eye-stinging dyes, and the ever-present threat of scorpion fish whenever we were forced out into a boat, the word *purple* had attracted a host of unsavory new meanings. I tried to explain away my distaste by reminding myself that purple highlights in a cat's fur had no connection with predatory shellfish . . . sometimes I listened to myself, but mostly I didn't.

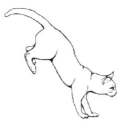

26

Stones Falling from the Sky

Purple Gleaming in Shadow speaks

*W*e'd just returned to the dye yard to watch the women finish the first dye lots when the black horror from my dream exploded in my head. The slave women were lifting the first length of dripping fabric out of the dye vat to hang it over the ropes strung along the side of the yard. Blood-dark dye spattered the ground, and like the blast of odor from the dye hut, the unmistakable reek of fresh blood bloomed in the air.

I sank my claws into Aeliana's robes to keep from falling to the ground, but realized that both she and Tirzah were falling with me, their screams rending the air and piercing my ears with their pain. The servants in the dye yard froze like statues in the Acco temples, their tools falling from nerveless fingers as they gaped at us, except for the purple hangers: even struck dumb with surprise, they held the priceless fabric high off the ground, bloody dye dripping unheeded on their feet.

"Yeshua!" Aeliana groaned, while Tirzah's cry of "Ben Adamah! Lord!" twisted around my human's voice until the two were one wordless wail.

"What's happening?" I gasped.

I could feel darkness billowing like choking smoke, and ben Adamah's threads unraveling from the One's loom into ragged shreds of kinked fleece, but I didn't understand. My friends saw something I couldn't, however terrifying it might be.

"Tell me!" I pleaded.

But as Tirzah reached out to me, lowering skies suddenly hurled a barrage of hailstones at our heads. Aeliana screamed with the anguish of a pinioned rabbit, her shrieks echoing around the walled yard and spiraling up into the sky like the wails of a chorus of madwomen. Blood flowed down her face and arms where hailstones had broken her skin. Tearing the cloth from her hair and the stained tunic from her breast, she fled out into the storm before we could gather our wits to follow.

"Lord God, have mercy!" Tirzah moaned in a despairing keen that frightened me as much as her first cry.

Hail soon gave way to sheets of freezing rain, but still she knelt there in the piles of melting ice, her face lifted into the downpour.

"The waters are rising, Lord! The flood carries me away! Yet even though my eyes grow dim, still I will wait for you. You are my rock and my shelter. You alone will I trust, even though the waters of death roll over me."

Then she bowed her head beneath the torrent of water and wept.

"Tirzah!" I yowled, "please!"

Like the blind woman she'd once been, she reached out with trembling hands and pulled me to her breast, staggering to her feet, oblivious to the chaos in the dye yard all around us. But instead of returning to the robing room or even to her house, she fought her way through the downpour to the pitiful shelter of Aqhat's colonnaded terrace overlooking the beach. There she turned and searched the shore for any sign of Aeliana, but the beach had vanished behind dense bursts of torrential rain, and what glimpses we caught were empty of human life.

I was desperate. At last I bit her hand, not hard, but enough to raise beads of blood on her aged skin. "*Tirzah!*" I hissed.

"Oh, little one," she sobbed, pressing her face into my soaking fur, "he's dying. They're killing him."

"Killing ben Adamah?" I whispered.

Why was I pretending I didn't know? What else could my dream have meant? What other possible warning had it held?

"Tirzah?" I cried again, butting my head hard against her chin.

"Do you really wish to see what I see, kitten?" she looked at me with haunted eyes.

"I have to *know!*" I growled, in a frenzy of frustration.

So Tirzah opened her thoughts, and the images poured into my mind. I had no idea that a human could see events many days' travel from the place where she stood. Maybe it was one of those gifts she shared with ben Adamah. Yet she saw, and now I saw with her.

At first I didn't understand. I hadn't known that humans did such things to each other, nor did I see that the human male the Roman soldiers were tormenting was the son of Earth. Then in an appalling blaze of recognition, everything came clear.

I was only a cat, not yet full-grown. Yet even I could feel the Mother weeping bitterly for this one who had been guilty of nothing more than speaking her love to the human race. And Tirzah was right: they were killing him. But in such a way! They'd driven metal spikes through his wrists into a wooden crossbeam and were lifting him up, alive, to hang like a carcass in a killing shed! Mother of Cats, why didn't they sever his spine with their teeth or tear out his throat if they wanted him dead? Cats might play with their prey, but it was part of the joy of the hunt, never intended as torture! And still the pictures kept pouring from Tirzah's mind to mine. We curled together into a sodden ball of misery beneath the weeping skies. Yet we refused to wall ourselves off from the horror of his suffering. At least we could watch with him. With all that was in us, we reached out to him, offering strength, love, whatever we could muster from our ravaged hearts.

Then he breathed one last ragged breath, and no more. Ben Adamah's light flickered and died away from the world, and the mute darkness that followed might have been the cold womb of a Mother who had never known the kindling of life.

No matter where Tirzah turned her spirit's gaze, she couldn't find Aeliana. With ben Adamah's death all the world's light had been quenched. Vision, kindness, faith, and hope had died with him into the darkness. We who remained were no more than prey for the vipers of our dreams. We sat in silence, together, but isolated in our grief.

Nothing made sense to me. Ben Adamah had walked into my world, reached down like the Mother's own hand, plucked me from certain death, and created a safe nest for me where I could grow up unmolested. His hand was safety, shelter, food, love. And now that hand was dead and cold, his heart's blood as black as the horrible dye in Aqhat's pots.

I had no idea what Tirzah might be thinking: at some point she'd closed her mind to me. So we sat on in the gathering dusk numbly scanning the shore for a friend who never came.

The rain thinned to a drizzle and the drizzle to a mist. As true dark fell, we answered Chariton's knock at the garden door. His face glowed with the anticipated pleasure of seeing the one person who wasn't there. A quick glance at Tirzah's expression loosed his fears in a violent flood.

"What's wrong?" he cried, his weathered skin blanching to an ashy pallor. His hands trembled as he reached out to clutch Tirzah's shoulders. I watched his eyes as anxiety passed into terror and then trembled on the verge of panic.

"The storm," Tirzah whispered, "blood dripping . . . Yeshua died . . . hailstones . . . Aeliana ran . . ."

Tirzah tried to find words to explain to him, but Chariton interrupted each stumbling attempt she made, unable to hear or understand. Every word she spoke merely added to the shadows of his nightmares. All he could grasp of the true events was that Aeliana had run away in terror and was lost. He could find no strength to mourn for ben Adamah, although his death grieved him. Aeliana's danger consumed his whole being, body and soul. Where was she? What damage had the son of Earth's death done to her fragile balance? Had she found shelter in the storm? Had storm waves overwhelmed her? And where was Ahumm?

At last Tirzah managed to herd him into the room overlooking Aqhat's terrace, where Alba and Elissa waited, but he refused to sit down. Round and round, back and forth, he paced, until Elissa finally shouted, "Sit!"

Shocked as much by her sudden boldness as by the command, he sat. Once down, all resolve vanished. He slumped in his chair, flung his mantle over his head, and said no more for a long dreary time.

All of us could feel the malevolent glee that rode the dark tides that night. No one knew what it might mean. Who had he truly been, this gentle man who had held me in the palm of his hand, that the Earth's demon shadows should rejoice so at his defeat?

"We *must* search for her," Chariton insisted, staring out beyond the terrace to the dark sea, where heavy breakers still rolled over the reefs. I couldn't tell if the first dim hint of dawn was actually touching the heavy overcast, or I was imagining it.

"She won't come back here," he growled. "Don't you understand? She'll find some dank burrow and dig herself in, hiding there until she dies of her own terror. We must *find* her!"

"But Chariton," Tirzah murmured, going over the same argument yet again, "where should we look? Your sight as well as mine is darkened. Aeliana is young and strong, and she was running as if all the demons of hell pursued her. She could be anywhere: on her way back to the Galilee, halfway to Tyre, on the cliffs of Carmel. Where do you suggest we search?"

"Anywhere!" he bellowed, and then muttered something indistinct in apology.

Listen! The voice suddenly spoke into my mind, repeating ben Adamah's word like a flaming talisman. But this voice spoke softly, with the sweetness of a summer breeze, bright with sunlight, fecund as the Earth herself. Long after the word sighed into silence the voice vibrated in the air, and perhaps through the very heavens. I might never have heard her speak before, but I had no doubt that the mighty Mother of Cats was calling to me, least of her daughters.

"*Listen, small Purple!*" she said, again choosing the son of Earth's words. "You alone of all those who love this young human are not bound by the evil set loose in the world tonight, for you are a beast, suckled at *my* breast. *You*, small Purple! You alone can find her. Listen!"

Never mind the tumbling confusion of my thoughts after those words. It was beyond any imagining. But I could no more mistake the Lady's voice than overlook the light of the rising sun. Surely some spark of the son of Earth remained, for her to choose his words! But whatever mysteries moved abroad in this cold dawn, I knew one thing: she had given Aeliana's fate into my paws. "*Listen,*" she'd said. "*You alone!*"

So I crept out of the room, into the reluctant dawn, leaving the humans to their arguments. Guided by her breath, I leapt across the roofs to Tirzah's loom, settled on the coiled weaving at its top, sank my claws into the weave, closed my eyes, and listened.

At first I heard nothing. Then for a time I imagined the loom's shuttle moving back and forth between the warp threads, the small weights clicking together at the bottom. Then the clicking weights became panting breath, and I listened harder.

"Blood," I heard Aeliana croak, "blood falling from the skies, blood lapping at my feet, rising like a flood. Blood drowning the world in death . . ."

Her voice rasped in my ears, cracked and hoarse, as if she'd been raging against the storm for all the hours we'd been searching for her. I tried to *see* like Tirzah, instead of just listening, but no images came to me. If Aeliana was speaking of something she felt, and wasn't just imagining it, she *must* be walking in water. Seawater? If so, she had to be far away; at Chariton's insistence, we'd been out scouring the beaches half the night. We'd've seen her. She'd have to be all the way at the other end of the bay, beneath the cliffs of Carmel, for us to have missed her. Unless . . . maybe she walked in *river* water! I'd forgotten about the shallow river that ran down to the shore nearby, where ben Adamah had taken me with Wind on Water to hunt for water rats an eternity ago.

I calmed my pounding heart and listened again.

"Death!" my poor human rasped. "Stones falling from the sky, just like my dream, blood everywhere, rottenness squelching between my toes . . . death . . . am I dead? The son of Earth is dead, so surely I must be dead, too, a lost spirit on the face of a dead Earth . . . he was my life, he brought me back from Gehenna. Unless that was only a dream, too. And now the sharp spikes pierce my feet, just like his . . .

but why does it hurt so? Doesn't the pain ever stop, even when you die?"

Something soft was squelching between her toes, sharp spikes were hurting her feet . . . *She must be in the river!* Unless she'd gone mad. No, I refused to believe that. The Mother had said, "Listen!" It would be enough.

Then the soft voice spoke again, but this time she whispered urgently: "Run, small Purple! Run as fast as you can!"

I leapt down from the loom, over the roofs, along the garden wall and down to the shore. Over the dunes and around the canebrakes, I followed the river, listening and looking as far as my senses reached, but still I couldn't find her. I stopped, calmed my fears, and listened again.

"Why, I see tombs!" the cracked whisper in my mind mumbled in surprise. "My spirit must have wandered far in my frenzy, but I've found my way back. If only I can remember where they laid my body, I can lie down and forget. Like ben Adamah, though he won't be here . . . he's in some other tomb, far away . . . but what does it matter? All the dead alike are shadows, unknown and unknowing . . ."

Tombs? I didn't know enough about this stupid city! Where were the cemeteries? *Think, Purple!* There was the one along the seawall beyond the city, but if Aeliana were in the river, it couldn't be there. *Think!* No, this wasn't helping. I didn't know. *Just follow the river, foolish cat!* If she were in the river, the river would lead me to her.

"Tirzah!" I wailed in despair. "Can you hear me?"

Faint and far away, I thought heard a whisper of response. "Purple?"

"Tirzah!" I screamed with all my strength. "Follow the river! She's in the tombs by the river!"

But no answer came in return. Had she heard me? *Sweet Mother of Cats, let her have heard me!* I couldn't do this alone. But I ran on, keeping to the tops of the small dunes that rose along the riverbank, looking for anything that might be a human tomb. The grey dawn had slipped past me unnoticed long since, and a noisome mist hung between the swampy flatlands and the heavy skies. I could barely see the cliffs of the old city off to the side, between me and the sea. What did tombs look like, anyway? Had I ever seen one? Surely there'd been some on top of the old city hill, slabs of stone like paving tiles, and stone boxes. I ran on, and on, now panting with exhaustion. I was near collapse, slowing to catch my breath, when I glimpsed them in the hazy distance: tombs, at last! A few small stone buildings, with flat stones lying all over the ground. But where was Aeliana? I couldn't see her.

Then, just as the soft voice began to speak urgently in my mind, I felt Aeliana's rambling confusion blossom into terror.

"Hurry, sweet Purple!" the Mother cried. "He's here!"

He? Who? But then the Lady showed me: Ahumm, rimmed with the sullen glow of some evil presence, guided by who knew what sorcerous cunning. He'd found her. Found her alone, unprotected, and half-mad with grief.

"Where?" I screamed, as I picked myself up and stumbled across the uneven ground, only to sense at the last possible moment (with some divinely-gifted awareness) that a late-hunting owl was gliding swiftly out of the murky skies, her talons an eye's blink away from my flesh. I flung myself to one side, straining every last muscle in my small body to save myself, and Aeliana, from bloody destruction. But instead of tumbling across the sand, scrambling away from the owl's dive, I fell into darkness. I may have felt the vague tremor of the owl's collision with the sand. But still I fell, until my legs suddenly collapsed beneath me as they took the force of my weight hitting hewn stone. After blinking stupidly for a span of several heartbeats, I saw that I lay sprawled along the edge of a step part way down a flight of stone stairs

descending into an echoing underground chamber. I knew it echoed because I heard Ahumm's voice.

Cat tales and purple snails

I wished Wind on Water were here. Nothing seemed to disturb her calm. She'd know what to do. I didn't understand. Gods and demons? What use was a miserable black kitten in a struggle against a full-grown human male possessed by an evil spirit? I'd only just learned how to catch my own meals. My one dream in life was to understand how humans wove cloth, odd as that seemed. Heroic cats didn't spend their days draped over looms.

Tirzah's voice suddenly spoke out of my memories: *As clever as the daughter of the Great Cat Who Is Bast*, she had said. Ben Adamah's words. But he was dead. I'd watched him die through Tirzah's eyes . . . *As clever as the daughter of the Great Cat Who Is Bast* . . . Still, I could honor his memory by trusting his faith in me. I shivered slightly and lay still, waiting for my strength to return.

27

Into the Realm of Gods

Purple Gleaming in Shadow speaks

*H*uman hearing being what it is, neither Aeliana nor Ahumm had heard me fall into the chamber. Lying absolutely still, I listened for any sign of the owl's pursuit: not the slightest breath of air stirred in the murky haze above me, no winged shadow glided past my hole. Slowly, aching in every muscle, I pushed myself to my feet. I twitched one paw, and then another, and arched my back. My ears swiveled in one direction and then the other. No one body part screamed more loudly than another, so maybe I hadn't actually broken anything in my fall.

"*Lovely, clever hetairai,*" hissed a voice so heavy with menace that it must surely drip real venom. Ahumm. Was he, in truth, one of the vipers from my dream? I could see him across the dim chamber, lit by one greasy torch propped in a distant wall bracket. At least for now he wasn't making any sudden moves. I suspected he was gloating over the coveted prize suddenly within his grasp.

Aeliana crouched just beyond him, her stained tunic hanging in ribbons, her flesh crusted with river mud. She said nothing in reply; she looked to be beyond speech. With her voice worn to a faint rasp, she couldn't even scream. I didn't dare do more than brush her thoughts with mine, lest I be sucked down with her into the maelstrom of terror that spun around her. I crept down the steps carefully, black fur and the almost total darkness giving me my only advantage over my human enemy. To my disgust, my paws touched filthy water before I reached the bottom. Of course: if foolish humans dug holes in swamps and left the doors ajar, water would collect.

Everything in me shrank from going further into the foul pool. Death, both ancient and recent, breathed out of the very stone, each lending its peculiar nastiness to the water flooding the tomb's floor. All along the walls I saw shadowed alcoves where human remains undoubtedly lay. Two more arched corridors lined with similar cells disappeared into the gloom on each side of this main room. Carved stone columns like temple porticos guarded the cells' openings. Painted scenes of beasts and birds decorated every possible bit of empty wall and ceiling, although much of their paint had flaked away in the damp.

At last I turned my attention back to the humans in the room's center, and realized that Aeliana and Ahumm were standing on two separate stone boxes that rose above the filthy water. The torch's fitful flares threw delicate carved designs into relief on the stone. I knew humans went to mystifying lengths to provide for their dead; these boxes must be examples. Well, they had their uses today.

Judging from Ahumm's clothes, he must have waded through the pool to get where he was; Aeliana's clothes were so filthy already that any slime left by her passage through the tomb's water was indistinguishable from the rest. The water stains didn't reach above Ahumm's knees, but even such a shallow depth meant I'd have to swim. *No.* I refused. There must be another way.

I looked around carefully, and breathed a quiet sigh of relief: I might end up in the water before I was done, but I needn't climb into it of my own accord. Four short pillars stood in the corners of the chamber, possibly intended as tables of some sort. If my exhausted legs cooperated, I could leap to one of the pillars from where I stood now, and from there to Ahumm's box. The Mother alone knew what I'd do when I reached him.

"Trust me, sweet kit," her warm voice flowed through my frazzled mind.

So I sat down on the dry step above the water and cleaned my fur as best I could: in times of stress, bathing is always a good idea. Then I crouched down and breathed deeply, filling myself with the warmth that still held me close. Finally I rose to my feet, arched my back, and stretched each leg out to its furthest limit.

Then I leapt. Once. Twice. From the shadows beneath Ahumm's damp robe, I reached up and raked his leg with my claws from thigh to ankle, rending the flesh and spilling his blood over my paws. At the same time I sank my teeth into his ankle until I felt them grate on bone. As he screamed and thrashed, I threw myself blindly across the water toward Aeliana, silently thanking Wind on Water for her lesson in battle tactics.

Now I hummed softly into Aeliana's mind and rubbed against her ragged skirts before turning to face Ahumm, fur bristling, fangs bared, yowling in a voice any dueling tom would envy. My shadow leapt to the nearest wall, where it wavered like a Nubian lion. I felt Aeliana move forward to press against me, her mind slowly calming with the comfort of our contact.

"You!" Ahumm snarled in fury, but I noticed he didn't try to leap across to join us. Instead, his hand scrabbled at his throat and gripped something hanging from a chain. Puzzled, I watched closely as he finally released it: a round glass bead covered with eyes. A charm against the evil eye—said to be modeled on cats' eyes! My yowling rose higher into a feline scream of malevolent delight at this sign of human idiocy.

"Shut it, you filthy beast!" he snarled, reaching into his robes and withdrawing a well-honed throwing knife.

I hadn't thought of knives. If I stood still, I'd be an easy target; jump aside, and he'd hit Aeliana. As I considered my choices, my screams faded, and suddenly Ahumm was hurling himself across the water toward us. No sooner had he found his balance, than something large and heavy whistled toward me, slamming me against the wall and into the stinking water like a child's broken doll. I sank down beneath the surface, stunned. But only the briefest instant passed before a violent splash rocked the water, thundering in my ears, and Aeliana plucked me out of my watery tomb and into her arms.

I tried to struggle to my feet . . . but I couldn't move: not my legs, not my head, not my tail—I was as helpless as one of the many mice I'd dispatched myself. Aeliana was on her own now; I might whisper encouragement into her thoughts, but no more. At least I could still see, and with no feeling in my body (except for my head), I didn't have to suffer the foulness of the slime oozing under my fur.

I knew Aeliana had nowhere to go. The stone boxes blocked her only retreat. I could feel Ahumm's smugness radiating from his body like heat from an oven. His thoughts were as clear as a cruel child's: he was all-powerful! He charred lives with his smoldering passions! And he'd only just begun!

I whimpered with distress at my failure. When he'd broken my body, he might have quenched one tiny flicker of the Earth's light, but now he was about to humiliate and despoil a far brighter flame. I felt him savoring the taste of Aeliana's blood already. He stepped toward the edge of the stone box lid and leered down at her. But I was helpless, my body weakening, and my eyesight with it. Aeliana's trembling was no more than a distant flutter in a fading dream.

Then, beyond all possibility, I felt Aeliana take a deep breath, and speak into the deadly silence, her voice firm and clear.

"You shall not touch us. Your power is no more than a mask and a fraud, woven from the brittle kemp of greed. Even from the grave, the son of Earth will reach out to defy you if you try to harm us."

Through a dark mist, I saw Ahumm's face pale. He stepped back a pace, but then squared his shoulders and roared. His scornful laughter echoed around those chambers of death like ricocheting stones, but Aeliana didn't flinch. Ahumm stepped forward again.

"Who are you, or your dead Jew, to oppose *me* and the mighty Ba'al?" he sneered.

I thought I must be dying. I felt the Mother's glow filling the tomb with golden light, and the warmth of her presence thawing the deathly chill in my flesh. But then I heard her speak into my living ears. She was unraveling the echoes of Ahumm's words as if they'd never been spoken. I thought I recognized the same sad sternness in her voice that ben Adamah's had carried when he'd spoken to Aqhat's cats on the beach.

"I am the one with whom you must treat now, human, not these brave children. You've savaged one of my own, and you did so in the name of the demon you serve. What might have been no more than another vicious human crime has suddenly strayed into the realm of the gods. And I promise you, the ancient evil you serve will not prevail against me."

Aeliana turned toward the golden voice, and I saw with my own eyes the face of the Mother of Cats, just as ben Adamah had described her: the image of Cat hovering over the features of a Wonder too great for me to comprehend—hovering, but not fading, one with that Wonder . . . that One.

Aeliana turned back to see Ahumm's response, so by necessity, I turned too. Terror struggled with rage on his face. The cruel delights that had trembled on the brink of fulfillment had been dashed from his lips. His face was empurpled with rage, and, at the same time, he flinched away from the piercing brilliance of the Lady's light. But no sign did I see of regret. Instead, his jaw clenched, his body straightened, and the image of a fiery ram, great horns curling away into the darkness, overlaid the man.

"You have made your decision, then, human," the Lady said sadly, "even before I could offer you a choice. Just as Aqhat's cats chose to walk away from the light that illumines all true children of the One, so have you. You have honored Ba'al Hamon above all others through all your days, eager always to foster hate and shed blood, especially the blood of those weaker than yourself. So to him you shall go, witless and maddened as a sheep in rut.

"But the forsaken soul that might have been your salvation shall find nurture in a more fitting home."

The Lady turned toward Aeliana and me, reached out her golden hand, and laid it on my head. Fire like molten lightning flowed through my body until I was nothing but light. After an eternity of swimming through realms of impossible glory, I opened eyes of flesh on the glowing tomb, and stirred in Aeliana's arms to meet the Lady's smile.

"Welcome, daughter of the One, friend of the Beloved, and youngest of his children," her voice rang out. "Your days upon the Earth shall be blessed, and you shall dance through eternity in the light of the One."

The chills that rippled up and down my spine had nothing to do with Ahumm's violence.

Then the Lady glanced at Ahumm, and said merely: "Be gone, chaff of evil," and turned her back on him.

The one who had been a human man crawled down into the filthy water, muttering mindless gibberish, blundering aimlessly through the tomb's dark chambers. Aeliana climbed up the steps out of the water and turned to the Mother.

"Lady, who are you?" she whispered.

Cat tales and purple snails

I'd survived my own death and opened living eyes on the face of the Mother of Cats. How many life debts did I owe, I wondered drowsily? Ben Adamah had rescued me from Ebed Ubasti's cats—and the temple thief . . . Aeliana had plucked me out of the stinking water . . . and the Mother herself had lifted me out of the chill Silence into her golden warmth. That might be all. I wasn't sure.

If you owed a life debt to more than one person, did one of them have first claim? Could ben Adamah insist I repay my debts in a way that Aeliana would refuse? Nonsense . . . I was thinking nonsense. I must not be quite back in the world I knew. I supposed being almost dead could confuse anyone. And then there was something She'd said about a soul . . .

28

Mother of Cats

Purple Gleaming in Shadow speaks

"Ah, child, what a question!" she smiled. "And who will I be when this new day dawns? For already we have entered a night when all living will wake from a long dream to find themselves come to birth indeed."

A sudden disturbance outside the tomb interrupted her words, but she only smiled and spoke toward the dark opening.

"Come in, my children! We await a new dawning. Share our vigil."

I felt Tirzah's presence before I heard her dragging steps on the stairs. Chariton would have leapt down the staircase blindly, probably landing in the foul pool at its bottom, had his arm not been Tirzah's only support; without him, her weary body would have collapsed. But I watched as exhaustion and anxiety faded from both their faces when they entered the Lady's presence, replaced by wonder as great as my own. Tirzah stood alone now, perhaps, like me, filled with the Mother's own strength. Her eyes never strayed from the Wonder before her, even to acknowledge Aeliana's presence. Chariton frowned briefly as what had once been Ahumm floundered past the base of the stairs.

"Vengeance is not yours, Chariton," the Lady's voice spoke into his rising anger. "Your soul need not bear the stain of this one's destruction. He has already made his choice, and called ruin down upon his own head."

She turned her gaze toward Ahumm again, furrowed her brow slightly, and glanced up the stairs toward the tomb's opening. Apparently having received his orders, the witless creature splashed his clumsy way up the steps and out into the night.

She regarded Chariton with a thoughtful smile. "You haven't done badly, son of the Mother of Mountains. Your gentleness has been sorely tried, but you never truly yielded to the darkness that stalked your heart."

"Lady," Chariton sighed, sinking to his knees before her.

He gazed up at her face for many long heartbeats before rising to descend the stairs toward Aeliana.

"You are well?" he asked my human, reaching out a tentative hand.

"I'm no longer sure what I am," she murmured, with a hesitant smile.

He approached her carefully, holding out ben Adamah's old mantle in his hands. Gently he draped its warm weight around her rags, and she smiled in gratitude, but then turned back to the Mother, who'd been watching them like an indulgent parent.

"Lady, you were telling us who you are," Aeliana murmured, almost whispering, as if fearful of giving offense.

The light blazing out from the Mother's presence gilded the sad tomb with its golden glow, lending a brief warmth to the gardens painted on the cold walls, and lifting the painted birds on wings of spirit they'd never known. To our eyes, the dreary tomb became an oasis of delight where any miracle seemed possible. I squirmed out of Aeliana's arms to test my new legs, or old legs, or, anyway, legs that did what a cat's legs should, and started licking the foulness from my fur.

"Perhaps I shall tell you a tale," the Mother smiled, "a tale of beginnings, and one your friend ben Adamah already began for me."

Like weary travelers around a campfire, the humans settled on the stairs to listen to the jeweled words of a master storyteller.

"When light first shone on the dark waters and smiled to see itself filling the new creation with the vision of its own beauty, the Creator rejoiced greatly," she began.

Her words rang with the deep resonance that rises up through the recounting of all true mysteries.

"From the Creator's joy bloomed wonders never before conceived. Each image that rose into the Creator's mind, he—or she," the Lady smiled, "considered carefully, and shaped with love.

"Now when each new piece of the great cosmos arose and presented itself, its shape hovered about the One until he seemed to take upon himself the likeness of that thought. He gazed upon the thought that would be "sun," and for a brief moment he *was* sun. So it was for every thought that found its way into creation, from the wheeling galaxies to the smallest spider. Each had its moment when the Creator took its form upon himself and approved its fitness. And creation remembered those images, when for an instant each simple life shone with the glory of the One. They were burned into creation's memory like impressions made in the cooling glory of molten stone.

"Now, the images creation holds in its memory drift forever through the dreams and visions of its children. So, as humankind became more self-aware, they thought to worship these bright images that visited their dreams, glowing with the light of eternity. After all, was it not easier to speak to a god who takes on a shape from the known world than a Being greater than the unbounded universe?

"I cannot say what the Creator knew from the beginning and what she did not, for I am no more than one of her bright images, called by some 'the Mother of Cats.' I am she who speaks with the voice of the

One to the feline peoples of the Earth, and upon whom the One has laid her power and light brightly enough for me to speak with you here. But whether the One intended it or not, we images discovered that the more humankind adored us, the stronger we became, and the more power we wielded on the Earth. Some of us accepted human worship reluctantly, quickly passing it on to the One, to whom it rightly belonged. In doing so, we also became conduits of the One's love and care for her creation.

"But there were other spirits who coveted the worship of humankind, and consumed it like strong wine, becoming bloated and cruel with power not rightfully their own. Greed ruled their spirits, and they closed themselves off from the memory of the One. These spirits became the dark gods, demons hungry for blood and sacrifice, who throve on fear and misery, and could never be satisfied.

"In time, the Creator's grief for his suffering creation overshadowed his joy, and he decided to put an end to these old evils. So he allowed the Beloved to enter the world, flesh as you are flesh, human as you are human, yet brimming with the love and compassion of the One. He walked your roads, suffered hunger and thirst, and knew the joys and pains of humanity, but he also bore in his spirit the power to heal, and to recall men and women to their true selves, as sons and daughters of the mighty One who had created them.

"The coming of the Beloved was not hidden from the small, greedy gods, and they gathered their forces to seek to destroy him, not realizing that by his coming alone they had already been undone. For when the One joined himself to the flesh of his creation, he entered this world in a way never before imagined. For the first time in eternity, the One took human joy, pain and fear into himself. Terror of death almost extinguished his light. He endured the agony of torture as if the bleeding flesh were his own. He fell to his knees beneath the weight of your human dread of nothingness. He tasted the bittersweet delight of your brief sojourn on the Earth. And his compassion poured out like streams of milk and honey. What had been separate was joined eternally: physical life and pure Spirit mingled.

"But in a further miracle of that joining, the creatures of the Earth are being gathered in with humanity—dust of the same dust as they are. With the Beloved's coming, the beasts of the Mother will look up and begin to understand the love of the Creator and yearn toward him. In time all divisions will be healed, all dualities made whole. Beasts will glow with the One's fire, the dark gods will fade into nothingness, and the bright spirits will be united with the brilliance of the One whence we had our birth.

"Without the coming of the Beloved, I would not have been sent to speak to you now, because I am the Mother of Cats, not humans; and neither this brave kitten nor her elder sister Mari could have entered into the joy of the One as the first fruits of their kind. From this day forward, all creation is bound together with humankind, capable of being ennobled and restored to the glory of the One, or, like that sad broken wreck who just fled my presence, reduced to something far less than any of my beasts has ever been. For with the possibility of great good comes the temptation to terrible evil. The difference now is that both will rise from the hearts of the One's children by their own choice.

"The Beloved has put into your hands (and paws) the greatest gift of all time: the freedom to choose in love to share the joy of your Creator . . . or to refuse it and go down into darkness. Neither voracious spirits who stalk the nights nor laws that shrivel the heart and possess the mind will rule over you. You are children of the One, and free."

Like me, the others sat in silence, momentarily stunned by the rolling cadences of the Mother's voice, and not quite certain that they had understood everything she'd said. I suppose I recovered first: the chill of my damp fur was tying me to my physical senses irksomely.

"But what of ben Adamah?" I cried. "I thought he was the Beloved you spoke of! How can the One have let him die, and die so cruelly, in such terrible pain? How can he be dead if he is the one who bears the Mother's love between the heavens and the Earth?"

"Ah, clever Purple!" the Lady laughed, but then her face grew grave. "The One and all the hosts of heaven covered their heads and wept for the Beloved's suffering and death, but he chose it freely. By taking on human flesh, he bridged the infinite chasm between the foolishness of humankind and the loving Spirit of the One. Yet he believed that only by offering his own death freely to a skeptical human race could he convince them of the depth of the Creator's love. This he did by his own choice, drinking that grievous cup to its last bitter dregs.

"But even as I speak, grief is turning to joy! Did you think the One would abandon the Beloved to the grave? No, death will never hold the son of Earth in thrall! Like all those whose hearts beat in rhythm with the great pulse of creation, we stand breathless before the miracle that approaches."

I didn't see the Mother of Cats leave us. One moment she was speaking of the approaching miracle, and my heart was full of the wonder of her presence, and the next, the tomb was a dank, stinking hole, lit by a guttering torch. At the top of the stairs, I glimpsed the first pale glow of dawn dimming the stars of a brilliant night sky.

Even as I put a tentative paw on the step above me, the tomb's painted walls shivered and cracked, and a single ray of light pierced the tomb's darkness. The first gleam of dawn? The Lady returning? While I hesitated, uncertain, Aeliana passed me, pulling herself up the stairs as if each step were a boulder her exhausted body must scale.

The ray of light seemed to be her climbing rope, lending her strength through what was clearly the agonizing pain of her ascent. Yet her face shone as brightly as the vanished Lady's, although it held more of the moon than the sun in its glow. Tenaciously she dragged herself up the long flight of stairs, the three of us following at her heels. The stairs finally emerged from the tomb into a rough pit overhung by shelving rock. No door secured the entrance. No wonder it had seemed to open out of nowhere! How would I ever have found it on my own? I supposed I should honor that owl as a messenger of the Mother and be grateful for my bruises.

When Tirzah, last of all, stepped off the stairs onto the soft expanse of the earth's surface, the ground rumbled beneath our feet, and the tomb, with its flooded chambers, collapsed in on itself, leaving only a few crumbling steps to mark its fallen vanity.

Better, I thought to myself, *to let the dead vanish into the Earth*.

Then I turned toward Aeliana, and found her still clasping the ray of light that had guided her from the tomb, light I now saw was streaming from ben Adamah's outstretched hands. Beyond all hope, Aeliana had conquered her despair to stand at last in the light of ben Adamah's smile. The rising sun threw his shadow like a mantle of glittering crystals across the scattered tombstones that stretched away into the western night.

Cat tales and purple snails

Ben Adamah? Alive? My heartbeat marked the passing moments like a terrified bird's, while the One's miracle tempted my thoughts into outrageous leaps of longing. I wobbled on my long-suffering legs, blinked my eyes, and looked again. I *did* see him, with my own eyes . . . or at least with the eyes the Mother had given me. Did her eyes see ghosts and spirits, where my old ones hadn't? After all, I'd prayed for Tirzah's sight. Maybe it hadn't been a very wise prayer.

But then I looked at Aeliana: I couldn't mistake her awe, or the confidence in her gaze. The son of Earth must be alive! I could see it in her delight. The loom was rewoven, the vipers destroyed! Humans talked about hosts of angels singing praises: could that be what I was hearing now? Because the whole Earth seemed to be singing with joy.

29

Dreams

Purple Gleaming in Shadow speaks

"*T*irakemah," he smiled.

"Ben Adamah," she whispered in response.

"Not-so-small Purple," he nodded with mock seriousness, and I ran up to him, rubbing roughly against his robe, hungry for the reassurance of his touch. Softly, for my ears alone, he murmured, with the careless joy of a bubbling spring, "Your weaving is much improved, small one."

Then, "Tirzah," he said, and inclined his head slightly, as if to do her honor. Last, he looked long at Chariton, who finally dropped his eyes in confusion.

"All will be well in the end, my friend," the son of Earth said, laying his hand on Chariton's shoulder.

Turning again toward Aeliana, he held out the hand that had just rested on Chariton's shoulder and called, "Walk with me, child."

Where the spike had been driven through his flesh a scar showed clearly on his wrist in the brilliance of the morning light, but the horror and grief that had bound us in cords of agony had dispersed like a violent storm blown out to sea. Although my stinking fur assured me that it had been no dream, somehow the pain was flowing away in the streaming light. I didn't understand how any of it could be. How could I? But since the Mother of Cats had never given her kits a gift for make-believe—and this extraordinary morning was no dream—then it must be real.

Stumbling over her feet in a whirl of astonished joy, Aeliana joined ben Adamah, and they turned aside together, her exhaustion vanishing as if it had never been. Yet when the son of Earth turned away from me, I saw that the world's dawn was still only a spreading glow beneath the eastern horizon: the earth lay in darkness. The light we had followed was the glory of the One shining through the son of Earth like sunlight through clear water. Determined not to be separated from that light, I ran after them, clawing my way up Aeliana's mantle until I reached her shoulder.

Ben Adamah smiled at me briefly, but then looked back to Aeliana. "Do you remember now, child?" he murmured.

"I remember, Lord," she replied with a shudder. "All this . . . the journey to Acco, your time with Aqhat . . . you did it for me, didn't you? Shabtit had found me in Cana."

Ben Adamah looked at her steadily, his eyes glowing with love.

"Yes, child, I did all of it for you," he smiled. "All for you."

"Now you must tell me what you remember," he said softly, but the iron of his command lay only lightly sheathed in his gentle tone.

"Tell you, Lord?" she gasped, backing away.

"Yes, Tirakemah. You must tell me, because once you have spoken the words to me, the memories cannot vanish again into a fog of forgetfulness. The terrors you give into my hands I will bear into the light, where their power will crumble into dust and drift away like pollen on a breeze."

For many long moments she stood facing him, struggling with her fear. I purred softly, pressing myself against her neck, reminding her of the courage she had summoned to deliver me from Ahumm, and to make her way out of the tomb. At last, she bent her head, and nodded briefly. They resumed their walk, while the words bubbled out of her heart like poisoned groundwater flushed from hidden caverns by the sudden inundation of a mighty river in spate.

I listened, and stored her words in my heart, but they need no repetition. To speak them again would give them greater weight than they deserve, for by the grace of the One, Aeliana's pain is no more.

The son of Earth met Aeliana's gaze, and as his eyes met hers, the sun rose indeed. "I greet your courage with gladness, Tirakemah," he smiled, and then laughed for sheer delight, raising his scarred hands toward her in blessing. "Joy cannot take root in the shadow of fear, my daughter."

"You mean I'm truly healed, Lord?"

"Of your fear, yes, child. For the rest, let each day's task be sufficient unto itself. Remember that you are beloved of the One, walk with your eyes fixed on his light, and the rest will follow . . . with the help of these others who love you. And I will never be further than a breath away."

He smiled at me again, and gazed back toward Tirzah and Chariton. To my amazement, they lay asleep on the rough ground, curled like children in their beds, heads pillowed on their arms. Then in the brief instant that it took me to wonder at this unexpected scene, I dropped into sleep with the suddenness of a falling stone.

When I awoke, the sun was bright in the sky. I was still curled around Aeliana's neck, although she was sitting on one of the stone slabs, fingering the worn fabric of ben Adamah's old mantle. The son of Earth was nowhere to be seen.

Tirzah and Chariton were struggling to push themselves up from the ground, their eyes heavy with sleep. The task appeared a difficult one for them. I'd always wondered why humans sank into sleep as if they were drowning in fathoms of deep water rather than slipping into the pool of light that cats know as sleep. So many human behaviors puzzled me! If I were fortunate, perhaps I'd live long enough to discover some of the answers.

But Chariton finally rose, and approached Aeliana hesitantly. She looked up and smiled, but her smile was distracted, offering no more than polite greeting.

"The son of Earth said many things to me, Chariton, and I need time to think about them," she said softly, recognizing the hurt on his face.

He was nodding, his disappointment plain, when he suddenly froze in place, his brows drawing together in a puzzled frown. In the next instant, a similar puzzlement came over Tirzah's face, quickly replaced by a smile. Last of all, *I* realized what they were seeing: while we'd slept, the son of Earth had given each of us a dream, dreams that only now were slipping quietly into the light.

But my curiosity was greater than the pull of my own dream. *Listen!* ben Adamah had said to me, and the Lady had repeated it. So listen I would, if the son of Earth permitted it.

First I turned to Chariton, and discovered that I already walked beside him in his dream as if it were mine. I hadn't expected it to be so easy! Either ben Adamah was indulging my curiosity, or my curiosity had its roots in the will of the One, or both. Or maybe it was a distinction with no difference.

Ben Adamah and Chariton were walking through a forest of towering fir trees, more massive than any I'd ever imagined. Their bark was rough like the crumbling stone of a weathered cliff, their scent rich as desert spice, and their needles smooth to the touch. Where the trees parted, I caught glimpses of stony heights falling away to misty valleys and distant hills.

"Chariton," the son of Earth said gently, "you stumbled at this first test because your roots are sunk deep into the old ways of your people, and the dark gods knew this. You chose to forget the words I spoke to you beside the seawall: 'Who serves whom? Does the child obey the parent or the parent the child?' Your love for Aeliana has its being within the love of the One, but you separated the two, as if they were alien, each inimical to the other.

"Instead of seeking to protect your beloved with the One's wisdom, you turned your back on the Creator, set Aeliana herself up as a god, and delivered your will back to the dark ones you had served for so long. Do you see how futile your haunting of Ahumm was in the end? Had this *mere* kitten not intervened, Aeliana would have been lost.

"And even if Ahumm had not threatened her, you had set your own feet on a path that could only have led to her destruction. As a goddess enthroned in your mind, Aeliana would have become an abomination and a mockery of the One, or a lifeless idol cast from the covetous model of your dreams, like Aqhat's golden statue of Bast: hollow but for the substance leant by your desires. You are a powerful man, Chariton, while Aeliana is still only a lovely image of the woman she must *choose* to become.

"I thank the One that these near disasters never took on flesh. What you must understand, in your bones and in the blood pulsing in your veins, is that you are a son of the One, just as Aeliana is a daughter. You crave power and control, but remember . . . as I told Aqhat's cats to remember . . . you are the son, not the father; the creature, not the Creator. Continue as you began with Aeliana. Hold your heart with patience, in love: allow her the space she needs to heal and grow. Your strength and endurance are not tools of domination, but gifts to equip you for your road, and to carve out shelter and safety for those you love.

"I tell you, Chariton, if you nurture the love emerging between you and Aeliana, it will bear fruit that will nourish the whole world! And do not be too proud to seek my help when you need it, my friend."

Chariton opened his mouth to speak, but his image faded, along with ben Adamah's and the mountains where they walked. Apparently my curiosity's satisfaction had limits.

Still, instead of joining the others, I found myself slipping into Tirzah's dream. Where she walked with the son of Earth I couldn't say, because the light burned too brightly for my eyes. I walked blindly on a dazzling path, following the sound of ben Adamah's voice.

"I must ask a great gift of you, daughter," he was saying.

Daughter? Tirzah? But I had no time to puzzle this out before he continued.

"You have walked a weary road learning to release the hate you carried for those who enslaved you and spilled the blood of your loved ones. Your peace is hard-won and precious to you, and no one can take it from you.

"But today I am asking you to lay it down for a little while . . . and remember the hate that threatened to burn the very flesh from your bones. For Aeliana's sake.

"The horror that was yours must soon be hers; she cannot escape it. Young as she was when her life was shattered, she hasn't yet recognized the hate that hid beneath her fear these last years: hate for those who betrayed her so cruelly. With her memory restored, soon or late rage will follow, and I am asking you to be there to take her in your arms when it does, to show her the way through it to the One's peace."

Perhaps ben Adamah's words shadowed Tirzah's joy, because suddenly I could see her face in the midst of the blazing light. Her eyes grew grave as she held his request in her mind. Then she laughed aloud.

"If I refuse you, will I not cast myself into darkness of another kind? Do you think me such a child that I cannot see the trap?" Her voice bubbled with the rich chuckles of a young girl, and her face disappeared into the light once more.

"I will do you this favor, but you must grant me one in return."

I felt ben Adamah's smile, although I couldn't see it.

"Hold my peace in your hand like a lamp, Lord, where I may see its light and visit it from time to time, lest I lose myself in the darkness."

"I shall do better than that, beloved," he promised. "I will hold *you* in my hand. My strength will be your own. You shall not lose yourway."

Cat tales and purple snails

I felt like a young kitten trying to stand on my head in the loose sand of the dunes along the shore. The world I'd known had not only turned on its head, but it kept slipping away from me every time I thought I'd found my footing. I could never regret the miracle of the son of Earth's return, but how could I ever begin to make sense of everything else that had changed with him?

Would I be able to *see* like Tirzah now, or was I just riding along on the fringes of ben Adamah's robes? Were dreams no longer stories wandering through my sleeping mind, or had they all been conscripted like unwilling sailors onto fearsome voyages with the One? I'd once believed my life a simple thing. I certainly hadn't ever imagined that my thoughts might not be my own. But when did the change come about? Did I choose it? Had I made some momentous decision unawares—thinking I was merely choosing between an appetizer of mouse or mole?

30

A Small Scholar

Purple Gleaming in Shadow speaks

Suddenly it was my turn. I admit, by now my curiosity had all but disappeared. The son of Earth wasn't laying hands on my friends' heads in blessing, or offering them sparkling visions of paradise, but sending them back into the world with near-impossible tasks. I found myself wondering if what I'd imagined as ben Adamah's indulgence of my curiosity was more like the deceptively simple leading threads of an appallingly complex weaving.

"Your world is about to change more than you can possibly imagine," the son of Earth said to my dreaming self.

Here it came: I could feel it. We were sitting on a rock jutting up out of the sand on the shore of a deep blue sea, but it didn't feel like the sea I knew.

"The One, by the gift of the Mother of Cats, has given you a soul, Purple kit."

I didn't respond, and after a moment's pause, ben Adamah laughed, and added, "Calm yourself, small Purple! You knew this already. It was by my will, and the One's, as well as by that of the bright guardian of cats. We chose to honor your courage, your determination to understand, and your passionate devotion to those who win your love."

"Thank you, son of Earth," I replied in a small voice. "I am honored by your gift. But . . . I'm sorry, what is a soul?"

Ben Adamah's laugh seemed to shake the very roots of the Earth.

"A very proper question, little one! How could you know? If only Mari were here! I should have thought of that."

For an instant, the air around me grew hazy, and the sea's voice fell silent. When sight and sound returned, Wind on Water was sitting beside the son of Earth, her tail curled neatly around her toes.

"A soul, Purple Shadow, is something that human beings are born with, but beasts are not, although I believe that may be changing."

"But what is it?" I persisted.

Ben Adamah shook his head, smiled, and leaned back against the warm stone, leaving Wind on Water to answer my question.

"It's a lot of trouble, in my opinion, both good and bad. You'll have choices you never had before, but also the responsibility to choose carefully. The One will consider you her own kit, just like a human being, but she'll also expect you to behave like the very best of them.

"Ben Adamah once told me that as a beast of the Mother, I was incapable of choosing evil, because the Mother's expectations were part of my flesh and bone. As a beast I merely followed the Creator's pattern for cats, moment by moment, without worry or fear for the future. But as you saw in Acco, the balance is changing. Beasts are taking on the evil habits of humankind, and humans are becoming mindless beasts. I don't understand what it means, but I suspect ben Adamah does."

"But what IS it?" I almost yowled.

"Ah. It's hard to explain, Purple."

"Wind on Water!"

Abruptly she twisted around to address an itch at the base of her tail. Feline etiquette demanded I at least *pretend* to look elsewhere while she tended to her grooming. No cat would dare question the supreme importance of personal hygiene.

I sat and fumed. Ben Adamah looked amused.

When Wind on Water settled herself again, she said, "You know that when a cat dies, she just closes her eyes and falls into Silence in the Mother's paws?"

"Of course!" I huffed. I wasn't stupid.

"Well, if you have a soul, you don't just go to sleep when you die . . . it's sort of like when I jump up into ben Adamah's arms, and he catches me. You leap, and the One catches you. And then you go on. Only differently. I haven't done it yet, so I'm not exactly sure what happens."

I sat and thought about what she'd said.

"So, for most cats it's like when the weft thread runs out and the weaver decides to let it hang. That's the end of that thread. It's finished. But if you have a soul, it's like the weaver takes another thread, spins the ends together, and the weaving goes on. Is that it?"

Wind on Water stared at me the same way she'd stared when I'd told her how Aqhat's cats had rejected the Grandmothers: like I'd lost my mind.

"Ben Adamah, you talk to this kitten!" she said in disgust.

Was it my fault if Wind on Water didn't understand weaving?

"It's a clever comparison, small Purple," he smiled. "You have the idea, although it might be clearer if you imagined the new thread being made of something finer and more subtle than wool, silk perhaps.

"But that's not really the most important difference between a beast with a soul and one without. An ordinary beast has the Mother's expectations embedded in her flesh and bone. She is the reflection of the Creator's thought and altogether lovable. But with a soul . . .

"No, let's look at this in a different way. A soul isn't a *thing* so much as a way of being. It's a possibility that lives inside you. Human beings are created so that they can speak with their Creator. You might describe a soul as the ability to understand her language in their beating hearts . . . Or you might imagine the Creator's presence as a great river delta, with an endless number of trickling streams flowing into the hearts of humankind; each human being has a soul bubbling up inside her like a desert spring . . . Or, again, the soul might be a sand lily growing in each human heart, with the possibility of great beauty in its blossoms. But the sand lily cannot grow and reproduce unless, in the stillness of the night, one sole species of moth alights in the blossom's heart, bringing the pollen that gives new life.

"So if a human refuses to heed the Creator's language pulsing through her body, she may forget that there was ever a language at all. Likewise, if the bubbling spring of life in a human's depths is buried under layers of busyness and greed, it can sink away until the water fails and even the memory of its flow is lost. And if the sand lily's blossom is shut away from its winged guest, even the original blossom will shrivel, and no more flowers will bloom.

"In each of these examples, human beings have a choice: to take up their souls and live a life filled with the Creator's love, or deny the very thing that makes them fully human, and let their souls shrivel away into dust.

"But beasts, small Purple, were not created with this possibility within them. Their paths were laid out for them, their choices small, and their joys and sufferings limited. In the Earth's song, human voices led the choir and carried the melody; the beasts hummed the flow of harmony that gave depth and beauty to whole.

"As of today, you, small Purple, will hear and understand the One's voice. You may feel the Creator urging you in one direction or another, and if you listen, you will *always* know when you have chosen darkness over light.

"*Chosen*, you notice, Purple kit. You will now choose your own path among a bewildering number of possible paths. And that means that you may lose yourself along the way, just as humans do, although if you listen, the One will always call you back to herself. But if you choose darkness often enough, and keep refusing to recognize the warning that flares in your heart, you may lose your ability to hear the Creator's voice. Then, like Aqhat's cats, your choice becomes permanent, and you go down into darkness, into oblivion, not into the Mother's comforting arms."

"Can I give it back?" I asked worriedly.

"Of course, little one. Mari asked the same question once, and I will tell you what I told her: all the wisdom you've accumulated by my side, all the listening you've learned to do, you will lose, even the inborn gifts of a sacred cat of the Mother. You will become an ordinary cat. You will bear your kits, hunt your food, sleep in the sun, and die into the Mother's paws—but you won't remember these short months of your life. You will forget Mari, Aeliana, Tirzah, and me. You will forget looms and the struggle of light against darkness. But you will also lose sight of the future, and with it, fear. Your memory will hold only practical matters of survival and the uncomplicated loves of a simple beast. Still, it is no bad thing to be a beast in the pastures of the Mother."

I turned agonized eyes toward Wind on Water, but she was staring at the waves breaking against the reef. The decision was mine. The son of Earth waited patiently for my choice. After all, it was the privilege of a cat who possessed a soul to choose her path.

In a flash I knew my answer: I would keep this mighty gift the One had given me, and I would *learn*! If even the Beloved trusted my small store of wisdom enough to wait upon my decision, what wonders might I learn in time? What mysteries might I unravel among the threads of the One's loom of creation?

"I do not wish to forget you, son of Earth," I replied formally, and crouching at his feet, I prepared to spring.

When I leapt, he caught me in his arms.

"Welcome, small scholar!" he laughed.

"One thing remains between us, Purple kit," he said at length.

"Yes, ben Adamah?" I replied.

No fear lay in my waiting. As long as I held to his light within me, fear was only an evil memory of the past.

"You and Aeliana share many wounds in common," ben Adamah's soft voice hummed.

"Wounds, son of Earth?" I repeated, puzzled.

"Grief crushed you both beneath its heavy load before you were old enough to understand: grief, and betrayal by those whose love should have been a shield between you and a world you were not yet ready to face.

"Chariton and Tirzah will do their best for her as she struggles to free herself from the chains of her past, but you will walk beside her in her thoughts, *listening* . . . answering, and asking questions. Together you will find healing. For nothing comforts the heart like the certainty that another understands your pain."

Cat tales and purple snails

I spent a lot of time thinking about that last comment. Hadn't the Mother of Cats said something like that when she talked about the One's learning what it was like to be flesh? That the fullness of her compassion was rooted in discovering what a beast's, or a human's, life was like in all its joy and misery? In fact, hadn't she said that ben Adamah's experience of creation's pain and suffering had prepared the ground so that compassion could truly flower in the One's heart?

So wasn't the son of Earth asking me to do something similar for Aeliana? To help her understand herself by sharing my experiences with her? In fact, wasn't that the same thing he'd asked of Tirzah? And even in a way of Chariton? Rather like a master weaver passing along the secrets of his craft to those who followed after.

I hoped I wouldn't have to do demonstrations. Surely ben Adamah's model would suffice.

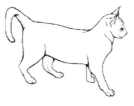

31

Gates of Heaven

Purple Gleaming in Shadow speaks

*M*any peaceful days passed after that morning when He Who Brings Life to the Earth returned to us from the tomb, hands brimming with light. We met him in our dreams each night, but we didn't see him with our waking eyes.

Aqhat returned from his voyage, devastated to have missed the wonders we'd witnessed, but the new partnership he and Chariton's father had agreed upon comforted him in his loss. Ahumm disappeared completely, although a few fragments of richly woven red fabric and gnawed bones littering the river tombs convinced the people of Acco that he must have met his death. No one mourned Ahumm's going, except perhaps his parents, whom I never met. For the four of us who had witnessed his change, his physical death had little meaning. The man called Ahumm had been uncreated, reabsorbed into the Creator's mind like an unborn kit. I tried not to think too much about possible connections between the drooling horror shambling out of the tomb and my acquiring a soul.

Even in Acco, rumors reached us of the amazing events surrounding the death of Yeshua ben Yosef. But perhaps half a moon's cycle came and went before we were summoned to the garden gate in the dim pre-dawn light by Chariton's frenzied pounding.

"He's here!" he shouted, almost dancing with impatience. "Come! Come now! He's waiting for us on the beach! Hurry!"

In no more time than it took humans to throw mantles over sleeping shifts, Aqhat's household was streaming out across the terrace and down to the shore toward the holding pools. Riding on Aeliana's shoulder, I could see the son of Earth's unmistakable silhouette, the rising sun just warming his robes with its glow.

Cats and humans, runner birds and gulls, dogs and even great lizards streamed across the dunes and along the shore to greet him. They came running from the flat lands and the city streets, darkening the beach with their numbers. Who would have thought that ben Adamah could have touched so many lives, human and beast, in his brief visit?

Just as the crowds parted to let Aqhat's household approach, the sun's slim disc crept above hills of the Galilee, striking some hidden reservoir of light in the son of Earth. His face and hands blazed out like the sun itself, their light racing through his body as the sun's rays stream across the Earth. His robes proved no greater impediment to the light within him than finely woven gauze would to the noonday sun. He stood before us, his arms outstretched in welcome—or in a reminder of his death—the glory of heaven come to Earth, his light streaming across the sea as far as I could see. I leapt to the cool sand and took a few hesitant steps toward him.

I, like everyone else in that silent throng, held my breath in anticipation. What would he say? What news had he brought?

At last he looked up into the brilliant sky and called aloud in a voice that roused vibrations in my flesh and spread through my feet into the sand, where it flowed away in rolling waves, traveling with the speed of his rejoicing through stone and water alike.

In the blink of a cat's eye, the dawn light began to fill with glowing shapes, translucent like reflections on a still pool, pressing around him where he stood. Some hovered in the air, while others drifted in the foaming waves beside him. All who intended to answer his call were soon present, and for a moment the shore grew absolutely still. Perhaps the waves themselves ceased their restless flow. I didn't notice.

In that moment of utter stillness I suddenly understood what I saw: the bright images of creation, those lesser gods who had always honored their Creator, were gathered around the son of Earth, their faces glowing with joy—beast and ocean spawn, rolling ocean and flowing river, fertile earth and mountain stone, mighty winds and singing stars—far more than I could grasp. Their hands raised in adoration, they flowed together in a swirl of golden light too swift to perceive, and vanished into the luminous wonder of the Beloved.

In that same instant, on the very edge of my vision, I thought I saw a dark cloud similar in kind to the golden spirits before us, but as it swirled, it dispersed in the growing light of day and settled onto the ground like a dust devil's spinning sand slowly sinks exhausted onto the parched Earth.

"Creatures of the One!" the son of Earth cried, his voice edged with the accents of the small powers who had flowed into his light. "This day you are joined to the One Creator who formed you. No more will these bright spirits stand between yourselves and the One, except as his emissaries and comforters, sent to ease your hearts. The demons are dissolved into the dust of greed that spawned them. Their shades may haunt the dark places of the Earth for a time, but their day is done. Creation is now one, flesh and spirit, spirit and flesh, knit together in the miracle of the One's compassion.

"All that remains is for humankind to reach out to the Creator in love, as the beasts of the Mother and elements of the Earth have always done without thought. And those beasts who strive toward the One with all the passion of their great hearts will find new wonder and delight in the days to come. The gates of heaven are open, and creation's long groaning shall finally find a balm.

"With my coming, the gap between spirit and flesh closes. Yet the fate of all flesh is bound together with humankind, for they are the firstborn children of the One . . . and their choices will bring grace and growth—or diminishment—to all. If humankind fails in their simple act of love, then all of creation will fall with them.

"As for you, human sons and daughters of the One, never have you known such glory as the One bestows upon you this day: I reach out my hand to each of you, asking only that you accept your Creator's love as a child accepts the love of father or mother. Wherever the One's children walk beneath the sun, whatever face the One shows to them, this summons will ring in their ears: Grasp my hand, and step into the light of the Creator's glory, for now and forever.

"Yet unlike the long faithfulness of the beasts, and the great spinning cosmos, you are free to destroy what you have been given, and to drag all creation into the abyss with you. You are free: it lies in your power to turn your back on the Father's love, revile his compassion, and embrace the cruel lies of the Evil One . . . for he endures, and he is always seeking new paths into human hearts. Yes, you are free to turn the Earth into a wasteland, destroying in your madness all the innocent lives nourished at her breast. I tell you, beware! For the rage of greed and hate I have tasted in your hearts is as deadly to the Earth as any sorcerous evil—as is the despair that haunts your willful emptiness.

"What unimaginable act of love the One holds as a last resort if that day should come, even I do not know. Perhaps extinction will be the only grace possible by then, apart from comforting the few who still cry to their Creator.

"I summoned you to meet me here beside these holding pools for a reason. In these round pools, carved in the circled shape of eternity, evil brews its poison in tiny isolated worlds. Here you can see the nature of the wasteland *you* will create if you turn your backs on the One. In these pools humankind preys upon one of nature's cruelest predators—the purple murex, who drills its way through the shells of its prey and sucks the living flesh from their bodies. But once snared by human predators, the murex live out their last days in captivity, and then find their own shells drilled in turn, and their flesh ripped living from their shells to feed the vanity of human tyrants and the petty parasites who grow fat on the crumbs of their banquets. Slaves and divers, dyers and washerwomen, spinners and weavers, all are sacrificed to this industry that circles endlessly round the lust for a dye resembling the clotted blood of a newly dead heart—a color that if worn by common people is punishable by death.

"An industry of death, built upon death, celebrating death, and dealing death. Is the world blind, that it cannot see this depravity? Here is evil, laid out before you in its fullness. What are the fruits of this labor? Death and despair for the murex! Death and despair for the slaves shackled to the stench and horror of its endless slaughter! Greed and scrabbling for status among those who control its spread, and bloated pretensions to divinity by those who wear it. I say to you, you shall know a tree by its fruit, and this fruit has a foul stink.

"Here is a miniature portrait of creation without the compassionate hand of the One. Left to yourselves, so you may ever choose. I say to you, look, and quake in fear, for such is the end of all the designs of the Evil One: misery and cruelty among the powerful, and misery and abuse cascading down to stifle the poor who have nowhere to flee, and the tendrils of his dark spirit penetrating every part of the One's creation.

"Are you no better than the cruel murex? Where is your delight in honest labor and the fair treatment of your brothers and sisters? What can be worth this traffic in horror? The color is even ugly to the eye, and rank to the nose of the wearer! Why do you not cry out at the wrongness of this thing?

"Honoring the One and receiving his love in return is more than a matter of prayer and psalms. Look, and see the beauty and nobility of kindness and fair dealing. Let the wonder of the One's love flood your senses and transform your hearts, summoning you to share his compassion with those around you. What is the purpose of the One's spirit in your hearts if you ignore his voice? I say to you, listen, and remember: Let justice roll down like waters, and righteousness like an ever-flowing stream!"

Then he paused, and looked around at the gathered crowd. Most of the beasts had wandered off, and some of the humans as well. Miracles were all very well, but no one enjoys being told they need to change their ways.

Aqhat hadn't moved from his place, but his eyes were glazed, and his mouth hung slack. No doubt hearing himself described as either a parasite or a sacrifice to his chosen trade was unsettling. But his daughters had gathered around him, and little Arisha was doing her best to distract him from his distress.

I pressed hard against ben Adamah's legs and purred. He smiled down at me and at each of our small circle of friends, touching each of us with his warmth.

Chariton tore his eyes away from ben Adamah's face and touched Aeliana's cheek lightly.

"Shall we fly to the hills, Lady, where sheep may safely graze, and purple is found only in the roots of madder flowers?"

I leapt up onto her shoulder and purred.

Aeliana turned, smiled into Chariton's eyes, and placed her hand in his. "How can I refuse to share your path, friend of the Beloved? I—we," she laughed, rubbing her cheek against me—"shall gladly go with you to seek these green hills where compassion takes root in the midst of purple."

Epilogue

*N*one of those who remained on the beach showed any signs of leaving. Instead, they waited patiently, their eyes fixed on the son of Earth's shining image. He swept their faces with his gaze, smiling at each of them in turn, before striding closer.

"Rejoice with me in this new day!" he cried, his voice a mighty exaltation. "Death's tyranny is broken! Whatever evil may lie ahead, the final victory is certain. All creation rests in the One's hand, and his faithfulness never fails."

Then he raised his hands in blessing and lifted his face to the bright sky.

Praise Him, all you creatures of the Earth,

he sang,

for his breath fills the laboring breast with hope!

Praise him in the desert places of the heart,
for he pours himself out like water for those who thirst.

Praise him in the dark places of the soul,
for his love redeems even the bitterness of despair.

Praise him in the innocence of childhood,
for he is the vision dancing in a child's eyes.

Praise him in the strength of your youth,
for he is the joy that gives you wings to fly.

Praise him in the anguish of your flesh,
for his compassion sustains you when all else fails.

Praise him in the trembling palsy of age,
for his wisdom is your staff and support.

Praise him in the midst of death,
for he is the light that pierces even the grave.

Praise him, all you ends of the Earth,
for one day he will welcome you into his rest.

As his words fell into silence, the brilliance of his light dimmed, and he walked out among the people, laying his hands on the sick and lame, and sowing hope wherever his feet touched the Earth.

ΑΩ

About the Author

C. L. Francisco has always chosen fiction for her downtime reading: "Fiction sneaks up on me, gets under my guard, and touches my heart in a way that non-fiction can't," she says. "It opens up new possibilities and sets me dreaming. For me, life-changing books have always been fiction. That's probably why I chose to write a book like Yeshua's Cat."

A retired college professor, Francisco found her faith again several years ago after a time of radical doubt. Her conservative Christian upbringing, undergraduate study at Mount Holyoke College, year's stay at L'Abri, early career years in art therapy, and PhD in world religions had all contributed to her questions. But as a woman whose life had always been grounded in faith, she struggled to find her way again. Oddly enough, the voice of non-human nature spoke more clearly than any other—except for C. S. Lewis' fiction, which she never abandoned. The whispers were faint at first, and often resulted in dead ends, but when they finally spoke clear, she found herself in the presence of the Christ who lives beyond all walls.

The Gospel According to Yeshua's Cat had its roots in Francisco's desire to offer fellow strugglers a fresh perspective on Jesus of Nazareth. The book's feline narrator speaks with the wise voice of a young cat whose death after a devastating wildfire provided Francisco with the impetus to begin the book.

A Cat Out of Egypt emerged from readers' eagerness for Francisco to write another book in the same series after *The Gospel According to Yeshua's Cat*—something she had never planned to do. But once the idea took hold, *A Cat Out of Egypt* came to life almost as if it had been waiting fully formed just below the surface of her thoughts. A stand-alone prequel to *Yeshua's Cat*, *A Cat Out of Egypt* introduces Francisco's original feline character's many-times great-grandmother Miw, beloved of the child Yeshua.

The Cats of Rekem is the third volume in the series. Several characters from the two earlier books—human and feline—appear in a richly layered story set in ancient Petra, culminating in the early ministry of Paul the apostle.

Now, with *Cat Born to the Purple*, a second sequel has emerged from *Yeshua's Cat*. Like *Rekem*, *Purple* follows the life of a character introduced in an earlier book: this time, the young woman Eliana, whom Yeshua healed after finding her stoned by a mob and left to die in the stifling smoke of a Galilean wildfire. Forced to flee her native Sepphoris, she follows Yeshua to the home of a merchant and weaver in the Phoenician city of Acco (today, Akko), where, with the help of an extraordinary young cat, she begins her journey toward true healing.

Join *Tracking Yeshua's Cats*, C. L. Francisco's bi-monthly newsletter, and get behind-the-scenes previews of all her upcoming books! Sign up at http://clfrancisco.com/contact/.

Acknowledgements

The following resources were invaluable in helping me understand Aeliana's world:

Books:

Barber, E. J. W. *Prehistoric Textiles: The Development of Cloth in the Neolithic and Bronze Ages with Special Reference to the Aegean.* Princeton, NJ: Princeton University Press, 1991.

Barber, Elizabeth Wayland. *Women's Work: The First 20,000 Years.* New York: W.W. Norton and Company, 1994.

Gleba, Margarita and Judit Pásztókai-Szeöke. *Making Textiles in Pre-Roman and Roman Times:* People, Places, Identities. Oxbow Books, 2013.

Jeremias, Joachim. *Jerusalem in the Time of Jesus: An Investigation into Economic and Social Conditions during the New Testament Period.* Philadelphia: Fortress Press, 1967.

Stern, Ephraim. *Archaeology of the Land of the Bible, Volume II: The Assyrian, Babylonian, and Persian Periods.* New York: Random House, 2001.

Stern, Ephraim. *Dor: Ruler of the Seas.* Israel Exploration Society, 2000.

Essays and Journal Articles:

Ron Beeri, "Hellenistic Akko," in *In the Hill-Country, and in the Shephelah, and in the Arabah (Joshua 12,8): Studies and Researches Presented to Adam Zertal in the Thirtieth Anniversary of the Manasseh Hill-Country Survey*, ed. Shay Bar, Jerusalem: Ariel Publishing House (2008), 195-210.

Deborah Ruscillo, "Reconstructing Murex Royal Purple and Biblical Blue in the Aegean," in *Archaeomalacology: Molluscs in Former Environments of Human Behaviour*, ed. Daniella E. Bar-Yosef Mayer, Oxbow Books, 2005.

Charles C. Torrey, "A Phoenician Necropolis at Sidon," *Annual of the American School of Oriental Research in Jerusalem*, Vol 1 (1919), 1-32.

Coming in 2017: Volume 5 of Yeshua's Cats

Many scholars say that the woman named Lydia in *The Acts of the Apostles* was only called by that name because she once lived in the city of Thyatira, in the old kingdom of Lydia; Luke may not have known her real name. Both Thyatira and Lydia lay in the heart of Asia Minor, or Anatolia—Chariton's home. As "a seller of purple," this unnamed woman made her living in one of the most widespread industries in the Roman Empire. Who can say where her journey had taken her in the years before her meeting with Paul the Apostle? Perhaps she'd even been called Aeliana . . .

Made in the USA
Columbia, SC
23 May 2017